Lethal Beauty: Special Edition Discreet Paperback

Accardi Tactical, Book 1 (Special Edition Discreet Cover)

K.C. Ramsey

K.C. Ramsey

Copyright

This book is a work of fiction. Names, characters, places, and incidents are the brainchild of the author. Any resemblance to actual persons, living or dead, events, or locales are entirely coincidental.

ISBN print: 979-8-9873493-8-0

Created with Atticus   Cover by: Y'all That Graphic

Book Blurb: Briggs Consulting, LLC

Developmental and Line Edits by: Olivia Kalb Editing

Proofing by: Lawrence Editing

Dedication

To my family, both by blood and through words. Without you all, this book would never have been written, let alone published. Thank you with all of my heart for encouraging me to dream big and follow my passion.

Contents

Chapter 1

Alessia

Temper coursed through me in waves, making my hands tremble and cheeks flush. If looks could kill, then Tony Romero was a dead man walking and I was about to be arrested for his murder. Considering my plans for the night, being arrested right now would be more than a little problematic. I drew a breath in slowly before letting it out, reining in my anger and burying it. Around me, people laughed and talked with each other, the fake giggling adding to my irritation. Despite the laughter, no one was having a good time, but I expected nothing less. It was our job. Well, it was supposed to be a job, but somehow, over the years, it had morphed into a soul-sucking monster, consuming me one tiny nibble at a time.

Behind me, the ocean waves crashed into the shore, spraying my skin with a salty mist. The briny smell mixed with seaweed, sand, and perfume. Despite the cold droplets clinging to the ridiculous dress, plastering the skin-tight material to me like a second skin, most of the people loitering around barely glanced in my direction, too focused on either their own jobs or the flirting and ass-kissing that inevitably happened when you mixed the powerful with the power-hungry.

"Hold that position," Tony called from behind the camera that, by all rights, should have grown attached to his face years ago. "Now, give me more heat. Lose the ice bitch look and give me the sweet seductress we both know you're incapable of being in real life."

He wasn't wrong—sweet was not even a word my family would use to describe me—but irritating me with insults to make me lose my bad mood was not the best tactic. Tony wasn't a bad guy, for a photographer anyway, but I'd learned when I first met him eight years ago that his genius behind the lens didn't extend to his mouth. And it had been in rare form today. Loud, obnoxious, and cutting for hours. Most people would have run off set hours ago, crying and contemplating their career choices. I had thicker skin, but despite my efforts, the words affected me. Instead of self-doubt, my confidence and anger issues turned the emotion into seething irritation. I'd bitten my tongue so often today that if I didn't end up with one giant canker sore, I would be surprised.

Tired, beyond hungry, and more than ready to turn to the real reason I was on the soft white sand of Fiji, I gave him five more minutes of what he needed. "Done?" I tried not to snap or whine—it really wasn't my style. I was a seasoned professional. Being able to keep my emotions under control and focus on my work was the reason I could do what I did. It worked for modeling as well.

My head was pounding, a result of staring directly at the sunlight for hours, combined with barely eating enough to keep a rabbit alive. It was yet another reason I hated being out on modeling assignments—I could pretty much eat normal meals at home as long as I exercised enough and ate healthily, but on location, I was subjected to a negative fifty-calorie count and expected not to have an issue with it. I was pretty sure I'd trade my favorite knife for a burger at this point, but eating red meat in front of this crowd would cause a riot. The last time I'd eaten some jerky that one of my brothers had sent me on a set, Melissa Karmichael had cried actual tears over the dead cow sacrificed for my snack and Kasia Alaynna just about jumped me to get a piece.

Tony was looking at his camera, his focus on the tiny screen so intense I wasn't sure he had heard me. "What?" he looked up after several long moments, his brown eyes barely meeting mine before he looked back at his equipment. "Oh." He glanced around, noting the people packing up the contents of the tent we had used as a base the entire day and the sun beginning to set on the other side of the private cove we were using. "Yeah, light's starting to go anyway." His bottom lip jutted out, every bit a pout, and I knew that if it weren't for that fact—not the people packing up or the twelve hours we'd been out there, I would be fighting him over calling it a day.

Not bothering to reply, I spun on my heel, my long legs eating up the ground as I made my way to the tent. Knowing the crew wouldn't wait for me to change before they started taking the tent down—the assholes—I stepped up to the small platform that allowed easier access for them to peel the ridiculous gown off me. The strapless straight-jacket of a dress required two others to help me get out of it. The sea-foam blue-green material of the bodice clung to me like a second skin, trailing down my curves like a lover before loosening at my knees to trail at my feet. I'd glanced at myself in the mirror that morning and knew it was a good choice for Valencia. The expensive material complemented my golden skin and black hair—curtesy of my Italian grandmother—and set off my eyes—my trademark as a model. My father's mother might have been Italian, but my mother's family, according to her, were all Romani ... or gypsies. My violet eyes were so vivid they often startled people. I frequently received double takes when meeting people's gazes for the first time. It often amused me that gossip magazines posted articles a few times a year questioning their legitimacy and accusing me of wearing contacts to play them up when, in all reality, I used contacts to cover them up from time to time.

As the gown came off, I took my first real breath in hours, then snatched up the offered jeans and tank top. My hair had so much product in it I was afraid if I tried to tie it up, it would just break off, so I left it loose and jammed my feet into a pair of heeled sandals as the sides of the tent fell to the ground around me.

"Ready, Miss Accardi?" The question had me rolling my eyes before turning to stare up at the behemoth standing just outside where the tent had been. Valencia, the powerhouse brand responsible for today's poor mood, had insisted that I be assigned a bodyguard while on the island for the photoshoot. As with anyone who had their picture plastered on billboards, magazines, and the internet, I had my fair share of crazies. The luxury brand was not about to have the face of their new line mixed up in any sort of sordid scandal, and a bodyguard to keep the wolves at bay was their answer. The colossus of testosterone they'd hired looked like they'd plucked him off the door to a nightclub, and I was still fairly certain that was where they'd found him. Of course, I couldn't admit that the idea I needed protection was laughable and that if I had needed assistance, he was the last one I'd trust to protect me from anything, but it was another instance where I had to take a breath and keep my mouth shut. Keeping with the appearance of being compliant made my job, my actual job, easier. Especially as the idiot, who apparently had learned all of his bodyguard duties from watching blockbuster movies, was going to provide me with a great alibi and, with any luck, help keep my brothers off my back. They might not know that I was better prepared to deal with an intruder than the so-called bodyguard, but on paper, he looked like he would suffice, and it would give them—Gideon, in particular—peace of mind that I had someone watching my back. I hated that I couldn't tell them just how capable I was, but keeping my cover intact was more important than screaming at the top of my lungs just how well I could take care of myself.

Keeping my senses on high alert, I pretended to text on my phone as Hammer—yes, that was the name said action-hero-wannabe introduced himself as—played up his role, looking around as he exited my car, eyeing everything in exaggerated suspicion before allowing me to get out. I almost ran into him when, as I was about to step off the elevator, he jutted an arm out, preventing me from moving forward as he leaned into the hall, looking both ways even though the bank of elevators only had one entry point and the other was a solid brick wall. Then I waited impatiently at the door as he investigated my suite, again impersonating every Hollywood rendition my brothers and I had ever ridiculed with his exaggerated movements and shoddy work checking places someone could hide before coming back to let me know I was safe to move around my rooms.

"I've got to rehydrate my skin," I complained, walking toward my bedroom. "All this sun has done countless damage to my complexion." I heard Hammer snort as he went to the couch in the main room, which had a direct line of sight to the only door to the hallway and, more importantly for him, a clear view of the big screen television. It would amaze the teenage me, the things that came out of my mouth. Of course, I didn't care about my skin any more now than I had then. If you had told the thirteen-year-old me that I would be a world-renowned model, I would have asked you if someone was holding a gun to my head. I'd been clueless that love could be just as forceful as a weapon in motivating you to do something you absolutely hated. If it wasn't for times like I was about to have, I wondered if I could have stuck with modeling as long as I had. I blew out a breath, reminding myself to set my daddy issues aside and focus on the work I actually looked forward to before my time window closed.

Shutting the door to my bedroom, I carefully evaluated the room, ensuring everything was as I'd left it. I checked the windows and drawers and kept my eyes peeled, looking for any sort of electronic surveillance. The room was clear, as I'd expected. But it wouldn't have been the first time a crazy fan or creepy so-called paparazzi snuck into the room of a beautiful woman and placed a camera or two, trying to make a buck by selling nude pictures. And with my private profession being what it was, habits of safety and security rode me hard. I practically ran to the shower as soon as I was done, my scalp and face itching from the products the makeup artists had used on my skin and hair in the name of selling beauty. On a timeline now, I gave myself three minutes to wash the day away, braiding my thick, wet hair while I was in there before carefully drying off in the corner of the shower that was mostly dry, leaving the water running. An advantage of being one of the highest-paid models in the world was the digs. I could have had a party for six in this thing. I got out and hung the towel back up on the rack—I would need it again in a few minutes.

The natural light in the bathroom was much dimmer compared to the light entering my bedroom. I'd requested a suite with a view of the morning sunrise, which put the bathroom in the prime location to be bathed in shadow, given the shape of the hotel.

Pulling out my makeup case, I opened the enormous box on the vanity counter. Grabbing a can of shaving cream, I carefully twisted the lid and pressed down hard while fingering the bottom. With a quiet snick, the bottom dropped into my hand. I pulled out the contents and quickly applied the contacts that would turn my almost purple eyes into a muddy brown in case of witnesses. I hadn't made a mistake yet, and discovery was unlikely in my mission, but better safe than sorry was my motto. Gloves came next, though I didn't put them on until I'd accessed the hidden compartment in the makeup case and pulled on the super lightweight specialized suit that covered me from head to toe. The hood covered my hair and much of my face. Despite being tighter than the dress—I was essentially wearing a black, huge condom—I felt freer than I had in months. I was doing what I was meant to do, my purpose and passion in life. My heart wanted to race in anticipation, but training and control kept its rhythm steady. I grabbed one last necessary item. The razor looked ordinary enough, but like the can, it held its own secrets. Twisting the base in one hand and the disposable blade head in the other, I pulled, revealing the single scalpel hidden within. I smiled, not able to contain my excitement. My handler had told me to make a statement, and a statement was what they would get.

Padding over to the window, which was now completely cloaked in shadow, I removed the screen and set it aside. Taking a careful peek at the surrounding landscape, I was pleased to see it deserted. They'd cultivated thick vegetation to cater to the island's remote feel, and pairing that with the darkness made most people's instincts steer them away from this area once the sun had set.

Hoisting myself onto the window ledge, I grasped at the window above mine with my fingertips. My gloves assisted me in the climb, but nothing but my own strength and determination would get the job done. Already five stories above the ground, the only thing keeping me from falling would be my own abilities. I pulled myself, inch by inch, until I could get my feet onto the windowsill above my suite. Now was the fun part. I jumped, grabbing the underside of the deck that made up the floor of the balcony above me. Looking down, I idly noted that I was close to ninety feet off the ground, with nothing between my feet and the island floor. I hung for another moment, making sure I could hear no sound above me before moving closer to the side of the balcony, traversing it as easily as a child would the monkey bars at recess. Taking a deep breath, I used my body's momentum, swinging a few times to gain what I needed, thankful that the hotel had outfitted its balconies with modern horizontal wire to minimize the effect on the view. With one last swing, I curled my body around the side of the deck, bending at the waist to allow my legs to slide between the top of the balcony and the bottom wire. In a move that would make a gymnast proud, I pushed off with my hands, my torso following my legs until I rested flat on the bottom of the deck.

With my internal clock ticking away, I moved to the sliding glass door, a gossamer curtain blowing in the breeze, hiding me from the occupant inside. The floor plan I'd been provided was correct—instead of a bathroom like my suite and the floor between mine and this one, there was an office attached to the bedroom.

"Well"—the man's Slavic accent was thick, but the English was recognizable—"if you need another shipment of toys, I can certainly assist you. I do agree that they ... diminish ... over time and need to be replaced occasionally. Plus, creating a collection is a great hobby to have. Do you need assistance throwing them out, too, or just need a product replacement?"

I stood stock-still, listening intently as the monster disguised as a human made arrangements for the sale of women his organization had kidnapped from their homes. Revulsion and fury swirled within me, but I tapped it down, waiting with a patience I didn't want to have as he wrapped up the phone call.

Thankfully, it didn't take long before he hung up before getting to his feet to stretch, his back to me, providing the opportunity I needed to do what I was there to do. For his crimes against humanity, they sentenced that piece of filth to death, and I was his executioner. The price was only another piece of my soul and a bit of time.

I was back in the shower, all evidence hidden in their compartments, scrubbing my skin fiercely with a loofa, when a knock sounded at the door. Cursing in irritation, I yanked the towel from the rack, wrapped it around me as I scattered water everywhere, and stomped to the door. "What?" I asked, my ire exactly in line with what one would expect from a temperamental model.

Hammer stood in the doorway; his jaw was slightly open at the sight I made. I'd applied a green seaweed mask to my face and a body scrub that shimmered, turning my tanned skin into something more than human. The towel was small and was purposely gaping at the bottom, giving Hammer a hint of a view of my curves.

"Hello." I snapped my fingers in his face, returning his attention to my face. "What did you want?" I said the words slowly, as if he couldn't understand me, and his face flushed.

"I, um ..." he stammered. "You were in there a while, and I wasn't sure if you—"

I cut him off. "Do you have any idea how hard it is to reverse sun damage?" I snipped, though I didn't know the answer any more than he did. "Thank God I'm leaving tomorrow morning. It'll take weeks to recover from this. I'm going to have to schedule an appointment with my dermatologist—for all I know, I contracted skin cancer." My words were outrageous, but they did the trick, reminding the man that I might be pretty, but my attitude was anything but. "But since you're here, call and order some food to be delivered. I couldn't eat this morning, or I would have looked bloated for the shoot, and I'm starving." I slammed the door in his face before he could respond, then headed back to the shower with a smile. Hammer's timing couldn't have been any better, though he didn't know it, and now I had an even more solid alibi in place. Not that I needed it. After all, who would suspect me?

Chapter 2

ALESSIA

I was jetlagged, still craving red meat, and beyond exhausted by the time I strolled into my brothers' offices the next day. I was glad to be back in Texas—the smell of sunshine and barbeque practically swirled on the breeze, mixing with ocean salt and red dirt, relaxing me in a way very few things could. My morning flight was delayed due to engine trouble, and after spending almost the entire day at the airport, the flight had been yet another irritation. First class should have afforded me some time to relax, but the man seated next to me had other ideas. Granted, he was pretty in a polished polo-crowd kind of way, but like most men, he hadn't bothered to look past my face. He also hadn't shut up about his favorite subject the entire flight—himself. And trust me, he was *not* that interesting.

I glanced at my watch as I entered the lobby, noting it was already almost five. The empty front desk was unusual, but Maria, my brothers' silver-haired miracle worker of a receptionist, might have taken off early if the grandkids were in town. Taking the opportunity to snoop, I walked around the desk to pull out her chair, waking the computer as I did so. Maria had been with our family since before I was born, having started with my father shortly after he'd married my mother. My brothers wouldn't hear of anyone taking her place, and she spoiled them rotten.

Her birthday was next month, and for reasons that continued to escape me, my brothers, apparently thinking that gift-giving was somehow a female-only appointed task, stuck me with coming up with a present from the whole family. More accurately, they knew my gift would be kick-ass and her favorite, and they wanted to jump on that bandwagon. Pulling up her browser history, I clicked through the pages, not at all feeling like I was infringing on her privacy. It was a company computer, after all—if Maria didn't want me to know what she looked at during her downtime, she should have at least deleted her user history.

I'd just finished committing the beach house rental in Maine that she'd looked at repeatedly to memory when the door to the lobby opened, and two men stepped in from the hall. Both were well-muscled, but one was definitely a gym rat while the other was rougher, illustrating in vivid lines that he'd actually gained his through need and use, not just by filling his time with endless reps in front of a mirror.

The first man, Mr. Gym Muscles, was short, likely an inch or two shorter than my five-foot-eleven. His All-American typical good looks—blond hair and brown eyes—didn't detract from the sneer that twisted his lips as he laid eyes on me, sizing me up and stereotyping me in a glance. I did the former and tried very hard not to do the latter, but his collared black shirt, two sizes too small, made it hard not to. I gave him points for the police shield proudly displayed on his shoulder, though I wondered if he had to control his breathing for fear his shirt would rip in two. He walked toward me, and I automatically evaluated him for weaknesses, his attitude putting me on alert. He limped slightly on his left leg, revealing a previous knee injury that I could capitalize on if needed. His movements illustrated his aggression and attack style—he would come at me hard and fast but was a brawler at best. I could take him with minimal effort if needed. After dismissing him, I focused on the man with him.

Now there's a worthy opponent, I thought in appreciation. The second man was taller, much taller. He wasn't stocky like Mr. Gym Muscles, but had solid corded muscle and a lanky physique that was deceptively strong. He, too, wore black tactical pants, but his simple black tee shirt was free of any decoration and actually fit correctly. His dark brown hair was cut short, just over military regulation, and I wondered if it was long enough for me to grip in my hands. His mossy green eyes were evaluating every inch of the interior layout of the lobby, barely touching me before going back to look at the room, cementing my former military guess. He fell a few steps behind the first man, slightly to the man's left, his walk much more balanced and controlled, belaying an extensive history of martial arts and experience in fights where one wrong move could result in death. His square jaw and slightly crooked nose made him too rugged to be called handsome, but he was definitely a looker, his magnetism more visceral than appearance-driven. So much so, I had a hard time looking away from him and back at the other man.

"Your boss still in?" Mr. Gym Muscles' words were an attempt at being polite, but his perusal of my body as he spoke was completely inappropriate as he leaned into the desk, an impressive monstrosity that dominated the entry and separated the lobby from the maze of offices. It was obvious as he scanned me slowly up and down. I hated to say I was used to it, but at this point, it was nothing new.

Grateful I was wearing pants instead of a skirt, I cocked an eyebrow at him. "And you are?" My patented ice-bitch persona was front and center. My bored expression, paired with completely ignoring his blatant behavior, had him flushing in irritation. I wasn't sure what he was there for, but I knew three things immediately. One, I didn't like him. Two, he wouldn't make it through our hiring process, and three, he was an asshole.

"Mike Tomleson." He didn't offer a hand. "I'm here for the Tactical Firearms instructor position."

I snorted, not at all concerned with trying to hide my amusement. There was no way in hell he would teach a class for Accardi Tactical. No matter how qualified he was to teach firearms, "tactical" was a key—not just in how you handled your weapon. It was clear in the time it had taken him to cross the room that he wasn't up to our standards and had no interest in working to improve to get there. We were a family at Accardi Tactical, and if you couldn't fit with our standards both personally and professionally, you weren't welcome.

"And," I prompted again, waiting for a beat before I continued, "if memory serves me correctly, everyone receives an itinerary prior to arriving here for evaluation." It had been more than a hot minute since I was involved in the administration side of the business, or any part of it, for that matter, but I couldn't imagine anything had changed that much.

His hands dropped off the counter, balling into fists at his sides. I was egging him on, I admitted it, but I hadn't had some fun in a while—unless you called cutting off a human trafficker's dick and shoving it down his throat fun. And since my appointed psychiatrist got more than a little squirmy when I admitted things like that, I tried not to get as much enjoyment from the wet work anymore for fear she'd pull me from the field.

The man behind him cleared his throat a few steps away from us. "I'm sorry to interrupt, ma'am," he began, and I was relieved to discover he wasn't with the idiot in front of me. "Keene asked me to give him a few minutes of my time when I had the chance. Does he happen to still be in?"

I dismissed the hothead, pretending to give the other man my full attention. I smirked at him; my expression was much friendlier, but my professional mask was still firmly in place.

"Keene?" I certainly hoped he was since all my brothers were supposed to be here somewhere. It might be close to bankers' hours, but it was rare for my brothers to cut out of work before seven. My plan was to put them all on the spot and have no option but to say yes to us imposing on Gideon and leaving early to have a cookout at his place. I missed them and wanted some family time. "I'm afraid I'm not completely sure. You're more than welcome to check, though. Take the second hallway down on the right. He's the third door on the left." It was a major breach in protocol, but I wanted to push the jerk in front of me further. Besides, he would be much more apt to do something if it were just the two of us. The man smirked, seeming to follow my thoughts, and took a step back.

"Thank you for the information," he said, leaning back on his heels, "but I'm fine waiting here." Until the asshole left remained unsaid.

I sighed in irritation—the man just had to be a buzzkill—before turning back to Mr. Gym Muscles in front of me, who looked like he was about to have an aneurism over being ignored. He might be handsome to most, but I was around the most beautiful and handsome regularly, and as the saying goes, beauty was only skin deep.

"As I was saying," I let my voice ice over again. "You would have been provided an itinerary. Any questions should be directed to your Human Resources liaison."

"Look, sweetheart—"

My eyes narrowed at him. I hated pet names. Especially from men who thought they could take liberties because I had a pretty face and they thought they were God's gift to women. I stood and snagged a pen that Maria had on her desk. My heels, a necessary part of the ensemble I wore to maintain my image, would be a hindrance in an actual fight, but I didn't have much hope things would get that interesting with Keene's military buddy in the room. If he were truly Keene's friend, he wouldn't be able to stop himself from saving me—after all, being a hero was pretty much ingrained into any good military personnel, active duty or not. I was betting on very recently active, judging by his awareness. It took a while for the edge to wear off, but his over-regulation haircut clued me into his likely change in status.

Cutting Mr. Gym Muscles off, I waved a hand toward the door. "Mr. ... I'm sorry, I've forgotten your name. You have your way forward. The office is closed for the day, and I have plans, so I'm sorry to say you're going to need to leave now."

His jaw opened and shut as he stood there, stunned, before pointing to the second man. "He's still here," he argued, his face turning red and his fist flexing. I felt my spark of hope for a good fight grow. Looking over at the stranger, I made a show of studying him.

"You look trustworthy. If I give you a key, will you lock up behind you?" I asked, making a show of looking around for the stuff I didn't bring in with me.

He smirked, clearly understanding my game, nodding once. "Sure. Anything I can do to help a pretty lady. Should I—"

Asshole took one step toward me, his aggravation past the point of being contained. The stranger for Keene broke off, coming toward us as if to stop Mike, but I was quicker. I grabbed a handful of blond hair and, in a blur, slammed the idiot's head against the counter. The sound of skull against marble was satisfying, as was the man's yell of hurt and surprise. Holding the pen in my hand like a weapon, I balanced on the balls of my feet, waiting for the charge I knew was coming.

"What's going on out here?" My brother Boone appeared in the hallway, walking toward us.

Mike the Asshole was holding his nose, muttering something about an assault, but I put on my most innocent expression.

"Just trying to stay occupied, waiting on all y'all to finish up for the day. I was just about to take out the trash." Seeing my brother was the last missing piece I needed to settle back into the "home me," bringing my Texas accent back in full force.

The other man snorted, and Boone looked at him. "Brody, right?" he asked, extending a hand and ignoring me for the moment.

Brody returned the handshake. "Nice to see you again. Keene still here?" he asked, and my brother nodded, pointing him in the direction he needed to go. The stranger—Brody—glanced at me, giving me a respectful nod before disappearing down the hall. I resisted the urge—barely—to check out his ass to see if it was as spectacular as his front. My brother was present after all, and apparently, I'd missed him enough to give him a break and not get him worked up any more than he was already.

Boone turned his attention back to me, sighing. "Does trouble have to follow you everywhere you go?"

Not about to admit that I created it on purpose more often than not, I put my hands on my hips indignantly.

"Strictly speaking, you brought this one here," I drawled. "He claims to be here for a job interview but, assuming he hasn't been washed out of the selection process already, I think I did your job for you and illustrated why he wouldn't qualify based on our code of conduct." Because I was right, and at that point the possibility of getting a good tussle in was pretty much zero—no way would Boone let me play at the office—I changed subjects. "Oh, and I figured out what we're getting Maria for her birthday. We're going to give her and her family a vacation on the East Coast. We'll have to plan pretty quickly to get the right rental and in time for the whale migration, but I know she'll love it."

Boone ran a hand down his face, the picture of exasperation, but really, he grew up with me, so he should be used to my antics. "What did he do?" He pointed to the still bent-over man between us.

"This asshole? Besides being in a piss-poor mood, he called me sweetheart." I might have to deal with misogynistic attitudes modeling, but at home, I could be myself. Me, myself, and I had little tolerance for shitty behavior.

"Well, then," Boone nodded in sarcastic sympathy, "he totally deserved it." Finally, he pulled me in for a hug, waiting until I squeaked in protest before kissing me on the head and pulling back.

I smiled at him and tilted my head back to give him a wink. "I'm glad you agree. Now, what are your thoughts on dinner?"

Chapter 3

Brody

I took a breath before rapping on Keene's door. The goddess at the front desk had certainly gotten me off balance, that was for sure. It shouldn't surprise me that someone working for Accardi Tactical, paper pusher or not, would have at least the basics of self-defense, and I was a little ashamed to admit that I'd been thrown off by the stunning woman. Just because someone was pretty, or in her case, the most beautiful woman I'd ever seen, didn't mean they also couldn't throw a punch or shoot a gun. I was ready to jump in to save her, the hero to her damsel in distress. At least until she'd risen from her chair. Her stance, the pen, and the look in her eye had all but screamed that not only could she take care of herself—a good and likely necessary thing considering the mouth on her and the package it was attached to—but that she had expert training. Most couldn't size someone up that quickly, but I'd survived on this planet for thirty-three hard-as-fuck years by making quick assessments and believing my gut. They were necessities for someone like me, and they were skills I'd kept honed. They were also nagging me at that moment. I knew that woman from somewhere, but try as I might, I couldn't place her. It was rare for me to forget a face or a name, and I couldn't remember either in that case, but again, my gut jabbed at my brain, telling it to get in gear. Someone that beautiful was not forgettable, not by a man who had any brain cells and a healthy sex drive, at least.

Shaking my head to clear it, I banged my knuckles against the closed door in front of me, the irritation I felt at being summoned like a kid to the principal's office coming back full force. Hearing a muffled yell, I opened the door and closed it behind me.

Keene, the second eldest in the Accardi clan, sat behind his desk, his suit jacket thrown carelessly across the back of his chair and his dress shirt rolled up his forearms. It always surprised me to see him in a suit—or the remnants of one. Whether it was because I was used to seeing him in uniform or he just never seemed like the suit-type, I wasn't sure.

"You summoned," I drawled, letting my deep Texas twang come out full force, and Keene rolled his eyes.

"Dramatic much?" he asked, looking away from his computer and hitting a button, blacking out the screen. I wasn't offended—I wasn't an employee, though not for lack of trying on his part. Rising, he stalked across the room, and I met him halfway, pulling it in for a bro-hug before we both flopped down into our respective chairs.

"Have a situation," I repeated his text from memory. "Need to see you as soon as you can clear your schedule. Meet me at the office tonight or the training complex tomorrow morning." My lip curled in humor. "You presumed an awful lot. For all you knew, I could have been backpacking in the Himalayas."

Keene snorted. "Like you would take vacation time."

I raised an eyebrow, "I haven't done anything *but* take vacation since I got out." Six months of rehabbing and trying to get my head on straight.

Keene gave me a look, telling me he knew I was feeding him shit, but he would let it pass. "I guess you're wondering why I asked you here."

"No," I deadpanned, "never had the thought. I just drove my ass an hour to see you 'cause I missed your ugly mug."

Keene laughed, and I relaxed. If he still had his humor, no one was dead or dying. Oddly enough, we hadn't been close when we served, though I was closer to him now than anyone else. We were part of different teams, and Keene got out a few years ago, but when I was released from the hospital and went home, he was the first visitor I had. Realizing that I didn't have much—as in nothing—in the way of support, he stopped by several days a week, making sure I had groceries and didn't drown myself down the bottle so far that I couldn't pull myself out of it. After life started to look a little brighter, he made sure to bully me back into the land of the living. Hell, he continued to drag my ass to a monthly poker night with some of our mutual buddies.

Leaning back, he ran a hand over his hair. It was longer than I'd ever seen it, styled and cut in a way that screamed wealthy businessman instead of the military man I knew him to be. His blue eyes looked weary and confused. He barked out a laugh, but it was self-directed and had no humor. "I need to hire you."

"You've been trying to hire me since I got my official discharge papers. My decision won't change. I might work well *with* a team, but I don't do well working *for* a team." Never again would I take orders from someone, even if it was someone I respected. My last assignment had resulted in several good men losing their lives and a few more of us lucky to still be breathing, all because two politicians got in a pissing match over territory neither of their countries had a claim to. And despite knowing the shitty situation, the commanding officer let us walk into a death trap without so much as a warning.

"No, not A.T. *I* need to hire you."

I cocked my head. Accardi Tactical was widely considered the best advanced tactical training school in the country, if not the world. SWAT teams across the country came there to train, as did the Secret Service, and I personally knew that the wait list for top-tier operators to come in for additional training was a mile long. Not only did they hire the best, but they trained the best. Keene's list of contacts was assuredly a who's who of military and civilian contractors, again assuming he didn't have over a hundred individuals on his payroll that could and would jump to do his and his brothers' bidding.

He saw my expression and continued, "I have a situation brewing. At least, I think I do." He looked a bit bewildered. "I have a family member who I believe needs additional protection."

"And you can't use your own company because ..." I let the question hang in the air.

He snorted, his look of confusion still in place. "Two reasons, one making more sense to me than the other."

"And," I pressed again, feeling like I was pulling teeth. Keene was tight-lipped. His business and our past service made it a necessity, but he was being extra tight today. "Look," I said when he hesitated again. "You asked me here, clearly needing help. But I can't help you if I don't understand the situation. If you don't feel comfortable talking to me, I can leave, and we both can forget this entire day, no harm, no foul." I offered the out, and I meant it. I didn't want to deal with drama, and even knowing as much as I did told me it was a stickier situation than I wanted to get involved in. But he was already shaking his head.

"The first reason is that the family member in question apparently has it in their contract that neither A.T. nor anyone trained or employed by us may be hired on their behalf without their expressed permission, which will not be granted."

I grunted. While I didn't understand why, the reason itself made sense.

"And the second is that my brother doesn't think it's necessary."

Before I could ask for clarification, the door opened, and Boone stepped inside. "Lessia's home, and we've been summoned to Gideon's for burgers," he said as he closed the door. "Royce is on crowd control, so we probably have about twenty minutes before both of our phones blow up and twenty-one before they get suspicious." He spoke to Keene but kept his eyes on me, clearly assessing me.

I'd lived in and around alpha males long enough, and was old enough, that even though my natural knee-jerk reaction called for me to match his challenge stare for stare, I kept my attitude in check, letting him look his fill before turning back to Keene. "So, your brother Gideon is the one who's in trouble?" I asked, remembering enough poker gossip and venting to know he had three brothers.

Keene shook his head. "Gideon is the one who thinks protection isn't necessary, which makes no sense." He looked over at his brother, who nodded in agreement. "Gideon is the most protective of all of us. He's the oldest and a pain in all of our asses. He's the reason we all have our own security protocols. I—we—don't understand why he'd allow a family member to run loose with threats against them without doing something about it."

"Who's the family member?" Curiosity had gotten the better of me, and I snapped my mouth shut, wishing I could take the words back. It didn't matter in the long run, and I still hoped I could get out of the conversation without being backed into a corner and forced to accept a job the client didn't want anyone to have and one I certainly didn't want.

Keene started to answer, but his brother cut him off. "That information is need-to-know. Unless you agree to the assignment, you don't."

"So, why haven't you talked to Gideon? You know, asked him why he's acting out of character?" I was grasping at straws, but I knew if push came to shove, I would do this favor for Keene if he asked. I owed him that. Owed him so much more than that. But damn if I wanted to. I might not be ready to join the dead, but I sure as hell wasn't sure I wanted to be part of the living again.

Boone spoke up, "Told us to leave it be, that he had it handled. But we checked. The guard assigned to them wasn't qualified to get a job as a mall cop, let alone protect someone like—" He cut himself off, took a breath, and paced over to his brother's side table to pour himself three fingers worth of whatever alcohol was in the decanter before starting again. "The person in question has received quite a bit of hate mail, fans have tried and failed to gain access to their home in the past, and several groups have recently targeted them, protesting at events they attend. The threats have turned more and more serious as time has gone on. Now, particularly, they seem to have an individual whose obsession and focus has become past the point of creepy and deep into disturbed and dangerous. We've gotten reports of this person getting through security into what should have been secure dressing rooms and hotels. They've even snuck in and left 'gifts' at random locations that are not common knowledge or easy to access, like seats of vehicles or tables at restaurants."

He downed the contents in the shot glass in one go, motioning to Keene and me in an unspoken question. We both shook our heads, and Keene continued. "I don't understand why our brother is acting so out of character. But we aren't going to sit back and let something happen to—"

Boone cut him off. "I know it's not fair to saddle you with this, but Keene and I were able to strong-arm the company they work for into hiring you full-time. You don't work for us, nor have you officially trained here, so we aren't breaching any contract parameters. Make no mistake, the people who hired you are worried about the danger, but our family member is going to throw a fit that we interfered. This isn't necessarily going to be pleasant."

I took the warning for what it was, but there wasn't anything I could do about it. I sighed, looking at Keene. "You calling a marker in for this?" I asked, wanting it crystal clear that I wasn't accepting the job happily but that I would do it honorably. Our code might be archaic to some, but anyone who had fought in combat lived by it. Keene had saved my life—I knew that without a doubt. I literally owed him for every breath I took. He was my brother, though not by blood. If he wanted me on babysitter duty, I would take the mission on with as much gusto and attention as I had anyone assigned to me when I was enlisted.

"Yes." The answer was immediate and resolute. I stood, extending my hand to his, grasping it at the wrist in a warrior's hold. "Then I guess you have yourselves a personal security officer, gentleman."

Boone plopped down in the seat next to me, and I realized just how worried he was. Whomever they were concerned about, they really loved them. "Now, can I know who exactly I'm supposed to be protecting?" I asked.

Keene smirked, his humor returning now that he knew I was on board. "Our baby sister."

Fuck.

Chapter 4
Alessia

Something was up. I wasn't sure what it was yet, but you could be damn sure I would get to the bottom of it. Boone had disappeared immediately after assisting me in taking out the trash—not that he'd let me join in on any of the fun. Royce hadn't even let me say hi to Keene or get a better look at the excellent male specimen who was his friend, whisking Gideon and me out of the building before I had a chance to do much more than blink. Gideon looked just as suspicious as I did, and that in itself was a red flag. My brothers were like the four musketeers. All for one and one for all or, more accurately, all against one when it came to them and anyone else. That their leader was left out of the loop boded poorly for at least one of us. Normally, I would say that would be Gideon, but the looks Royce gave me when he thought I wasn't looking had me worried.

"Aunt Lessia!" I turned at the excited shout, leaning down to hug the bouncing little girl and stumbling back a step as she flung herself at me.

"Hello, my darlin'," I cooed, wrapping her in a tight hug. "How is it you grow even prettier every time I see you? And I hear you aced your science quiz. I'm so proud of you." It was important to me that my niece saw herself as capable and smart as well as beautiful. We were born with our genetics—to me, that wasn't something to be proud of. It was something one used, like wealth you inherited or knowledge your parents passed down to you, like learning how to change a tire. In my case, it was my father teaching me how to dismantle and reassemble a Glock when I was eight in less time than some people could blink.

She smiled at me, her deep blue eyes a carbon copy of her dad's, and my heart jerked a bit. Family was everything, and that right there was what I needed. "How long are you in town this time? Do we have time for mani-pedis tomorrow?" She practically bounced from foot to foot in excitement, with my arms still wrapped around her, causing us both to sway.

Gideon rolled his eyes, and I forced myself to hold my family persona in place. I might need my family, but they didn't know me, the real me, anymore. For a family that valued each other more than anything, we certainly kept a lot of secrets. We hadn't even realized Gideon was married all those years ago—let alone expecting a baby—until he called to tell us that his wife had died in childbirth. I didn't even know he was seeing someone, but considering it was ten years ago and I was just a teenager in high school, that wasn't completely unexpected. Though I certainly got a crash course in baby rearing. With Gideon's hands full of learning everything he could in anticipation of taking over Accardi Tactical, child care had been left largely to me. There was no better birth control for a sixteen-year-old than a newborn baby to take care of, that was for sure.

Diapers and sleepless nights and endless crying were better than any sex-ed class.

"Do you need some girl time?" I asked with sympathy. We were two against a horde, and the overprotectiveness I had to deal with, having four older brothers, was almost as bad as being the only grandchild and niece surrounded by male relatives.

She nodded. "Do you think they can get us in last minute?"

I smiled and finally let her loose from my arms. "I think we can persuade them." I winked at her before looking over her head at my brother. "As long as your dad says I can steal you away after school tomorrow."

Gia laughed. "Tomorrow is Saturday, Aunt Lessia."

Gideon looked grumpy, but I knew he realized how much his daughter needed a female role model, and heaven help her, I was it. If he knew what happened during our so-called "spa days" I wouldn't be allowed to see the little munchkin until she turned eighteen.

"Of course, you can spend time with your aunt," he said. "Though why a ten-year-old needs a mani-pedi, I will never understand or agree with. Can't you guys just go to the movies or get ice cream, like you did when you were six?"

He would never know that those ice cream dates began with lessons in self-defense. I changed the subject before Gia could say anything that might give us away. "I'm thinking of taking a step back from modeling. Not quitting," I said in a rush before anyone could cheer. It was no secret my brothers disapproved of my public profession, and Gia would love to have me around on a more permanent basis. "Just cutting back a bit. My contracted photoshoots with Valencia wrap up soon, and after that there are some public events I need to attend. But I'm not going to renew my contract with them. I'm going to start being pickier with what I do and who I do it with."

"Getting burned out?" Royce asked, looking at me critically. Gideon did the same, and I averted my eyes, staring at the roaring fire Gideon had started. I loved his backyard—it was large, private, and comfortable. I could be myself there, apart from the rest of the world. But even being myself personality-wise, I couldn't fail to remember that there were pieces of me even my loved ones couldn't know about. Like the reason I was pulling back was that my popularity was too much. It was hard to do your work for your country when your cover persona was front and center in everyone's minds. I couldn't risk anyone piecing together my travel habits with the kills I made. True, I only completed a few assignments a year, and most were made to look like accidents or natural causes, but the fact was I walked a tightrope between being popular enough to get the jobs that took me to the places I needed to go and so recognizable that I couldn't continue to do my current job. Though, Royce's words made my chest tighten for just a moment.

"Something like that," I said finally, seeing Royce shoot another glance at Gideon. Only instead of looking at each other in that silent language that all my brothers seemed to be fluent in, Royce looked almost irritated with Gideon. Maybe he was the one on the chopping block after all.

"Are we too late?" Boone's voice boomed across the yard as he and Keene came walking over from the side of the house. "I'm starving." He swung Gia up in a hug, whirling her off her feet before plopping her back down. Keene was quick to do the same, and I smiled, loving her giggles.

"We were waiting for you," Gia said as she grabbed both her uncles by the hand and dragged them to the firepit with the rest of us. Gideon was cooking burgers and manning the grill while I and everyone else relaxed in our chairs by the fire. No one cooked like Gideon, and I fully intended on taking advantage of his culinary expertise by eating myself sick.

"Awesome!" Boone didn't pause before heading into the house. "I'm grabbing a beer. Does anyone need anything?"

Keene frowned at his back but didn't say anything. "I'll take a glass of wine," I called. What was going on with the family tonight? Keene, Royce, and Gideon exchanged glances, silently communicating in the way that drove me crazy. I could never understand their wordless language, which was probably why they created the damn thing in the first place.

When Boone returned, a half-empty beer in one hand and a glass of red wine for me in the other, I saw him shoot his own look at Royce and nod almost imperceptibly. All the hidden currents put a damper on my mood. I'd been gone a lot, especially the last two years—building my reputation as a model was a lot more work than most realized—and once you were successful, you had to stay in the eye of those who mattered to keep your spot at the top. But the main reason I'd been gone was my fear that I would slip. Even now, especially now, I had to think about ensuring that my brothers didn't know what I did for a living. My ability to continue to do what I did best revolved around them believing I was nothing more than a beauty-product, spa-day-loving fiend who sold her body by way of pictures to make her living. Life just sucked sometimes.

A few hours later, I'd devoured two burgers, two glasses of wine, and zero green vegetables. As much as I wanted a s'more, I didn't have the room, so I just ate the chocolate bar because—hello ... chocolate. God, I loved being home.

Gia, pouting because she had a bedtime that Gideon made her stick to, had said goodnight a while ago. She'd tried to bargain for more time, but my brother had held firm. He made an outstanding dad, even if he was a bit of a hard-ass. Lord knew that little girl wanted for nothing save a mother. Gia and I had had a serious conversation when I started our "girl time adventures" regarding that very subject. She wanted her dad to marry for love, not because he thought she was missing out on the company of someone with breasts. My words, not hers, but I understood her, mainly because it was my opinion about my dad as well. My mother died from cancer when I was thirteen, and there wasn't a day that went by that her presence wasn't missed by all of us.

"Y'all going to tell me what's going on here?" I finally asked, feeling like I'd given them enough time to let their guard down. They had expected the inquisition to start the moment Gia was sent to bed or possibly after Gideon returned from checking on her a few minutes ago. I hoped to get more reaction out of them by stalling.

"What makes you think anything has been going on? Beyond the norm, that is?" Boone asked, bringing his beer bottle to his lips. I'd lost count of how many he'd had throughout the night, but his speech wasn't slurred, and his eyes were only slightly glassy, so while I wasn't about to let him drive himself home, I wasn't worried about him getting wasted.

"There were so many conversations about people without them being a part of the conversation my ears are ringing, although none of y'all said so much as a word. So, spill." I narrowed my eyes at Royce, who flushed. Gideon was the leader of their little troop, and Keene was his second-in-command. I knew they wouldn't break, but Royce and Boone were the weak links. Going after Boone when I was completely sober and he wasn't felt wrong, so Royce was in my crosshairs. I glanced at the two eldest, gauging if they would stop my interrogation, when I noticed Keene also refraining from meeting my eye or anyone else's.

That tidbit, which cemented my thought that their ranks were fractured, no matter how slight, allowed me to pounce. "Why would the boys be keeping secrets from you?" I stared straight at Gideon.

His jaw tightened, and I knew I hit a bull's-eye on my first volley. He knew he was out of the loop, and he didn't like it any more than I did. I might not like them ganging up on me, but at least when they all agreed, I knew whatever they were doing had been both discussed and well-planned. Anyone going rogue did not bode well for anyone because it meant they were acting rashly and without much forethought.

"And you three," I pointed to him, Keene, and Royce, "are mad at him for some reason." My finger had moved to Boone, who was finishing off the beer bottle.

"And," I moved back the original three I'd singled out, "you three have been giving me weird looks all day. I want to know what's going on. Is it Daddy?"

I knew it didn't make sense. They wouldn't have kept Gideon out of the loop if it was, but my thoughts always went to the worst-case scenario. My relationship with our father was strained, but it didn't mean I didn't love him wholeheartedly and worry about him as he got older.

"Just worried about you, is all." Boone was staring at me, studying me. It took everything in me to act normal, not to freeze or flinch. His eyes were a lighter blue than the rest of my brothers', more like the summer sky on a sunny day. Gideon's eyes were so dark they almost looked black when he was irritated or angry, which was most of the time. Keene and Royce both had shades in between those two. Not sure which brother was which in the birth order, just look at their eyes, I thought, not for the first time.

Raising an eyebrow, I tossed a smirk his way. "I'm a big girl. I'm one of the most in-demand models in the world. I go where I want, when I want, how I want. Feeling the urge to go clubbing, I can hop on a plane and check out the hottest clubs in Germany. Want to do some gambling? Monte Carlo by morning. If I need some R and R? I can get into the best spa Europe offers. I have enough money to retire in the lap of luxury if I play my cards right and more than enough to keep me out of trouble when I put my fist in someone's face for being a dick because my brothers taught me how to defend myself and not to take shit from anyone. What is there to worry about?"

Keene spoke up, and I knew trouble was brewing when he suddenly stared down Gideon even as he spoke to me. "We know you have threats against you. You've been pulling away the last few years. From the company, from us."

I flinched, unable to help myself.

"You have problems, princess—you come to your family, not run from them." The anger in his voice wasn't directed at me exactly, but I felt it all the same.

"My not being here has nothing to do with my family and everything to do with my modeling schedule." I defended myself. I wasn't about to tell them it had everything to do with me—I was splitting hairs with that one, and I wasn't going to discuss it. "And threats are nothing new. I've been dealing with them since I pushed Bitsy Merkle down into a mud puddle when I was in kindergarten."

"Preschool," Gideon corrected.

"Regardless," I plowed on—my brothers remembered the highlight reel of my early years better than I did. Mainly because they had to pull my ass out of the fire every time I jumped in it with both feet until I was old enough to do it myself. "At Gideon's insistence, I agreed to a bodyguard on my last shoot. I also promised him I would allow Valencia to keep one with me from the time I got off the plane until I was wheels up for home. Not that it's needed," I defended, "but the guy they hired has my back."

Boone snorted, his lips loose from the alcohol. "And is as qualified to protect your ass as a rent-a-cop working at a strip mall."

I wasn't about to tell him how right he was. "The individual was a complete professional. He cleared every room prior to me entering and slept with a clear line of sight to the only entry and exit point to my suite." Falling asleep on the couch in the middle of channel surfing, even though he snored loud enough to wake the dead, still counted. I wasn't about to admit that I'd walked right past him to hit the gym that morning, coming back, showering, and packing before Hammer had even stirred.

"And if you want to know, I've been pulling away from the company because I don't feel like I have much to contribute. I don't have anything to do with A.T., so I guess I don't feel comfortable at board meetings. I mean, how can I vote on pertinent items when I have no idea how they would affect the company? I've pretty much voted with the four of you anyway the last few years, so I don't see much point in clearing my schedule to attend the quarterly meetings." All of it was true, just not the whole truth.

"Would you like to? Contribute more, or at least catch up on what's going on with the business?" Gideon asked shrewdly.

More than anything. I shrugged. "I have time this week. Maybe I'll stop by and pester y'all at work."

"Can you come by Monday morning?" Keene asked, and Boone went still. I sensed a trap but didn't have enough information to figure out whom it was for—me, Gideon, or Boone.

"Sure." I shrugged, rising to my feet. "Is nine going to be too early for the rug rat?" I asked Gideon, stretching my arms over my head.

He shook his head. "You haven't even called to make the appointment yet."

Placing a hand on my hip, I struck a pose. "Brother-mine," I said, sliding into my model persona as easily as other women put on heels. "There is no way in hell anyone is going to tell me no." I toned down the attitude, serious now. "Besides, I miss our girl-time as much as she does. I figured we would make a day of it if you don't mind? Mani-pedi, facials, and maybe end with some ice cream and princess movies at my place. I can turn it into a sleepover if you need me to." I made the offer, even though I knew he wouldn't take it. As far as I could tell, Gideon had slept with only a handful of women since his wife had died, and none of them more than once. But I wanted him to know I had his back if he wanted to cut loose for the night.

Gideon smiled at me, shaking his head. "A day with her is enough time for one weekend. You'll probably be counting the last few hours until I pick her up. I love her to death, but she has more energy than that pink bunny on TV."

He wasn't wrong about the energy part, but I had a secret weapon in my arsenal. Odds were that she would be asleep before the opening line of the movie ended. "I can handle my niece for a day," I sniffed, giving all of my brothers a hug goodbye. "Face it, big brother, she might be a handful, but she's got nothing on me."

I pulled into my driveway a few minutes later. All of us Accardi siblings lived within ten minutes of each other, and I loved how easily it was to pop in and out. I sighed as I waited for the garage door to close, feeling the comfort of my sanctuary swirl around me like a warm hug. I loved my house. It was a sprawling single-story with vaulted ceilings and large doorways. I was tall for a woman, but I felt small in it. The entire interior was open space decorated in what I called cozy elegance. It was flashy enough to feel like a finished home but comfortable enough that I could put my feet on the furniture without feeling like I had committed a grave sin. The entire house was decorated in gray and white. White cabinetry, baseboards, and framing complemented the white-washed-looking wood floors. I balanced out the white with various shades of warm gray tones on the walls. It gave the home a classic look, and the touches of bright, bold color in the throw pillows and décor made it feel homey.

But just like me, the house had secrets. After disarming my alarm and clearing the rooms, I checked to ensure no one had planted listening devices or surveillance equipment before returning to the car and grabbing my luggage. As much as I would love to fall into my bed, I had a job to finish. I wheeled the suitcase into the mudroom, closing the door and locking it. Pulling out the makeup case, I tossed my personal clothes—because I sure as shit wasn't owning something that I couldn't toss into the regular wash unless it was for work—into the washer, starting the load. Once the water started filling the washer, I grabbed the case and turned to the large cabinet that held coats and dresses. Pushing the few garments in there aside, I stepped in. When I got to the back of the closet, I reached up, placing my fingers on the ledge at the top. Feeling the back panel swing open, I stepped down carefully, securing the hidden door behind me before reaching for the light switch.

Lights hummed to life, flooding the narrow stairway. I made my way down, scanning my fingerprints again before punching in a code when I reached the bottom, where another door slid open. As homey as the main floor was, the lower level was the polar opposite—stark and sterile. The harsh lights illuminated a basement that ran the entire length of the house. My office was tucked away in the far corner, a safe the size of a walk-in closet, with my room of weapons next to it. Other than those rooms, the entire thing was one big open space. A kitchenette setup lined one wall, with a comfy couch and living area next to it. I had another couch in my office that I could sleep on if needed, making the entire downstairs one large panic room.

Not in the mood to waste time, I walked to the corner that housed what I needed most at the moment—my incinerator. Built into the wall, it was large enough to burn a body. Not that I had the occasion to need it, but I liked being prepared for various scenarios. Placing my bag on the counter, I zipped it open and removed my body suit, gloves, and scalpel. The material was sticky with blood—the scalpel covered in it—but there was no way I could have disposed of it before now. I certainly wasn't leaving DNA evidence behind in my suite. The suit and gloves were specially designed for my purposes—they absorbed a lot of blood without dripping and attracted loose or falling fibers, hair, and skin cells. The material also didn't bleed through to the skin, which was why I could make such a bloody mess and yet scale a building and jump back into my shower with minimal mess and effort.

I fired up the incinerator, waiting for it to heat. While I did, I screwed off the top of a hole in the floor nearby, careful not to touch anything but the lid. Gingerly, I lowered the scalpel into the liquid. Hissing, it started bubbling immediately, and I quickly re-screwed the top back on. The acid would eat away at the metal until nothing remained. I would check tomorrow just to be thorough, of course. The clothing burned up quickly, turning to ash in seconds. I ran the unit a few more minutes, then turned it off. Tomorrow, once everything cooled, I would sweep up the ash and dump it down the drain, running the water to ensure it was just a memory.

With my cleanup complete, I turned on my heel to the office where my secure line was. Picking up the phone, I hit a button on the side. The screen on the base of the phone pulsed red for a few beats before turning green, letting me know the line was secure. I keyed in the number I knew by heart, waiting as it rang twice before someone picked up the phone on the other end.

"Shield," the gruff voice said, sounding like rocks in a blender. The familiar sound soothed me as few things could.

"Sword," I replied, both of us letting the other know we were uncompromised and alone. While I talked, I keyed up my computer, going through the footage that the system stored from my home security system while I was out of the country.

"How was your trip?" he asked, and I could hear classical music in the background. Try as he might, I never could tell Mozart, Handel, and all his other favorites apart. Give me country music any day of the week. Classic didn't necessarily mean good, and in my opinion, some of that music should have been buried with its composers.

"Successful. Other than the fact I might have picked up skin cancer from spending the entire day trying not to fry like eggs in a diner. My bodyguard practically had to peel me out of the shower." I smiled, thinking about Hammer's expression when he saw me covered in beauty goop in that tiny towel when I answered the door. I clicked through the video clips. Other than a few birds landing in the yard, it hadn't noted any movement. Not even my brothers stopped by to snoop while I was gone.

"How was he?"

"Perfect." He hung up with little fanfare, liking to keep things short and to the point.

I sighed, hating that most of the males in my life seemed to have difficulty ending a phone conversation. My handler was probably the worst offender. In the almost nine years I'd worked for the U.S. government, I couldn't name a time he'd actually ended a phone call with the word "goodbye." I seemed to be the only assassin who'd been raised with manners—my daddy would have given me a whooping had I ended a phone call by simply hanging up the phone—but no matter how many times I complained, it never changed. Of course, I'd known my handler for so long, much longer than when he'd recruited me at eighteen, and even in person, he never seemed to know how to "people" well, so maybe it wasn't manners as much as it was just the way his brain was wired.

Yawning, I powered down the computer. It had been a long few days with little sleep. I couldn't trust Hammer to have my back—he wasn't a true professional, after all. The trade-off of my profession—knowing how easily one could get into places they weren't supposed to—meant I didn't comfortably sleep without the full security I had at home. Catnaps sufficed to get me through, but I was wiped. And with Oliver escalating, I slept even less than I typically did. He wasn't to the stage of worry—for me, anyway. But he had me paying more attention, more on edge, than in previous encounters. The trick with the teddy bear in the car last month wasn't original or difficult since I could tell as soon as the driver was questioned that he'd lied when he denied leaving the car unattended. But the red rose on the table at Arnoldo's last week was more concerning. I'd made those reservations less than an hour before, and the rose was placed there sometime between the busboy setting the table and the maître d' leading me to it—a timetable of fewer than twenty minutes. He was lucky the cameras were down, but I'd stopped using Valencia's complementary service to make restaurant and event reservations and purchases. I was sure he'd somehow charmed someone into giving him my schedule. I hadn't even realized we'd been in the same country, let alone the same city. Mentally, I shrugged. If his parents didn't get him under control, I'd have to come up with a plan of action. Until then, I was heading up to my bed for a much-needed night of dreamless sleep.

Chapter 5

ALESSIA

Despite jetlag and my late night, I was up before sunrise. I tidied up the basement, finishing the laundry I had started last night. Changing into a sports bra and workout shorts, I made my way to the guesthouse. I had transformed it into a top-of-the-line workout room before I'd even moved into the house years ago, enabling me to get a ten-mile run on a treadmill before Matteo arrived without leaving my property.

Chipper as always, even though most barely considered it morning, he handed me a black coffee that was strong enough to stick a spoon in it straight up and kissed my cheek as he passed.

"How's my Belle?" he asked with the slightest hint of a French accent, smiling innocently as I grumbled into my coffee. He knew I hated when he called me that. "So," he said when I didn't answer him, instead scarring my vocal cords by downing half the cup of piping-hot nirvana in one swallow. "What's the plan today? You want to spar or just get a workout in?"

I considered my options. My hands hurt some from my free climb, mainly my fingers, but the idea of a worthy opponent in the ring was too much to pass up. I couldn't do it nearly as often as I liked, and I was afraid of losing my edge. We couldn't let ourselves go as much if I had a modeling gig—bruises that I couldn't easily cover or explain when I was on a modeling job were problematic. "Spar," I said, happy the next shoot required me in gowns that would cover me enough to hide most of the evidence of our bout, then sent him a wicked grin. "Then we'll have to have you prep for a little one-on-one if you have the time."

He groaned. "I already trained one generation. Do I have to help the next one, too?" Matteo wasn't that much older than I was, but the ten-year age gap was enough for him to act like he was an old man compared to me. Granted, he'd helped me develop, but he was around to help keep both of our skills sharp more than bring my skills along.

Rolling my eyes, I reached for the tape. Matteo was fine with just gloves and head protection, but I had to do everything I could to keep the damage to a minimum. "Come on, Matt," I taunted, knowing he hated when I called him that. "You know you love my niece. And more importantly, you want to claim responsibility for her abilities when she shows the world how kick-ass she is."

He shook his head, but I knew him too well to take anything he said seriously. Matteo loved Gia, and Gia loved having one other person besides me who was in her circle of secrets. We both focused on each other as we stepped into the middle of the room. Matteo didn't take the time to stretch; he just pulled off his shirt, telling me he had anticipated my choice and had done a quick warm-up before coming over. His dark brown hair was long, thick, and sticking out in every direction. His brown eyes were several shades warmer than his hair, but they were as sharp and serious as always as he looked me over, dropping into a ready position. Muscles rippled under his skin, which was decorated with tattoos. Army to his core, his service was clear to anyone who looked closely.

"I'm not going to take it easy on you, Belle," he warned, and I grinned, joy coursing through me at the thought of not having to hold back, to pretend I wasn't as capable as I was.

"Bring it," I taunted. "I need it." And I did, on so many levels. I needed the mindlessness of running on pure instinct, not worrying about revealing just how skilled I was or having to pretend to be an ice-bitch model or a beauty-queen sister. I could just be me, the deadly weapon that was honed and forged over years of blood and sweat and secrets. Sometimes I thought they might swallow me whole. Not wanting to waste a single moment of my time, I took the first swing.

I'm not sure how long we went at it, but I was far from done when a tiny alarm sounded. "Shit," I said, pulling away from where Matteo and I had been tussling. "I was supposed to pick her up at nine." I ripped the Velcro on the gloves with my teeth, throwing them to Matteo, who caught them and stuffed them with his own in a drawer on the wall. We both looked at the screen hidden in a cabinet, which showed Gideon's SUV pulling down my winding driveway.

"Helmet," he said calmly, catching that as well and throwing them in with everything else. "It's not nine yet—your brother jumped the gun."

He closed the cabinet as I yanked the tape off my hands and disposed of it in the trash. I snatched for the mats I'd rolled in a corner, throwing them both out on the floor we'd vacated before rushing to the door to open it. "We're over here," I called to Gideon and Gia as they exited the vehicle. Gia waved, skipping over as her dad trailed a few steps behind. "You guys are early," I said, hugging Gia.

"Dad needed to get some work done, and even though I'm not a baby and am perfectly capable of staying at the house by myself," she said pointedly, "it was decided that it would be in everyone's best interest if I were dropped off at your house."

I bit my lip at her attitude, which skimmed just that side of respectful. "I see," I said, looking over at Gideon, who looked a little rough around the edges. Clearly, father and daughter had gone a round or two that morning despite the early hour. Gideon opened his mouth to say something when he noticed movement behind me. I saw his hand twitch, the only indication he fought the urge to grab his gun as Matteo came into view.

"Namaste," he said to my brother, nodding at him before looking at my niece. "And good morning to you too, mini Belle."

"Matteo, I didn't know you'd be here today!" She launched herself at him, and he leaned over to wrap her in a hug.

Gideon's jaw clenched. I knew all my brothers hated Matteo on principle. After all, they were fairly sure that my "personal trainer" also did some other "personal" things to me as well. It was a good way to explain the odd times they saw us together, but I neither confirmed nor denied the question every time they asked for several reasons. One, it worked out in my favor to make them think there was more to our relationship than just the one I claimed was gym-related. Two, I didn't want to have to lie to them any more than necessary, and I couldn't exactly divulge what he was without also spilling the beans on what *I* did. And three, it drove them crazy to think that their little sister had an on-again, off-again, sex-only relationship.

"I'm sorry if we ... interrupted anything," Gideon forced out, his jaw never relaxing.

I smirked. "We were just finishing up." I couldn't help but taunt him. "Yoga, I mean," I continued when his face flushed an angry red.

"When am I old enough for yoga?" Gia asked, looking between her father and me.

"Aren't spa days and nail polish enough?" Gideon asked, looking more than a bit aggrieved at how his morning was going.

"You wouldn't let me take kickboxing, taekwondo, or self-defense," Gia counted off her fingers. "I thought since apparently you think those aren't appropriate, something more girly would be more proper."

Someone's on a roll this morning, I thought, raising my eyebrow at my brother.

In an uncharacteristic move, he wiped his face with his hand, his weariness coming through loud and clear. "I don't know. I'll think about it."

"I just don't understand why you won't let me do active, boy things, like soccer or hiking club, or anything else I've asked to do, but you get mad when I want to do girly things. You make fun of Aunt Lessia for doing beauty things, but that's all I seem to be allowed to do."

The girl wasn't wrong, and I wanted to give her a high five for telling it like it was, without the extreme attitude and snark I would have, but I didn't think it would be appropriate. "Why don't you help Matteo move our mats, and you can show me what you've been learning in gymnastic class?" I offered the reprieve, and my brother looked at me gratefully as she rushed inside to get the floor cleared. Gymnastics was the only thing the two of them had agreed on.

"She's not wrong," I whispered when she was far enough away not to overhear. "You can't be upset at what she's becoming if it's due to your choices. You're molding her into this, not me. I understand how worried you were when she was born. I know you were terrified you would lose them both, but—"

He cut me off like he always did when the subject came up. "You don't have a child. You have no idea—"

It was my turn to cut him off. "Bullshit," I snapped. "I might not have birthed that child," I pointed behind me, "but I raised her just as much as you did. From day one, I loved that girl as if she were my own. Don't you dare tell me that again." I took a breath, more because I didn't want Gia to see us arguing than anything else. "You're going to have to make a choice," I continued, calmer now, "about what kind of adult you want her to become. Because two things are going to happen. She's going to fold and become that Barbie doll you're encouraging her to be, or she's going to rebel and pull away from you." I knew that with absolute certainty. I'd done the same, after all. They just hadn't realized it. None of them had. It made me feel like shit that I was doing it again with the next generation, but I knew what that little girl was going through, what it felt like to want to be one version of yourself while your loved ones wanted you to be another. And because they loved you, and you loved them, you couldn't say what needed to be said, couldn't explode with the hurt and anger that burned in the pit of your stomach like a volcano. Until one day, you had to make a choice, lest all that leashed emotion consumed you and burned you to ash.

If I hadn't been recruited by the government when I had, who knew how bad the fallout would have been. My parents had raised me to be myself, which, for me, meant loving to run the military obstacle course at A.T. and shoot guns. But when my mom died when I was thirteen, my dad forced me into a stereotype we used to ridicule. It made me cram my emotions into a box, lest I upset my father. He'd lost the love of his life, after all. How petty was I to deny him the opportunity to take me out shopping if it made him happy? The rationale of being a dutiful daughter, not to rock the boat, kept going, getting worse and worse while I kept more of myself—my real identity—away from him until I couldn't anymore. And when I tried to fix things, to show him just how far off his impression was about me and my likes and dislikes, I'd been betrayed in the worst possible way. Our relationship was strained to the breaking point even so many years later, and I wasn't sure if either of us realized just how close I was to severing ties completely. If it weren't for the rest of my family, I would have walked away years ago. Hell, I hadn't seen Daddy outside our dreaded Sunday dinners in years and, though I'd never admit it out loud, often planned my trips to make it in and out of Texas so that I'd miss the meal on purpose.

Afraid I would say something a little too revealing about my struggles, I took a step back and shut the door in his face with a resounding click. I took one more breath, putting my best "aunt-face" on, and turned around, dusting my hands dramatically. "He has so forth been banished until we complete our dastardly deeds for the day."

Gia giggled. "You're so funny sometimes, Aunt Lessia." She kicked her feet up into a handstand, holding it for several seconds before falling back to her feet.

"Great show of muscle control," Matteo complimented from his position next to her, spotting her in case she needed a save.

"It certainly was," I murmured, causing Gia to beam.

"Dad said we're supposed to have ice cream today. Does that mean we're practicing self-defense instead of karate?" she asked innocently. All our activities had code names. I hated teaching her to deceive her father, but I didn't know how else to balance Gia's desires in life with my brother's decrees.

"I thought I would let you decide," I said, forcing myself to focus on the person in front of me. "Though, Matteo here was hoping to see if you still remember how to throw him to the floor."

She beamed, and Matteo groaned but said nothing. That in itself indicated how much he cared for the little girl. Too bad no one could know what he was or what we were doing. The pictures from my surveillance camera would have been exceptional blackmail—the former Ranger super soldier taken down by a ten-year-old.

We spent two hours working with Gia before calling it quits for the day. I snuck in a quick phone call and booked us at the salon I liked in town—mainly because they had the best food for us to eat while they worked—so we both hurried to shower while Matteo left to do whatever it was he normally did when he wasn't hanging out with me.

I immediately noticed the tail—they weren't going through much trouble to hide it. "Kiddo, does your dad have security on you?" I asked. With a family as well-known, wealthy, and connected as ours, it wasn't unheard of for protection to be warranted. All my brothers really should have full-time security, but none of them save Gideon ever used it. Heck, even Gideon wasn't consistent. I could remember a handful of times in recent years, but with me not exactly present, I couldn't be sure if it was expected or not.

Gia sat up in the back seat, looking behind us at the black SUV. "That's one of Dad's, I think," she said finally, flopping back in her seat. "Usually, he has someone watching me if he's not here." She snickered. "Though it beats me why he did today. He doesn't have anyone assigned to me if I'm with one of the uncles."

I bit my lip, unsure if they assigned the detail despite me or because of me. I would never put my niece in jeopardy, but the fact of the matter was I'd been getting more threats against me lately. Not for killing people, because, yeah, no one knew that part, but because of the modeling gig. Weirdos tended to fixate on pretty women, especially when that face was plastered across every known magazine and fashion line. They latched on to you and didn't want to let go. And the issues with Oliver lately had likely been leaked to Gideon, at least, if not all of them, despite my insistence on the contrary. Had Gideon stuck us with a babysitter as a precaution for that reason, or did he just not see me as being able to take care of myself and Gia the way he trusted my brothers to be able to?

Because either way sucked balls to think about, I kept my mouth shut. "Well, they're in for a pretty boring day today, aren't they?" I winked at her. "Because it's not like we did anything but hang out with Matteo, get beautified, then swung by Sweet Nothings for ice cream before going back to my house to pig out on more junk food and binge-watch some awesome movies."

Gia smiled. "Yep. Can I get nail polish this time?"

I cringed, thinking of Gideon. I didn't want the poor man to have an aneurysm, and she was only ten.

"Only if it's clear." I was firm, ready for an argument, but Gia only nodded. That was the great thing about the kid—she rarely bucked the system, and even then, only if she truly thought that whatever it was she was railing against was not fair. Not in a fit of pre-teen angst, but truly thought an injustice was occurring. She was a hell of a lot more level-headed than I was at her age—my brother's influence, for sure. Gideon always had to think about a situation from all angles before reacting. He was a gruff, borderline rude jerk most of the time, but he was a fair, honest, and caring one. Which was why his daughter's comments that morning had been such a direct hit.

I mentally prepared for the torture of having my hands and feet touched in the name of preserving my cover with my brothers and spending some quality time with my niece—who actually enjoyed it. I hoped she enjoyed my company more than the beauty treatment, but I was too scared to look too closely for fear that I had somehow corrupted her and was actually turning her into a girly girl.

A few hours later, stuffed with some outstanding tiny little cakes and sparkling grape juice—no way would I drink a drop of alcohol when entrusted with the care of my niece—we climbed back into the vehicle. I evaluated my nails as my hands wrapped around the steering wheel. The salon kept a bottle on hand, knowing it was my favorite color. Having Alessia Accardi, one of the top models in the country, frequent their establishment was a major score. But if coming in with almost no notice, having all-we-can-eat cakes, a bottle of sparkling juice served in champagne flutes, and a shade of just the right color red—a color I'd originally picked because it's the exact hue of freshly spilled blood—was all I asked for, I didn't think I was being too demanding.

We both decided we were too full from our spa meal to do ice cream justice, so we ordered to-go, taking it home to eat with our movie. Our ever-present shadow followed, doing a good job of being visible without intruding. A.T. was the best. It didn't surprise me they were exemplary. I pulled into the garage, waiting for the door to close completely before unlocking the car doors so we could exit. Gia waited, holding the bags as I disarmed the alarm and unlocked the entryway, then made herself at home in my living room. I grabbed the bag that had two containers of Rocky Road. "You pick the movie. I'll be right back," I called over my shoulder.

Walking out the front door, I didn't hide my destination. The SUV was still parked at the curb—the driver was on lookout while it looked like the passenger was taking a break, fidgeting with something that was likely a cell phone. They both jumped when the driver saw me, and he said something to his companion before rolling down the window.

"Hey, y'all. I know you probably came prepared with snacks and drinks and such, but I picked up some of the best ice cream this side of the state." I shook the bag for emphasis.

"That's right kind of you, ma'am," the driver said, smiling in appreciation, though he looked uneasy. I imagined it wasn't often that anyone acknowledged a security tail, let alone gave them anything.

He reached for the bag, but I pulled it back. "I have a question if you don't mind." I saw the men exchange looks. "Settle down. I'm not going to ask for anything that will get you in trouble." I resisted the urge to sigh. "Are you here for my niece or me?"

They both froze. "Uh, I don't think that's something we're authorized—"

I cut him off. "Look, I could find out with a phone call to my brothers. Hell, I could send Gia down the street and see if you follow her or stay here. I'm not asking for state secrets here."

"Who says we aren't supposed to be watching both of you?" the passenger spoke for the first time, his New York accent harsh compared to my deep Texas dialect.

I snorted. "Shovel that load of bullshit to someone who wasn't literally raised at A.T. I might not run the company like my brothers, but I grew up there. There's only ever one primary. If you were protecting both of us, I'd have two cars sitting out here, not one."

For a moment, they considered what I said. They might be good at their jobs, but I knew the fear of pissing any of my brothers—their bosses, bosses, boss, or whatever—was enough for them to consider before answering. They must have realized that what I was saying was true because the driver muttered, "You, they assigned us to you."

I absorbed the information, then handed them the bag with little fanfare. "Thank you, gentlemen," I said simply. "Now, the plan for the rest of the day is to stay here, eat ice cream, and watch movies with my niece. I see no reason for you two to stay out here, seeing as you can't even see the house from here. I've set my alarm, locked my doors, and have a fully charged cell phone that is never more than a foot away from me." I waved the device in question.

"That being said, I didn't ask for a protection detail, but I can guess where the order came from, so I'm not going to blame you for waiting for permission from someone with a—" I cut myself off, not wanting my mouth to unload on these two men simply because they had the misfortune of being in front of me when I was having a temper tantrum. I reminded myself to breathe. Patting the car door, I said, "Y'all have a good night now," with as much sweetness as I could muster before walking back into the house without a backward glance.

I heard the movie before I even stepped foot into the living room. Not at all surprised at Gia's movie pick, I grabbed a blanket and wrapped it around both of us before sitting down and taking the ice cream she handed me. Pigging out on sugar and happily ever afters, I smiled when she fell asleep before the movie ended. Gideon was right in saying she had more energy than she knew what to do with, but two hours of exercise, followed by a major sugar crash, would knock out anyone. Struggling not to yawn, I picked up my phone.

ME: MY CHI FEELS IMBALANCED. THINK WE CAN GET SOME MEDITATION IN TOMORROW?

MATTEO: YOU KNOW ME. ALWAYS UP FOR SOME MORE BALANCE AND HARMONY.

ME: CAN I MEET AT YOUR PLACE? I HAVEN'T HAD TIME TO GO SHOPPING YET, AND I'LL WANT BREAKFAST AFTER.

MATTEO: ISN'T SHOPPING WHAT YOU WOMEN LIVE FOR? BESIDES, WHO SAYS I'LL WANT TO COOK?

I sent him an emoji of a middle finger before setting my phone on the counter. I was just about to turn off the television when my home alarm chirped, letting me know someone was in the driveway. Pressing a button on the remote, I pulled up the feed in front of the house. Gideon, as expected. I could just make out the SUV, still parked at the curb at the base of the drive. Letting my anger build, I waited until Gideon unlocked the door, making him use his personal code to turn off the alarm before I got off the couch to meet him in the entryway.

"How did it go?" he asked, and I shushed him.

"Gia fell asleep on the couch," I said smugly, though I felt little of it.

His surprise at that should have amused me, but instead, it poured salt into a wound. He didn't know me as well as he thought he did.

"Any reason why I shouldn't be mad at you?" I asked, letting my temper rise a bit.

Gideon cocked his head, clearing his expression. "Can you be more specific?" he asked, and I gritted my teeth. Damn lawyer, never could give me a straight answer.

"I had a tail today. I thought they were for Gia, but they weren't." A tick in his jaw was his tell, though what it told me was unexpected. "You didn't know," I mused, pretending I wasn't as confused as I felt. "Never thought I'd see the day the four of you broke ranks."

He gritted his teeth. "It's not like that, Lessia. They're just worried about you."

"And you're not?" I questioned, curious to know where he stood.

"Of course, I am," he snapped, "but I also know the harder we try to hold on, the more you squirm away from us, and I like you home."

I startled at that. "I don't—"

He cut me off. "Do that? Hell yeah, you do. The more we try to be there for you, the farther you run. You've always done the opposite of what was expected of you."

That hurt, I wouldn't lie, but damned if I would let him see he drew first blood. "You ever stop to think that my choices have nothing to do with the rest of you?" I shot back, unable to keep my temper in check as I lashed out. "Do you make all the decisions in your life with the thought of the rest of the family? Feel like taking Gia on vacation—I better consult with the family. I think I need a new car—better ask everyone what they think. Hell, I think I might marry the woman who's pregnant with my child—I better ask the family's feelings about it." My anger was in full swing, but I kept my voice from rising too much, not wanting to wake Gia. "I do not make my decisions to spite you. They aren't personal. I'm sorry you don't approve of my job, but you know what—I'm good at it. It gives me a sense of purpose, and I'm proud to do what I do. Just because it wasn't in your plans for me doesn't make what I'm doing wrong or something to sneer at me over. You ever think that I stay away, not because y'all get too close, but because I get too smothered?" I pointed at the driveway. "No one even bothered to consult me before saddling me with a protection detail. Would you have done that if any of you got a threat or two? Hell, you probably have more security concerns than I do, but no one makes any of you get assigned under someone's watchful eye without input."

His eyes turned black, and I knew I'd succeeded in getting him riled, but before he could speak, we both heard Gia call out.

"Be right there," he said, and I took a step back, needing the space.

"You might not have known what they were doing," I whispered. "But I don't hear you all outraged on my behalf, either. You four are normally as thick as thieves. I don't know what's going on with all of you, but if you don't get them in hand, they're going to push me more than they realize, and not a single one of us is going to like the results."

With that, I spun on my heel, stomping back to the living room. "Ready to go, kiddo?" I asked, noticing she had cleaned up while her father and I were talking. The blanket we were wrapped in sat neatly on the back of the couch. Pillows that had littered the floor were back in their normal spots, and she had even thrown out the empty containers of ice cream.

Gia nodded, looking at her dad carefully, and I realized she'd been more affected by their discussion that morning than I'd known. Gideon, of course, clued into his daughter in a way he still hadn't with me and walked to her, enfolding her in a massive hug that pulled her up with him as he rose. "Sorry, baby," I heard him say against her hair. "Give your old man some time to get his head on straight, all right? We'll talk again about it in a few days."

I swallowed because, damn him, Gideon always tried so hard to do right by everyone, and there I was, placing him in the middle of yet another family squabble between my brothers and me. Granted, usually, he was leading the charge, so the change was unexpected. I studied him, a tender look on his face just an instant before his usual stone face replaced it. Maybe not so unexpected after all. Maybe he was starting to connect Gia's troubles with my past ones.

Chapter 6

Alessia

I arrived at Matteo's bright and early the next morning. Too keyed up to sleep in, I'd already gotten my workout in and replied to a few emails from my agent regarding upcoming travel arrangements—including the bodyguard I'd promised to allow. I'd expressed my desire for Hammer, but that hope was dashed. The replacement was supposed to be just as competent, my agent swore, and I almost laughed at what their idea of competent was, but overall, I didn't much care, agreeing to whomever they'd chosen in his place. We ditched my protection detail by hoofing it down to the basement of Matteo's apartment complex into the underground tunnel system. We then walked three blocks to what looked like an abandoned warehouse that was actually a combination of a safe house and storage unit—if a storage unit could be the size of a professional football stadium. Besides the gun range, we had a medical room, library, a room used to create fake documents, an armory, and a few bedrooms, among other things. It was the range I needed if I was going to make it through family dinner.

Several hours, about ten pounds of ammo, and a shower later, I strutted into my father's house, dressed in open-toed wedges that allowed my red toes to peek through. I had vetoed stilettos for two reasons; first, because the wedges were more comfortable, and second, because I really didn't need a viable weapon within easy reach. The silverware was enough of a temptation—I didn't need to add any others. The tan shoes complemented my cream white sundress, and the pearls Daddy gave me when I turned twenty-one hung from my ears and neck. As much as I loathed applying makeup, I made an effort for the formal meal, swiping my eyes with mascara and adding some lip gloss. The rest of the week might be informal, but God help you if you showed up for Sunday dinner without putting forth an effort to look civilized.

"There she is," my father said as I entered the drawing room. Every Sunday, come rain or shine, we all gathered at Daddy's for drinks and dinner if we were in town—yet another reason I traveled so much. Give me yoga pants and a home-cooked meal, and I'd be happy. My father's version of proper conduct—before dinner drinks, a four-course dinner with chillingly polite conversation, followed by the men retiring to the study while Gia and I had our version of a drawing room—wasn't the family day I preferred.

I let him gather me in a hug, his enormous frame swallowing mine, despite the fact I was anything but tiny. Bull Accardi earned every bit of his nickname. Even his sons, all warriors in their own right, failed to match his incredibly wide shoulders and massive bulk. He was a bit softer around the middle than my brothers, but he had too much pride to let himself go completely. I smelled his jacket, his cologne mixing with the faint hint of tobacco—his cigar habit a poorly kept secret. *Home*, I thought, taking in the comfort of his arms. It didn't matter how old you were or how independent you could be— your father's arms would always revert you to a time when your daddy could vanish monsters under your bed and take away nightmares without breaking a sweat.

"Hi, Daddy," I said, hugging him for all I was worth and ignoring my brothers for the time being. "I missed you." The truth sometimes sucked because I did miss him.

He pulled back, looking down at me. "You wouldn't miss me so much if you came home more often. We miss you, too, darlin'."

I couldn't argue that point, so I only smiled at him.

"But then Mrs. Mallery wouldn't make me all of my favorites for dinner," I joked, and his laughter boomed, echoing across the room. I reached for the glass of wine Keene offered, not so much as looking in his direction. Gideon and Gia weren't there yet, but the other three had been there long enough to have gotten a drink and made themselves comfortable.

"You going to say hello to your brothers?" Daddy asked, sitting back down in the gigantic wingback chair I had specially made for his six-foot-six frame a few years ago.

"Nope," I popped the "P." "I'm mad at them."

He chuckled again. "You haven't been home a few days. What could they have done so quickly to make you angry?"

"Assigned me security personnel without asking or telling me about it." I snorted. "They're lucky I was feeling mellow and didn't shake them on purpose." No one needed to know I'd shaken them, at least long enough to get my head on straight.

"You have threats against you," Keene said, sounding aggravated.

"Which are nothing new. Just because you want to act like the sky is falling doesn't mean it actually is," I countered, sipping the wine, hiding my curiosity at how much they really knew about what was going on.

"And you're so used to them," Royce piped up, "that you don't even realize they've escalated. You're a frog in a pot of water—completely ignorant of the fact that it's boiling you alive."

Ick, I twisted my face in disgust at that visual. *Just what I needed before dinner*. "You ever stop to think that I'm just lazing around in a hot tub and that you idiots just came in from the frozen tundra?" I snapped. "I'm not ignorant, never have been, never will be. Y'all just came in from the outside and are taking this completely out of context. And," I talked over Boone when he tried to cut in, "if y'all were a hundred percent confident in that thought, then you wouldn't have been sneaky about it."

Keene settled his glass on the table next to him. "We weren't sneaky about it. It's not like we told them to hide what they were doing. Otherwise, you wouldn't even know they were there."

That was a lie, but I wouldn't point it out. "I meant from Gideon. If you all were in agreement, you would have included him in ganging up on me like you always do."

"Your brothers just care about you," my father interjected, and I bit back a wince because I knew it was true. But I knew I was right, too.

"And I love them right back, but that doesn't mean they have the right to control my life with zero input from me," I sniffed, downing half of my glass of wine in one go. "If they pulled that shit with each other—"

"Language," my father cut in, but I continued talking.

"They would have beat the others bloody, and all y'all know it. Just because I'm a woman—"

"Your gender has nothing to do with it. If you had as much training as the rest of us, we wouldn't have as much as an issue, and *you* know it." Royce leaned forward, prepared to argue his stance.

"That's bullshit," I flung the words back, my temper getting the better of me, and my father snapped that time.

"That's enough, young lady. Your mother raised you better than to use such language. Your brothers worry about you, and they're well within their right to look after you as your older brothers. They're hardly keeping you from living your life, just trying to do their duty to keep you safe while you do what you were born to do."

I ignored him. My mother was the one I'd learned half of my vocabulary from, and I wasn't about to let him start guilt-tripping me that early in the meal. Besides, he had no idea what I'd really been born to do—he'd lost that right long ago—and it certainly wasn't posing for pictures. I stared Royce down, hating that he thought me so incapable but not able to rectify his incorrect assessment. "Regardless," I took a deep breath. "I'm no Bimbo Barbie.

Just because I make my living on my looks does not mean I don't have a brain. If you had come to me and had an actual conversation—"

"You would have agreed to it?" Boone asked snidely, taking a large gulp of his drink.

"I might surprise you," I taunted. "After all, I agreed to the bodyguard Valencia has been requesting me to take for months after Gideon expressed concern a few weeks ago." As a unit, they all straightened, and I raised an eyebrow. "Didn't know that, did you?" I murmured. "Not sure why you started doubting him, but it has to tear at him that y'all thought you had to go around him." I let the reprimand linger, wanting it to hit home. I might not like being outvoted and run rough-shod over all the time, but I didn't like the change in dynamics and wanted it fixed.

"I hope you don't mind," a voice from the doorway pulled all of our attention to the newcomer, "but I was in town and thought I'd stop by."

"Uncle Harry," I said in surprise, rushing over to hug him. My father's younger brother lived in Houston but was always a welcome face. Not only was I fond of him, but his presence would keep Daddy in line for the evening. "Is everything okay?" I asked, looking at him carefully. He was as lean as my daddy was broad, his ice-blue eyes stark against his pasty skin. My family was all olive-skinned, sunshine-loving, dark-haired Italians, living life large and loud. Uncle Harry couldn't be more different. He would probably burst into flames if he spent more than a handful of minutes outside, and his cultured voice, void of the deep Texan accent the rest of us had, was soft and controlled, though his pack-a-day habit had taken a toll on him, its tone resembling sandpaper. I wasn't sure why the two brothers shared tobacco as a vice, but I was sure there was a story there somewhere.

"'Course it is." He patted my shoulder awkwardly. He never was good at showing affection. "I just heard you were home for a few days and wanted to see you with my own two eyes. How's everything going? I heard you secured a highly prized contract with a clothing company a while back."

I smiled, taking a step back so he could nod at his brother and nephews in greeting and trying to keep my weariness in check. "I did. It's probably the highlight of my modeling career to be selected by Valencia as the face of their new line."

"She said she's going to stop traveling so much after this," Gia announced from the hallway, running over to hug her grandpa before doing the same with her great-uncle. Gideon came in a second later, his dove-gray suit impeccable as always. "So that she can be home more."

"I said I'm going to be more selective about what I take," I corrected, not wanting anyone to put words in my mouth, noting my father's face was already reddening. "I didn't say I was going to be home more." As much as I wanted to, I wasn't sure I could be. To do my job, I had to maintain my skills, and being home never failed to spark the desire to relax my defenses in the worst possible way. I could be myself personality-wise, but in other aspects of who I was, I still had to hide. At least while modeling, everything I did was a cover. It was easier to be someone you weren't all the time than to be half that person.

Gia pouted. "I don't see why if you took on fewer jobs, you couldn't be here more. You live here."

I shook my head. "I live here sometimes, not all the time."

That had all the men in the room save Uncle Harry turning on me in an instant. "What the hell do you mean? You live here sometimes?" Boone demanded, and it wasn't lost on me that Daddy didn't correct his word choice.

"It means sometimes I live here, and sometimes I live elsewhere," I said with exaggerated patience. I hadn't meant to let that tidbit slip, but now that I had, I would have to live with the consequences, though damn if I was going to get into a fight over it with Uncle Harry in the room. At least I wouldn't start the fight, but I was willing to finish it if necessary.

"Your home is here. Where else would you be?" Royce asked, his frown dark.

"I have more than one home. Several, in fact." I kept my back to the room as I filled my wineglass, feeling the piercing stares of my brothers and father.

"I'd wager a guess that I'm not the only one in this room who has other residential properties," I said mildly, raising an eyebrow at Gideon. "Anyone else upset that Daddy has a house on the coast or Gideon has a townhome in D.C.?" I took a sip from my wineglass. "No? How about Keene's cabin in Colorado?"

"How do you know about—"

"I'm a little sister. Snooping is in the job description." I waved a hand in dismissal. "The important thing to note is that no one else is upset at the idea of them having other residences. Why should I be any different?" I challenged. "I have several homes in Europe. I'm often in Italy on shoots, and I own property in Milan and Paris and an apartment just outside Monte Carlo, close to the city of Nice. It makes sense for me to have a home of my own to recharge, even if the companies I work for would provide hotel accommodations." In reality, I also had properties in Switzerland, London, and New York, and a tiny cabin in the middle of nowhere Canada. But I didn't need to divulge that part, especially since they were buried in shell companies and fake identities. "Now, can we please move on to less-aggravating topics? I don't think this is appropriate dinner conversation. After all, discussing money, property, and investments is considered crass." I couldn't help the dig at Daddy's references to proper behavior, but it went over his head, though I saw Keene crack a smile.

Dinner progressed with little fanfare after that, largely because of Uncle Harry's presence. Daddy's attendance might not prevent a family brawl, but to do so in front of our very-proper uncle didn't sit right with any of us. And my uncle's view that I was an adult kept Daddy from laying into me for declaring I was pulling back from modeling. I knew he disagreed with the decision, and I'd catch an earful if he got the opportunity, but I'd distanced myself from him enough, both personally and professionally, that other than bluster and lecture, there wasn't much he could do. I only had to stop myself from brandishing my steak knife once when Gideon brought up the fact that he'd seen Matteo yesterday morning before most would consider it polite visiting hours at my house. I smoothed it over with everyone, laughingly telling him I was still jet-lagged and that Matteo had offered a four a.m. class since he couldn't fit me in later that day. "Yoga is excellent for the body," I'd announced, and I had to admit I'd added it to my workout routine years ago due to the excellent muscle control it incorporated.

Not one of us was foolish enough to think it was the end of the discussion, however. I knew our argument would continue tomorrow when I'd promised to stop by the offices. They hadn't told me a time, but I planned on coming in early. If I was going to storm out, I might as well do it early enough to get shit done afterward. And with any luck, I could avoid Daddy for at least a few weeks, delaying that showdown as long as possible. After all, one argument a visit really should be enough, and I could tell the one with my brothers was going to be a doozy.

Chapter 7

Brody

My weekend was jam-packed with preparations. After making sure my apartment was clean and emptied in anticipation of my absence and that I'd paid my bills since my promise to Keene was open-ended, I took several hours studying my primary. Alessia Accardi—the name to the face I'd admired in the lobby—and the reason she looked so familiar was because her face was plastered on just about every fashion magazine cover imaginable. I might not be up to date on my fashion, but I shopped in the grocery store as much as any other bachelor, and that face stared back at anyone waiting in the checkout line. Didn't it figure that the first woman I felt even an inkling of interest toward in months was none other than the little sister of one of my only friends? And I felt a hell of a lot more than an inkling. I drew a finger over the image in the file Keene had given me before I left the office. Alessia was walking, talking sin. From the top of her thick, luscious, black hair that begged a man to shove his fingers in it and hold on to her mile-long tanned legs, she screamed sex. Her impossibly purple eyes grabbed your attention even as they seemed to look into you, grasping at your soul. Despite being thin, a requisite for her career, she had curves, not the bony angles I was used to seeing on cover models. Her cheekbones were high, giving her a regal appearance, and, as I'd witnessed firsthand, she used her luscious mouth as a weapon—melting men left and right when she deemed them worthy of a smile and cutting them in two with a handful of words when they irritated her. Most of her weight resided in her breasts and ass, something other women wanted to kill her over, I was sure. Men, on the other hand, probably praised God and Jesus above for the sheer perfection of her body.

The lack of detail regarding her training puzzled me, though. Granted, I'd spent barely more than a few minutes in her presence, but I knew competency when I saw it. Alessia was more than capable of taking down that asshole in the lobby, meaning she had more than basic training—Mike the idiot was a SWAT commander, not some random Joe off the street. Yet, according to Keene's notes, the only mention of training was that the family had taught her some basic self-defense in her younger years and that she'd had a few years of karate as a child. No way in hell could she have handled herself that well, been that confident in her abilities with a highly trained police officer, if that were the case. Unless, of course, she was just bat-shit crazy, something that, according to her brother's tales, was a distinct possibility. More likely, she'd learned more at her family's company than her brothers realized, and anyone with a mouth that smart would probably constantly be backing it up, even if she looked like she was better suited for a runway than a cage match.

I closed the file with a snap and placed it in the bag that contained everything I needed to bring with me—clothes, weapons, security equipment, a case of energy drinks, and a box full of protein bars. A PSO, or personal security officer, never knew when they would get downtime, and it rarely occurred at a place convenient for eating.

Putting my truck in drive, I made my way down the near-empty expressway. It was barely light, but I knew I was better off getting to where I needed to be before rush hour descended with a vengeance. I could eat close to the A.T. offices if I needed to waste some time. It might be the last decent meal I had in a while. I couldn't imagine the eating habits of a model. I'd get a crash course, I was sure, over the next few days, but I didn't think it would involve the basic food groups a growing Texas boy needed to stay in top shape—meat, grease, and caffeine.

As luck would have it, Keene texted as I arrived at my exit, and I met him at the private entrance for employee vehicles. He spoke to the guard, then motioned me to follow him into the parking structure. I parked next to him, my ten-year-old pickup standing out against the dozens of black SUVs that made up the core of any security company I'd ever seen or dealt with. Keene stepped out and glanced at his watch, which probably cost more than I'd netted my last year in the service, before greeting me.

Then I followed him up the elevator, bringing my bag with me since I didn't want to have to retrieve it later on. "Good weekend?" I asked, seeing the tension on his face.

"It was something," he muttered, already pulling at the tie on his neck.

"Anything I need to know about?" I wondered if Alessia had any issues while I was back home over the weekend.

"We have a meeting with my brothers in two minutes," was all he said, stepping off as the door opened and making his way straight to this office. I followed, setting my stuff down by the door—it was as good a place as any to store it until I knew how the day would go down. There was a steaming cup of coffee on his desk, and he grabbed it, downing a third of it in one gulp. "Want some?" he asked, and I nodded. As far as I was concerned, coffee was the nectar of the gods, and I could never get enough of it.

He showed me to a small break room a few doors down from his office, filling up his cup while I snagged my own before we continued to the last door down the hall. Voices alerted me we were the last to arrive, and all talking stopped as I stepped into view.

"Y'all, this is Brody. Brody, you've already met Boone, but these are my brothers, Gideon and Royce." I nodded, noting the anger in Gideon, and mentally prepared myself for a front-row seat to a family argument. I knew enough to understand that Gideon wasn't included in the decision to bring me into the fold, so to speak, and looking at him, I realized they hadn't enlightened him over the weekend but must have as we walked in.

"Fuck," Gideon said, running a hand through his hair as he paced. "I told you I handled this," he practically snarled, not bothering to acknowledge me.

"With a no-neck, no-experience wannabe who couldn't get a job as a mall cop," Boone said, looking a little worse for wear.

Someone had a late night, I thought, keeping quiet as the drama unfolded in front of me.

Gideon shook his head. "You said something similar yesterday. I talked with Lessia and her agent. The company that hired her, Valencia, had several bodyguards on the payroll. I checked all of them out myself. Any of them would have been capable of protecting her, even if they weren't the same caliber as A.T. personnel. There was absolutely no reason to go around her like this, and if she finds out—" Royce pulled out a file, throwing it on the table in front of Gideon like a gauntlet.

"I'm not sure what you consider 'capable,' but this is the dossier on the guard they assigned her last week. He was actually an employee of the hotel she was staying at, not Valencia. And they pulled him from his regular detail of patrolling the grounds. No special skills, no experience at all, and other than a few bar fights, no prior knowledge of physically defending himself or anyone else."

"What?" Gideon snatched the file, thumbing through the papers in the folder. He shook his head after reading some of what was in there. "This guy wasn't on the list of possible employees. He isn't anything similar to the level of what Valencia sent over. They're professionals—Valencia is big enough and their security demands are constant enough to need experienced men."

"Well," Keene said, looking at his older brother, "it sounds like we need to ask Alessia what the fuck is going on."

"It appears I've arrived just in time," a sultry voice drifted from the door, the woman in question draping herself against the frame. Surprisingly, instead of a dress or casual wear, she was the epitome of a businesswoman in simple black slacks, short black heels, and a blue three-quarter sleeve shirt that flowed over her curves. She had her hair pulled up in a neat bun and a black suit coat draped over her arm. It was clear by how she matched her brothers in appearance that she was in the building to work, though I wasn't aware she had anything to do with Accardi Tactical.

"What's this?" Gideon was still holding the papers Royce had given him.

She raised an eyebrow, looking at her brother like he was one card short of a full deck. "Papers? The things made from poor, defenseless trees. I really don't understand why all y'all print everything off when technological advances no longer require you to do so."

Gideon slapped the papers on the desk, the noise making Boone wince. "Why is the bodyguard from your last photoshoot not on the list of potentials you sent me to vet?"

If I hadn't been watching intently, I would have missed her almost imperceptible intake of breath. Her pupils dilated, and I watched her mind fly in the space it took her to blink. "I don't know what you're talking about. You have the list of guards I sent you, not that it was any of your business to start with, but it got you off my back about my security. I swear, if my agent weren't as good as he was, I would fire him. It's not his job to report anything to you at all. He works for me—"

Gideon raised a hand. "Don't change the subject. Why wasn't he on the list you sent me?" His voice was a rough, deep drawl that rivaled mine in full Southern twang now that he was riled, even though he was gritting out each word with precision.

She shrugged, stepping in to grab the file from him, thumbing through it. Cocking her head, she plastered a smirk on her face. "This is the assigned guard I had on my last shoot. The picture is right, but do you really think I wouldn't recognize if Hammer were as poorly hired as this?"

"What other option is there?" Boone spoke. "You just admitted he was the one you had. And what the fuck kind of name is Hammer?"

She closed the folder, setting it down on the table, her words precise and cutting. "I would think that perhaps, someone was sick of her brothers butting into her business and asked a friend to replace the employee files with some made-up bullshit in Valencia's internal server on the guards' in the event they stuck their noses where they didn't belong."

If I didn't think she was feeding them a line of bull, her answer would have impressed me. Something wasn't right, but I wasn't sure what. I didn't have time to find out as she turned. "Apparently, I'm not here for company business. I'm sure all y'all have more important things to do, but if not, feel free to continue trying to interfere with my life. After all, the only thing you've accomplished here is to remind me yet again just how much faith you have in me being able to handle my own life."

"Lessia," Gideon whispered, but she shook her head.

"No, Gideon. Y'all have made it abundantly clear just what your opinion of me is. As if, by becoming a model, I was required to hand over half of my IQ. I'm an adult." She was firm, meeting all her brothers, look for look. "And I clearly demonstrated the ability to reach out for advice when needed. You wonder why I'm gone so much? Why I spend more and more time away from my home? Take a look in the mirror." She didn't wait for any of them to respond before walking out the door.

I jumped up, hustling to catch up with her. "Miss Accardi?" I called, but she didn't slow. "Alessia?" She stopped then, turning around to look at me.

"Brody, right?" She offered me a tight smile, but it didn't reach her eyes or cover the hurt in them. "I'm sorry you had to witness that bit of family drama."

I extended my hand. "Can't change your family," I offered the reminder. God knew I wouldn't have chosen mine if I'd had a say in it. She looked at my hand for a moment in surprise as I shook it firmly, businesslike, and completely non-sexual. I supposed she was more used to pretty boys kissing her hand and acting all suave, but I was who I was. Couldn't see changing that now.

She gave a small laugh, but it was a sad attempt at humor. "Not sure I would even if I could, damn them." Shaking her head as if to clear it, she took a step back. "It was nice meeting you, but I best get going. I might as well not waste the day."

I stopped her before she could take a step. "Actually, I'm here for you."

The words stopped her short, her eyes flaming with suspicion, and her body jerked as if I'd touched her with a live wire. "I beg your pardon?" Her tone was polite, but I saw her guard go on full alert.

I winced. "Sorry, that didn't come out as intended." What the hell was wrong with me? I sounded like a deranged kidnapper. "What I meant to say is that I'm your new PSO." I reached into my bag, careful to keep my movements clear and slow, so I didn't rattle her any more than I had. I pulled out my contract with Valencia, another detail I'd finalized over the weekend, and handed it to her.

She reached for the papers, reading them line by line. "I'm sorry for the confusion," she said, handing them back to me. "But there must be some mistake. My contract stipulates that no one associated with A.T. can be hired on my behalf. As you just saw, conflict of interest is something I contend with on a regular basis, and anyone who worked or has worked with or for my brothers is not someone I can trust to have my back." Her contract stipulation Keene had mentioned in his office the other day made so much more sense after what I saw.

I nodded, and she gave me a relieved look when she thought she'd shaken me. "I agree, but since I have not worked for or ever have plans to work for your brothers in any capacity, I nor Valencia have violated your agreement."

That froze her, and for the first time, I saw panic in her eyes. Then, just like in the conference room, she cleared her expression in a single blink of her eerily purple eyes. "When you came in on Friday, you said it was to talk to

Keene. Sounds like you have some sort of loyalty to him." Her snipped reply was understandable.

"I served some of the same time as Keene, and we have mutual friends in common." I'd planned my answer over the weekend, taking Keene and Boone's warning to heart that she wouldn't welcome me if she knew I had any ties with them. All of it was true, just not the whole truth. After what I just saw, I couldn't blame her thoughts and yet again wondered if it was even necessary for me to be there in place of the man who'd been in the position before me. "Since I knew him, I only felt it right to stop in and let him know I would be working with you, though I apologize for not introducing myself. I hadn't seen your picture yet and didn't realize you were the same person as the model that Valencia wanted me to protect."

A lie, but a small one in the grand scheme of things. Her assessing look was another clue that she was anything but stupid. She couldn't catch my lie but knew something wasn't completely on the up and up. "I'm sure you want to validate everything, and I also know you likely want to get out of here." I offered up the olive branch, hoping to gain some points in my favor, knowing I'd need as many as possible with this woman. "I will be happy to meet you somewhere if you would prefer that. Your brother offered a company SUV if I needed it since I'm not supposed to take over your detail officially until we leave tomorrow, but I can ride with you if you don't want me to use A.T. resources." I knew I made it sound like I didn't have a personal vehicle, but I also knew that my old truck would stand out like a Longhorn in a pen of Holsteins, and being as unobtrusive as possible was part of my objective. *You also want the chance to get close enough to her to wipe that look of hurt from her eyes.* I pushed that thought aside.

She looked unsure for a moment, but I was learning her brain was as fast as a computer, processing the situation and options in less than a second. "If you don't mind, let's head to my car. I can make some calls on our way down."

I nodded, grabbing my bag from Keene's office as we passed by it. I hoped she didn't pay any mind to it, but I knew her suspicion grew when I made the quick stop. She was playing it smart, keeping herself protected by the building's security before allowing herself to leave with me, and I was glad she took her safety seriously. It took less than five minutes for her to realize she was stuck with me. She herself had emailed her acceptance at a security replacement over the weekend, though she hadn't realized it was me she'd agreed to.

Alessia didn't look happy—I would go so far as to say she was fuming, but she didn't turn her fury on me, so I called it a win. Tossing me the keys to her black BMW sports car, she slammed the door as she settled into the passenger's seat. "Well, Mr. McCallister. We appear to be stuck with each other for the time being. But when I find out you're planted by my brothers, I'll kick you to the curb faster than you can blink."

I hid my smile at the *when*, not *if*, in her statement. "Where would you like to go?" I asked, backing out of the parking space.

"Just start driving. I'll tell you when to turn." She barely looked at me, typing furiously into her phone. I was happy to be directed to an Italian restaurant and parked in a spot well away from the other vehicles. She waited patiently as I circled to open the car door, obviously well versed in security protocols and not about to cause trouble for me. Her brothers had been clear that she was a handful—I was prepared for her to try to run on me or make my life difficult as I tried to protect her—but she'd done neither so far. She also hadn't run back to her house, home base, so to speak. Most people would want home field advantage when being thrown for a loop the way she was, already reeling from the curveball her brothers had lobbed her way that morning, but instead, she picked a small little restaurant off the beaten path.

Getting us a table for two, she settled in the booth with her back to the wall. Instead of challenging me, knowing I needed the position for her safety so I could see everyone coming and going, she slid over, making room for me to sit beside her. "I can't stand having my back to the room," she admitted when she saw my curious look. "Hazard of having brothers who loved to torment their little sister when we were kids."

Again, something about that statement didn't ring true. She wasn't lying, but I definitely wasn't getting the full story from her either. "I appreciate you not taking your surprise out on me. I can understand not being happy with the situation, but I assure you I'm here for your safety, not to spy on you for your brother."

I was being truthful. Keene might have asked me to watch her, but I wasn't about to spill her secrets to him just because he was a friend. I kept my work completely professional. Sure, I hadn't done it as a civilian, but I'd been assigned PSO duties in the past and was confident in my abilities and the lines I needed to stay within.

"I appreciate that," she said but seemed more preoccupied with her phone than what I had to say. I shut my mouth, nodding to the server in appreciation when she dropped off a basket of bread and two glasses of water on the table.

She put her phone aside—the food was clearly more interesting than I was—and grabbed a piece of bread. She tore it in half, putting part of it back in the basket before smothering it in butter and plopping it in her mouth. "I love bread." She sighed after swallowing it whole.

"I would have never guessed," I said wryly, taking my own slice of the steaming goodness and tearing off a piece, then taking a bite.

"So, why did you decide to become a PSO?" she asked, looking at the basket with a forlorn expression but not making a move to take another piece of bread. I tore a small chunk of the one in my hand, giving her another small bite. Surprise registered on her face as our hands touched. Whether it was because I'd given her what she'd clearly been about to deny herself or the zing I'd certainly felt when our hands touched, I wasn't certain.

I shrugged. "I like the challenge of it, the constant change of pace. I take the jobs I want, but I'm a private contractor, so I'm not stuck with anyone I don't like." Winking at her, I continued, "Though I'm hoping you will be easier to work with than some of my past clients." Okay, I might be going a little far in making it sound like I had experience outside the Marine Corps, but if she found out I hadn't done this since getting out, I knew my goose was cooked. And I was hoping she would be easier to handle than some assignments I'd had in the past. Guarding dignitaries and high-profile business executives who thought they were untouchable were not my best days spent in the military.

"What about you? Why did you decide to become a model?" I could have cut off my tongue. Her face closed, a door slamming on her emotions, replaced with an icy mask. I recognized the look as one she had on most of the candid pictures taken of her on modeling sets.

"I've always dreamed of becoming a model," she said, but I could tell it was a line. "What girl wouldn't want to travel to some of the most beautiful places in the world, wearing gorgeous dresses, and see her face on the cover of magazines?"

Apparently not this one, I thought. I was saved from answering when the server returned to take our order. She ordered a large chicken Caesar salad, dressing on the side, and, deciding lunch sounded better than breakfast anyway, I chose the fettuccini. The server gave us a quizzical look, probably because of the early hour, but I figured there probably weren't many choices for a model counting calories in a place that was known for their homemade baked goods for breakfast.

"So, what's our schedule like after we land tomorrow?" I asked. "I understand this is the last photoshoot for a while. Do you do anything differently than the others? Retake shots or something?"

She shook her head. "Each shoot is its own. This one is forest-themed. Thank goodness it's not back at the beach."

I almost choked, thinking about her in a bikini, and took a long sip of water to cool myself off. "That sounds ... interesting."

She laughed. "Really, it's going to be pretty boring for you. I just stand around all day."

I highly doubted it was that easy or boring, at least when it came to her. "It makes more sense to know why we're flying to Germany. I'm guessing they aren't using a set?"

Alessia shook her head. "No, the photographer refused to use them. Says he can tell they're staged, and he needs to be 'authentic to his artistic talent.'" She snorted. "He's full of himself, but he does a good job. It's the only reason I tolerate his mouth."

I narrowed my eyes. "How so?"

She waved a hand in dismissal. "It doesn't really bother me. I have a thick skin and a very real sense of self-worth. But I wouldn't put up with it regardless if he wasn't such a genius when it comes to lighting."

I couldn't believe how quickly the morning turned into the afternoon. After devouring her salad, I took pity on her envious glances toward my pasta, giving her the last bite off my plate. The conversation started light—the typical getting-to-know-you things but quickly turned more personal as we relaxed in each other's company. I surprised myself by telling her about how I'd grown up in South Texas with my alcoholic father. My mother had died in childbirth when I was six, and I'd had to grow up hard and fast. I'd joined the Marines as quickly as I could, determined to never look back. He'd died when I was in boot camp, finally succeeding in drinking himself to death. We bonded over the loss of our mothers, though she was older when hers had died from cancer. My father had gone even harder after she'd gone, and any money he made went straight to the bottle. She skimmed around the subject, but it seemed hers had changed in ways that caused a rift between them. After that, she talked about her job, favorite movies, books, and childhood memories, clearly wanting to change the subject. She was regaling me with uproarious stories of getting back at her overprotective brothers when her phone pinged, making her jump.

"I didn't realize we'd been here for so long," she said, looking self-conscious and a little aggravated. We'd talked well into the afternoon, and I was more than a little pleased that she seemed to be having as good of a time as I was. "I never lose track of time." She sounded more upset than I thought the situation called for. True, we'd been there for a few hours, but she'd admitted she didn't have any real plans for the day, and we'd both been enjoying our conversation. There was a sexual tension both of us were trying to ignore, but the heat and chemistry had weaved back and forth, probably another reason we'd lost track of time.

"I didn't have anywhere else to be," I said magnanimously, rising and letting her out in front of me before escorting her out the door with a hand on her back. She shuddered at the contact as heat rose between us. I snatched my hand back, determined to keep things professional. "Where to next?" I asked when we were back in the car, but she was back to closing me out, keeping her head down, focused on her phone.

"A.T. so that I can drop you off." Her tight smile didn't reach her eyes. "I have plans for the rest of the day, and I'm sure you want some time ... visiting ... before we leave tomorrow."

I frowned. "My job is to assist in your security."

"Starting tomorrow morning at the airport," she said lightly. "And just until we get back here. Four days total, so by Friday, we'll just be distant memories of each other."

"Until the next engagement." I matched her tone. "I've been informed that I'm assigned to you for the foreseeable future."

I saw her irritation out of the corner of my eye.

"That may be, but I only agreed to security while I'm officially working. I don't need a babysitter at home," she spoke firmly, clearly preparing for an argument, but I wasn't in a position to argue with her, nor did I want to. While I had copies of all the accumulated information on the threats, logs of attempted contact, and protests that occurred at places she'd been over the last few years, it wasn't my place to tell her she was being pig-headed, even if she was. And that again didn't make sense. If she was reasonable enough to realize she was vulnerable while working, surely she realized she was even more so at home, where she, and more importantly, her routine were easy to evaluate.

"I'm not here to argue." I avoided the subject, returning to the original question. "And I don't have anywhere else to go. I planned to spend the day catching up with your brother and begging to get a pass into the training complex to get some shooting in, but knowing you aren't happy with Keene makes me feel a bit like a traitor for thinking about doing it now." It felt like one of those times when the truth was best, even if it reminded her she had a good reason to be wary of my motives.

She sighed. "Just head back to A.T. I'll drop your bag off at Keene's since I'd bet money you planned on staying there. I have to exact some sisterly revenge anyway, so it's not like I'm going out of my way or anything."

I kept my mouth shut, not sure what I could say since she was correct, and I really didn't want to know what she had in store for her brothers. I was able to convince her to exchange phone numbers—at least I had a way to check in on her, and she could get ahold of me if need be—and then she was gone, not taking so much as a backward glance in the mirror as she drove off, leaving me at the entrance to the A.T. office building.

Blowing out a breath, I headed to Keene's office, not sure what else to do. He looked worse for wear, his tie gone and his shirt wrinkled. His attention was on me before I so much as walked through his door, clearly having been informed by security I was back in the building and anticipating my arrival.

"How is she?" he asked without preamble. His worry for his sister was honest and clear.

I shrugged. "She's not happy being saddled with me, but she was polite. We just came from lunch. She's more than a little pissed at you, though. And I think, even more, she's a whole lot of hurt."

He took the blow, not surprised in the least, but I could see my words had hit home. "She'll get over it." He said the words with false bravado, but I couldn't let it go.

"Why do you think she needs the interference?" I slouched in the chair opposite him, interested in his answer. "You made her sound like an ignorant teenage brat, sticking her head in the sand and pretending all is right in the world while carrying on without a worry."

He snorted. "Because she is. I've known that girl her whole life. She's that stupid Chihuahua who thinks she's as big and vicious as the room full of Rottweilers circling her, wanting to eat her whole."

It was my turn to snort. "Shelve your preconceived notion of your little sister for a moment and think objectively." I started counting on my fingers. "One ... assuming she wasn't bluffing this morning and did, in fact, change her bodyguard's file in case her brothers came snooping, she had qualified security. One who her eldest brother vetted at her request." I held up a second finger. "She took down that SWAT officer in a single move, without so much as blinking. You might think she's got an over-inflated opinion of her skills, but I'm telling you, no one is that confident taking down a skilled police officer without having at least some serious dedication to self-defense. And three," I held up the last finger, "she's a hell of a lot more aware of her surroundings than the average person. During lunch, she sat with her back to the wall, kept track of every move the entire restaurant made, evaluated exits and escape strategies, and never lost focus or awareness of where anyone was sitting in the room despite our conversation."

He scoffed at that, but I leveled a serious stare at him.

"She might not have formally trained at A.T., but she's absorbed a lot more than you thought while growing up or taken classes elsewhere. I'm not saying she's Superwoman, but she has more than basic knowledge of self-defense, awareness, and security protocols. She's clearly knowledgeable of the same content you offer in those courses set up for high-profile politicians and business executives. All of that tells me that not only is she aware of the danger she's in, but she might have an even better grasp of it than you do, and she's prepared to deal with it as best as she can." I shook my head. I was on a roll that I couldn't stop. "What does it say when I can come in, a total stranger to her, and see that in the space of hours, and y'all, who have the same training and know her better than anyone on the planet, have such a distorted view of her and her abilities."

For the first time, Keene looked shaken. He was silent for long minutes before whispering, "Gideon thinks she's seriously thinking about moving. She's been pulling away from us for a while. He thinks it's going to come to a head."

"Can you blame her?"

Chapter 8

Alessia

"Did you get it?" I asked as I was in the middle of pouring bottle after bottle of whiskey down the drain. I was at Boone's house since it was closest. He had entirely too much booze for one person, and I was about to remind him what happened when you pissed me off. As a two-for-one, I could not-so-subtly let him know what I thought of his new pastime. Pissed as I was, I'd still noticed his appearance, and it didn't take a rocket scientist to see he'd spent the night drinking.

As soon as I got in my car, I sent Matteo a text, trying to keep my panic under control. I was a trained professional, damn it, and I knew I could handle the situation. I wasn't sure how I would do it, but I prided myself on always getting the job done, and it would be no different. Thank God I just had some covert surveillance as my assignment for the Germany trip, though I might have to come at the information from a different angle. I couldn't see Brody being half as easy to get around as Hammer had been. That was the problem with PSOs. They weren't bodyguards. Hell, Hammer hadn't even been that, but I could have dealt with the run-of-a-mill guard if needed. Comparing PSOs to bodyguards was like comparing assassins to hit-men or a scalpel in the hand of a neurosurgeon to a butcher with a meat cleaver. Already he'd seen too much, and we hadn't even left the safety of home yet.

"He checks out," Matteo said in my ear as I opened yet another bottle of alcohol. I didn't discriminate, pouring out the ten-thousand-dollar bottle of bourbon as ruthlessly as I did the rest of his collection. My Bluetooth allowed me to move freely as I looked around, making sure I'd found all of it before putting the now-empty bottles back where I'd gotten them. In the back of his pantry, I had found a long-forgotten bottle of rot-gut whiskey. Careful to touch only the cap, so I didn't disturb the dust, I squeezed the eye dropper I'd brought in with me into the bottle. Looking at the whiskey with a critical eye, I added a few more drops. Granted, the drops were in my purse in case I needed to make a quick getaway from a hellacious date—not that I'd gotten them for that purpose—but they would do nicely in my current situation. The chemical itself could kill if given in the correct dose, and it was undetectable in an autopsy, which had come in handy for the weapons dealer I'd taken care of two years ago. I added just enough to kick in an hour or so after ingestion—I wouldn't want the fun to start too soon—before replacing the bottle in my pocket. One brother down, three more to go. I hadn't yet decided what to do with Gideon since, from what I had overheard, it seemed like they'd left him in the dark for the most part, but he had believed them when they'd shown him Hammer's file. How they'd gotten it was a mystery to me, but I knew they had more connections and contacts than I could count, so I shouldn't be surprised.

"I know he checks out," I snapped, resetting the security code and locking the door before jumping back into my BMW. *In more ways than one*, I thought. Brody was definitely a treat for the eyes, and the way his muscles flexed as he moved made me want to strip him for closer inspection. I made a mental note to up my vitamins. Apparently, I was missing something from my diet if my hormones were that amped up. "I already told you, he knows Keene personally. It's not like I thought he was using a fake identity or something."

Matteo ignored me, knowing my temper needed to flame out verbally since I could hardly circle back to his place for another few hours of shooting shit. Then he whistled at whatever he was reading on his computer across town. "You're fucked, Belle. And not even remotely in a good way."

I'd chosen a restaurant close to Matteo's apartment, allowing him to snag the water glass as soon as we were out of sight, taking Brody's prints to run so that we could get the lowdown on the newest ploy my brothers had enacted as a way to smother me to death. I could have just texted his name, but I wanted to make sure nothing fell through the cracks, leaving nothing to chance. Fortunately, Matteo knew me well enough that all it took was a few innocuous texts to him, complaining about what my high-handed brothers had pulled, for him to get his ass in gear and beeline it to the restaurant. As he ran the print, he also took me to task for not moving my ass along in eating and getting out of there. After all, there was absolutely no reason to have taken a several-hour lunch break when we needed the information as soon as possible. I was ashamed to admit I was having such a good time with Brody that I'd almost forgotten my reason for stopping for lunch. Not only was it embarrassing, but it was also alarming. Having spent the majority of my life living under one cover or another—very rarely being just Lessia—I never, ever forgot myself. And yet, for a brief time, I had.

"How so?" I asked, pushing my thoughts aside as I pulled into the drive at Royce's house and grabbed the supplies I needed from the car before entering through the side door. It really was convenient that my brothers and I lived so close together. It certainly made for quicker work for me.

"He's a former Raider."

The words stopped me cold, panic rolling over me in a tidal wave. That was bad, so very, very bad. Marine Raiders were the special operation force of the U.S. Marine Corps and were part of the Marine Corps Special Operations Command. They were the best of the best, the very top warriors the Marine Corps had to offer. Idly, I realized that if Brody McCallister hadn't been lying about how he knew Keene, it meant he, too, was a former Raider. I wasn't sure if I should be proud of that fact, angry that yet another highly trained individual who should know better underestimated me, or satisfied that I continued to fly below his radar. Deciding to be all three, I pushed it aside to listen as Matteo continued. "I can't get his individual records. Most of it is heavily redacted or missing, but what his exact missions were doesn't matter in the grand scheme of things. It's the training he received to get there."

I completely agreed, and for once, I wasn't sure what to do about it. It wasn't like I could buy him off or force him to quit. If he were doing this as a favor for Keene, a bomb wouldn't shake him loose from me unless one of us died or Keene called him off. "Well, shit." Yanking open the drawer beside Royce's bed with a jerk, I pulled out the box of condoms, making sure I checked the bathroom and his travel duffel as well. Then I replaced every condom I found with a brightly wrapped sucker. I couldn't decide whether it was a "Fuck you" or "Suck it" message, but you could bet my brother would receive it loud and clear when the moment was right. "As soon as I finish up here, I'm heading home. I'll make the call as soon as I get back." He hung up without so much as a goodbye, clearly as worried about the latest development as I was.

Because Royce would be suspicious if he didn't find something amiss as soon as he walked through the door, and I didn't want him to find anything until the time was right, I added bubble bath to his front fountain. By the time he arrived home, his entire front lawn would look like the world's largest washing machine had thrown up. Did I mention it was colored bubble bath?

Two down, I thought as I looked at my watch, making sure I was still within my budgeted timeframe. Keene's house was next. I remembered to place Brody's bag in the guesthouse—taking the time to snoop through the duffle, though I didn't find anything of merit. Then I grabbed a trash bag and took the extra bedding in the closet, leaving him only the towel hanging by the shower. In the main house, I stripped all the beds, from the comforters to the pillows, except for the master bedroom. In Keene's room, I pulled down the covers, sprinkling itching powder liberally in between every layer of material, including both sides of all the pillows. I gathered all the extra sheets and blankets, along with the towels, again leaving only one ready for use. Except that one was also liberally dosed with the powder. A quick stop at the top drawer of his bedroom dresser, and I was done. The bottle now empty, I grabbed his soap, shampoo, and body wash for good measure and put them in the bag before I stalked back to the living room, pulling up his Netflix account and changing the password before turning his iPad off and setting it back on the coffee table. No one looking at him would guess, but that man could binge-watch like you wouldn't believe. At least, he used to. Looking around, I mentally checked off my list. "Kitchen," I murmured, grabbing the three bags of coffee beans and adding them to my bag. Keene couldn't function without at least a full pot of coffee; his snobbery wouldn't allow him to swing through the countless coffee shops that dotted the city. I had to admit, he had excellent taste, though I took my caffeine any way I could get it.

Placing the evidence of my revenge in the trunk, I hopped back into my car, grateful for the air conditioning blowing out air so cold that, after the summer heat, it made me feel like I was breathing in the arctic. I drummed my fingers on the steering wheel as I contemplated what to do with Gideon. I considered my options, disregarding them as quickly as I thought them up until the thought hit me, and I grinned, pulling out my phone. When it came to sisterly revenge, it was always swift, harsh, and more than deserved.

When I got home, I practically ran into the house. I wasn't sure how much time I had before one of my brothers showed up—it could be today or when I arrived back home next week. With them, you never really knew how long it would take for their male brains to circle around to the fact that they were in the wrong and owed me an apology. I made quick work of clearing the house, turning my security system back on, and ensuring my perimeter alarms were all working before heading to the basement.

Not at all looking forward to the phone call, I went through my normal steps, waiting as the phone rang. "Shield," the gruff voice drifted over the connection, almost a whisper of sound, yet there was no question who spoke.

"Sword," I replied, leaning one hand against the desk, too keyed up to sit in my chair. "You heard?"

"Yes. This is an unfortunate turn of events, but one both of us should have foreseen."

I gritted my teeth because he was right. We knew my brothers had been a concern for a while—since I started, to be honest. Both of us thought that handling Gideon was enough, but neither of us considered my brothers' uncharacteristic mutiny. "We did expect this. We've been trying to offset it for years, and steps had just recently been put into place to prevent this very thing. None of us thought this move would happen this quickly." I wanted to remind him it wasn't like we sat on our asses trying to handle this situation. Who could have predicted a break in ranks?

"Regardless, we have to deal with the here and now. All your assignments from here on out are temporarily suspended."

"I can still gather intel on this trip." It irritated me to be pulled from the field, but I, more than anyone, understood that this problem took priority over my desires. "Just in a more ... visible ... way."

I waited as he thought it over, knowing not to rush his decision. "You're more vulnerable now. We cannot put your normal protocols into place. Your new security personnel will be alert and suspicious," he mused out loud.

I knew what he meant. Brody's presence alone meant I couldn't safeguard my rooms and person the way I normally would. Hammer might not have noticed the tricks of the trade I had on my windows and doors, as well as the surveillance equipment, to ensure no one had entered my rooms or placed electronic devices in my suite without me knowing about it, but Brody sure would, which meant I would have to forego my usual protection. Just his presence was leaving me more vulnerable than I was before his assignment. It irked me that my brothers' move to try to protect me was actually doing the opposite, and I couldn't even tell them.

"So I could let him do it," I pointed out. "If he's half as good as we expect him to be, he'll have his own equipment, if for no other reason than he isn't going to take chances with a friend's little sister when he knows the potential for problems is a given. I can get what we need during normal hours, doing what's expected of me in the public eye, so to speak."

"And delivery?"

I let my breath whoosh out as the interest in his tone told me I'd gotten my way.

"It will have to be delayed until I return." No way could I chance a handoff or send an encrypted email. Brody wouldn't have access to my computer, but thanks to my dumb-ass brothers, I couldn't take the chance that they weren't trying to snoop. I couldn't afford to have them come across something that wasn't exactly what they would expect to see in a civilian system. I swore to myself, realizing I couldn't even have my normal backup channels available to me. Matteo would be my only failsafe, and even that was tenuous at best.

"Very well. Proceed, but be cautious. You know what they say about hunters."

"They catch the best prey?"

"Sometimes they become the hunted."

"Not going to happen," I said with more bravado than I felt. I wasn't sure if he was talking about my mark or Brody, but either way, I wasn't about to have everything I'd fought for fall apart because of the actions of some well-meaning, irritating as fuck family members. They'd caused other shit storms that I had weathered. I would weather the newest one as well.

"I hope not." That was softer than the rest, and I wondered if I was meant to hear it at all.

Chapter 9

Brody

Keene and I were in the gym, beating out some of the aggression simmering in both of us, when Gideon walked in. I wouldn't admit it out loud, but if it wasn't for his interruption, I was pretty sure we would have continued trying to beat each other until we both passed out from exhaustion. Keene sure as shit hadn't let himself lose his edge, and part of my path to mental recovery over the last six months had involved a hearty amount of physical activity with a variety of teachers, instructors, and sensei. I wagered I was in even better shape physically now than I was when I was active military.

"Get ready," Gideon said, looking resigned.

"What?" Keene asked, and I was happy to see he looked as tired as I felt. At least my hands weren't trembling, I noticed, smirking at that detail. We pulled apart and looked at Keene's eldest brother, who, despite the late hour, looked as fresh and put together as he had that morning.

Gideon went to speak, but before he could get a word out, his phone rang. Reaching for his pocket, he pulled out his phone, pressed the button to answer it, and placed it on speakerphone for Keene and me to hear.

"Good evening, handsome," the syrupy sweet voice purred. "I'm so glad you reached out to Soulful Mates. I have someone here who is excited to meet with you—"

I bit back a laugh as Gideon pressed the red button, ending the call, but before he could say anything, it rang again. "Hi, Gideon, thank you for choosing—" The bubbly cheerleader-type was hung up on as harshly as the woman before her.

He swore. "I can't turn it off. Gia is supposed to call me after school."

"Alessia's revenge?" I asked, not able to hide my amusement, and Gideon snarled.

"She signed me up for every dating site, escort, and phone sex service known to man. I think I've had close to fifty phone calls in the last thirty minutes."

"I don't have any calls," Keene said, looking at his phone screen from where he had set it on the bench outside the ring.

"Of course not, because it would be too easy for you to get a new number. Besides, do you really think she would pull the same trick twice? This is our sister we're talking about," Gideon grumbled as his phone rang in his hand again. He looked at the screen before rejecting the call.

A ding of the elevator had the three of us looking up. Boone strode in, his jacket thrown carelessly over his shoulder. "You guys ready to get out of here? Royce left a few minutes ago to deal with a problem with his security system."

"Break-in?" Keene asked, concerned, but I noticed Gideon didn't bat an eyelash, more worried about his still-ringing phone than he was about Royce's house.

Boone shook his head. "I don't think so. An alarm went off about an obstructed camera." He took a step back, wrinkling his nose at Keene. "You stink, man. Why don't you take a shower? We can eat at my house. I think the housekeeper said she was leaving enchiladas in my fridge for dinner tonight."

Gideon was about to reply when his phone rang again—the fourth or fifth in as many minutes—but that time, he answered. "Hey, sweetheart. How was school?" he asked, turning on his heel, waving absentmindedly as he left, his attention fully on his daughter.

"Guess he's out," Boone said. "Go. I'll meet you at my house."

Keene and I hit the shower, and I jumped into his SUV a few minutes later. I was grateful I didn't have to find a place to park my pickup—Keene had told me to leave it in their lot while I was gone—but I hated not being the one driving.

We arrived a few minutes after Boone, and before Keene could even put the car in Park, we could hear Boone's shouts coming from the house.

"Alessia's revenge, part two?" I asked, sure the windows were rattling with the force of the swearing.

Keene ignored the question, taking the noise in stride as he pushed into the house without knocking. "What happened?"

"She poured out every bottle of alcohol I owned, including the Pappy Van Winkle!" Boone was positively livid, and I didn't blame him. Judging by the number and label of the bottles that lined the counter, she had dumped well over fifteen thousand dollars of liquor down the drain.

Keene raised an eyebrow, saying nothing, but I noticed he was beginning to look a little worried. He walked to the fridge, grabbed a foil-wrapped dish, popped it in the oven, and hit a timer. "Well, unless you want to make a liquor run—"

"Got it," Boone said triumphantly, holding up a half-used bottle of cheap whiskey that, judging from the amount of dust on the bottle, had been forgotten for years and left in the hidden depths of the pantry behind a box of rice. After grabbing a tumbler, he turned to us. "Want some?" he offered, but I shook my head, as did Keene. Something about the bottle didn't look right, and I stared harder, looking for what was off. He was about to open the bottle when it hit me—the entire bottle was filthy, save for the cap. I debated whether to say anything, but before I could decide, Boone poured a healthy three fingers into the glass and downed it. Shrugging, I consoled myself with the reminder that Alessia loved her brothers and wouldn't do something that would cause permanent harm.

Keene grabbed a bottle of water from the fridge, holding one up for me, but I shook my head. No way in hell would I take the chance she hadn't sabotaged more than the whiskey. I walked past Boone and grabbed a glass out of the cabinet, washing it in the sink before filling it from the tap. Who knew what else that hellcat had done while she was there, but I was going to follow the philosophy of "better safe than sorry" for the rest of the night.

Keene studied me, and I could see the wheels turning as he looked at the countless empty bottles of liquor Boone had pulled out in his quest for alcohol before landing on the remaining bit of whiskey. Awareness dawning, he placed his bottle of water carefully on the table, studying it as if it were a coiled snake.

"Want to take your chances, or should we get takeout?" I asked with a smirk. No way in hell would I eat there. I needed to be in top form for whatever tomorrow brought, and I had a feeling staying at Boone's was akin to rolling the dice on that outcome. Keene rose quickly, snatching the bottle as Boone began pouring more whiskey into his glass.

"Hey," Boone cried as Keene dumped it unceremoniously down the drain.

"You should thank me," Keene said over his brother's outrage. "You really think she missed a bottle?"

Boone straightened. "Well, shit."

I snickered. If he was lucky, that's all that would happen to him.

Keene chucked the glass into the recycling. "If you're planning to eat that," he pointed to the oven and the dinner bubbling away, "then you're either braver or stupider than I am."

Boone frowned sullenly. "Housekeeper was just here an hour ago. It's safe. And I only had one small drink."

I shook my head, following Keene to the door. I was going with stupid over brave. "Suit yourself," Keene called as we walked out the door. We'd just got into the car when his phone rang over the speakers, the SUV's Bluetooth taking over as he answered.

"That little witch," Royce said, his voice full of aggravation. "She put an entire bottle of bubble bath in my front fountain. Pink bubbles! It looks like a fucking princess cloud party in my front yard!" he practically yelled the last, and I lost control. Laughing, I tilted my head at Keene, who, despite himself, looked amused and intrigued.

"This isn't fucking funny." His voice boomed over the speakers. Keene winced, turning down the volume on the controls. "The police and fire department showed up."

"We're heading to pick up dinner. Want us to get you something?" he asked casually as he backed out of Boone's driveway.

"No, I don't fucking want dinner!" He was still swearing when Keene cut the call, the silence ringing in both of our ears.

"You afraid to go home yet?" I asked with a grin, loving Alessia's brand of justice. Keene grunted, clearly not about to admit it. "Can we make a quick stop before grabbing something to eat?" I was grinning like a fool, my cheeks hurting from the workout I was putting them through, the muscles weak with lack of use. He looked at me, seeing the humor in my eyes. It took a moment and was slow in growing, but a smile crossed his face as well. "Want to do a drive-by?" I asked, and he snorted.

"Fucking princess cloud party? Hell, yeah," he replied. I had a feeling my life just got a hell of a lot more interesting.

A few minutes later, after snapping a picture of what apparently was Royce's front yard, I grinned. He was right—the bubbles were so thick you could barely see the house, rising high enough to touch the roof. The pink color added more comedy to the whole thing, and even the police and firefighters were laughing from where they stood on the road beside the driveway.

Taking a picture of them as well, I pulled up my contacts, attaching both to the number Alessia had given me that afternoon.

ME: HAD SOME FUN THIS AFTERNOON?

ALESSIA: WOW! THAT'S AWESOME. WHY ISN'T IT SHUT OFF?

ME: MY GUESS ... TOO MANY BUBBLES TO SEE THE SHUT-OFF VALVE.

ALESSIA: LMAO, THE COPS AND FIREMEN BEING THERE IS ICING ON THE CAKE.

ME: PRINCESS CAKE??

ALESSIA: DON'T TEASE ME, CAKE ISN'T IN MY DIET PLAN.

ME: SHOULD I BE WORRIED BUNKING WITH KEENE TONIGHT?

ALESSIA: JUST STAY IN THE GUESTHOUSE AND YOU'LL BE FINE.

ME: IS BOONE GOING TO NEED MEDICAL ASSISTANCE TONIGHT?

ALESSIA: HOW SHOULD I KNOW? I'M THE INNOCENT ONE, REMEMBER?

I snorted at that but pocketed my phone. The enchilada at Boone's must have triggered cravings in Keene because he pulled into a Mexican restaurant a few minutes later. We both ordered a beer, sipping the cold brew appreciatingly when the server dropped them off with a basket of chips and salsa.

"Putting off the inevitable?" I asked, taking another pull of my beer.

Keene winced, shoving his bottle aside. "Let's just say I'm not in a hurry to get home today."

I grinned, thinking about the pranks Alessia had dolled out so far. "Is she always like this?" I wasn't sure exactly how to put my thoughts into words, but Keene seemed to know what I was asking.

"She's never been shy about letting you know where you stand with her. If she likes you, she likes you. If she hates you, stay the hell away, and when you mess up ..."

"Be prepared for the consequences." I finished his sentence, reaching for a chip. We ate in silence long enough to order, still working our way through the chips and salsa. I'd played enough poker with Keene to realize he was mulling things over and decided to give him the time and space to do it.

"I really fucked up, didn't I?" he asked suddenly, motioning for another beer.

"Yeah," I said, not about to sugarcoat it.

"Shit," he hunched over. "Didn't mean to hurt her. Gideon's pissed, and I don't blame him, either. We went around him and left him out of this. If she leaves for good over this, it will be on me."

"You didn't act alone," I reminded him. "And while I have no doubt you have some hefty damage control to do on several fronts, I think you have the ability to repair what's broken." I thought about our lunch conversation that afternoon. "Alessia loves y'all. She's angry and upset at your opinion of her." Keene flinched at that, but I wasn't about to shy away from it just because the truth hurt. "But I think what's worse is she's mad at herself for being blindsided by it."

Keene ran a hand over his face. "We picked on her for not caring enough about the company. She's been pulling away from us, from A.T. She thought she was coming in to spend the day catching up on what she's been missing."

Well, that explains the business attire, I thought. And added another tick in the box of ways her brothers had screwed her over.

"I did say you had some hefty damage control." I sipped my beer. We were quiet again as our server set our food in front of us. I was starving, but Keene barely picked at his meal, clearly upset. I could see what Alessia meant, how she loved them even though they'd hurt her feelings time and time again. The love Keene had for his sister was clear on his face. I had every confidence that the Accardi family could get past it, provided the brothers learned their lesson.

"Brody?"

"Yeah, Keene?"

"You really think I missed something?" His eyes bore into mine, and I knew instinctively he was talking about my observations that afternoon about Alessia's skills.

"Yeah, I really do."

Chapter 10

Alessia

Unable to get Brody out of my mind, I was ready to go so early the next morning most people would still consider it the middle of the night. I had hoped for another night of real rest before leaving, but instead, I'd woken after just a few hours, remembering snatches of dreams with Brody in various stages of undress. Grumpy and unable to go back to sleep, I'd packed and re-packed since I couldn't bring some of my more specialized items. Then I checked and rechecked that nothing in the contents was anything other than regular, everyday crap. Except for the garrote that was hidden in the lining of my suitcase, the knife hidden in one of the ridiculous high-heels women were expected to wear in the name of fashion, and my tracking implant—something that would only help me if someone knew I was in trouble since it wasn't like it had a panic button—I was completely naked. At least, I felt that way. I would feel better strutting down the street in my birthday suit than I was right now, getting ready for a mission with none of my normal equipment. Granted, it was just a little mission. It wasn't like I was planning a kill, just gathering intel, but I would have felt a lot better with my usual tools of the trade. I had just shoved a stun gun that looked like a tube of lipstick into my purse—because I figured the drops I typically carried would be a little too obvious with someone watching my every move—when the perimeter sensor chirped.

Slinging the purse over my shoulder, I grabbed my rolling bag and oversized purse before stepping onto the covered front porch as Keene's black SUV pulled to a stop. I waited, clearly expecting someone to get out and help me with my bags because, hello, manners were always expected—I was a lady, after all.

However, Keene sat stonily in his seat, glowering at me through the windshield, his face bright red and splotchy. Hiding my grin, I tapped my foot in a show of exasperation, looking at the delicate watch on my wrist. I couldn't read its face in the darkness, but I was making a point.

The door opened, but it was Brody who strode to the walkway to grab the bags. "Good morning," he said, barely glancing at me.

I pouted. I had hoped that my appearance would at least rate a double take. If he was bothering me—intentionally or not—the least I should be able to do was bother him right back. My minidress ended barely halfway down my thighs. I'd have to be careful how I moved, or I would flash my goodies to king and country, but I knew I looked good. Gold heels that added four inches to my already impressive height put me eye to eye with Brody. I'd left my hair loose to fall around me in gentle waves down my back. Other than the watch, the only piece of jewelry was the necklace Gia had made for me in art class. The plaster was rough, asymmetrical, and hung at an awkward angle from the chain, but Gia had been so proud to give it to me for my birthday last year that I couldn't help but love it. She'd chosen the color to be as close a match to my violet eyes as she could get, mixing several colors to get just the right shade. "Morning," I replied as he took both bags from me. "How was your night?"

I smirked as he tried to hide a smile as we walked to the SUV. "The yelling started about an hour after I retired for the night. What did you do to him? I can see the results, but he hasn't spoken an intelligible word yet."

I snuck another glance at Keene, who was studying the dash as if he'd have to recreate it from memory. "Itching powder on all of his bedding. He's slightly allergic. I also dusted it in his underwear drawer and stole his coffee supply."

Brody choked, coughing as he stopped at the trunk.

I left him to deal with the bags and got into the back seat. Between my still simmering anger, Keene's foul mood, and Brody's long legs, I figured giving him the front seat was a good move on all fronts. "Good morning," I said as I slid in, buckling my seat belt and avoiding so much as a glance at my brother.

"Boone called me," Keene said, ignoring my greeting completely. "He needs me to take all of his meetings today."

"Oh?" I faked concern. "Is he all right?"

"He's been up all night sick." Keene's voice was flat. "He ate enchiladas for dinner after drinking a shot of whiskey and spent the rest of the night alternating between running to the bathroom and praying to God."

"Poor thing." My sympathy sounded fake even to my ears. "He must have gotten a touch of food poisoning." I hadn't touched the food, so I knew good and well food poisoning wasn't the problem. Brody got into the passenger seat, shutting the door softly as he buckled up.

"A touch of something," Keene muttered, putting the car in reverse and backing out of the drive, reaching up to scratch his face. It was so irritated he hadn't even shaved, something my military-ridged brother never went without doing and was probably adding to his crabby mood.

"Are you okay?" I kept up the act. "You don't look so great either. I hope you aren't contagious."

The growl that rumbled from my brother's chest was impressive. "You know damn well I'm not contagious," he snapped.

"I'm sure I have no idea what you are talking about," I said innocently. "But if you want, I can lend you some of my makeup. Our skin tones are very similar, and I'm sure I have enough concealer to cover your face, at least." My phone chirped, and I looked down. "Oh, Matteo is so sweet. He wanted to wish me a safe journey and hopes to see me soon." I read off the text. He really meant that the plan was still a go and that he'd keep tabs on me via social media to ensure I was safe. That was what my world had dropped to, check-ins via social media and a lipstick stun-gun for protection.

Both men froze. "Just how close are you with this fucker?" Keene asked. Clearly, I had pulled the tiger's tail as much as I could get away with that morning.

I rolled my eyes as Brody twisted in his seat to look at me as I replied, "I told you countless times. Matteo is my personal trainer and a friend. A very ... personal ... friend."

"You mean you fuck," Keene clarified, yanking the wheel sharply as he directed the vehicle to the airport.

I looked out the window, not liking that Brody was still staring at me. "I mean that it's none of your fucking business. What's got your underwear in a twist? Do I ask you about your sex life?"

"You damn well know I'm not wearing any." Keene was on a roll that morning, and I made a mental note that taking his coffee might have gone a bit too far. "And Gideon would beg to differ about interfering with our sex lives."

I grinned, still staring at the landscape as we drove past, but didn't respond. Several long minutes passed in silence as I kept my gaze on the view outside the SUV before I couldn't take it anymore. I looked at Brody, not wanting to admit his attention was unnerving me as he hadn't stopped staring at me. "Do I have something on my face?" I asked, finally meeting his eyes.

"Nope," he said, giving me a lazy wink.

I refused to flush—a woman of my profession never lost her composure. Instead, I attacked. "What's the rule on fucking your brother's acquaintances?" I didn't let my stare waver from Brody as I spoke to my brother. "I mean, I know y'all have a rule about fooling around with your best friend's sister, but seeing as Brody swears you two don't know each other well, and you personally vetted him to guard my body—" I snapped my mouth shut as Keene stomped on the brake, the car screeching to a stop. Brody flew forward, his seat belt stopping him from flying into the dash. Before I could blink, Keene had the vehicle in Park, right in the middle of the road, opening his door and slamming it behind him. A second later, he ripped my door open, forcing me to scramble to undo my seat belt as he grabbed my arm, dragging me out of the car as I teetered on my sky-high heels before shutting it, leaving Brody sitting there stunned.

"Are you crazy?" I asked, looking behind us to make sure headlights weren't heading in our direction as I yanked my arm from his grip.

"I think that award goes to you, little sister," Keene said, throwing his hands up in exasperation before running them over his face.

My eyes narrowed as I crossed my arms. "I'm already mad at you. You really don't want to piss me off any more than y'all already have."

He turned away from me, pacing alongside his car before turning back to me. "I'm sorry."

I froze, certain I had to have heard him incorrectly. "Wh-what?" That certainly took the fight right out of me.

He rubbed the back of his neck. "I'm sorry. I shouldn't have forced Brody on you. And I shouldn't have interfered in your life without at least talking to you first, and I promise I will try to do better in the future." I wasn't sure if I was having an out-of-body experience, or maybe a seizure, because I couldn't have been hearing him correctly … could I? "And I would appreciate it if you wouldn't sleep with your PSO just to spite me." His words were sincere and solemn, a complete contrast to the fit of temper he'd arrived with that morning.

Just standing there, he stared at me as I struggled to figure out just what was happening. "O-okay," I managed to stammer out.

He nodded to me. "All right, then, let's get back into the car before we end up causing an accident."

I didn't say another word, simply let him open my door and assist me back into my seat.

I was still reeling close to twelve hours later when Brody opened the door to our suite in the hotel Valencia had secured for everyone roughly an hour outside of Berlin. Brody, his professionalism firmly in place, had escorted me from our plane to a waiting car. I'd waited silently as he vetted and verified that the driver was indeed the person responsible for getting us to our destination in one piece. We were staying at a charming hotel, which had been chosen as the staging area for everyone involved in tomorrow's production. I wasn't sure if he'd heard Keene and me, if I'd offended him in the car, or if it was due to my character change as I slipped into the model Alessia—no long Lessia the sister—but he'd barely said more than a handful of words to me since we'd arrived at the airport that morning. And, come to think of it, almost all of them revolved around asking if I needed something to eat, drink, or use the restroom.

He left me just inside the door to our suite, directing me to wait while he secured the rooms. I waited until he was out of sight before studying my surroundings, taking points of egress, blind spots, and the best possible placements for cover before he could catch my perusal. Then I buried my face in my phone, texting furiously when he returned.

"It's clear. If you don't mind holding out a few more minutes, I would like to put some additional security in place before leaving you alone in your rooms." I looked up, hating that he was acting so remote. I wished it were because I needed to make sure I had him firmly in my camp—he would be more apt to look the other way or grow lax if we were friendly—but I knew I was lying. For some reason, I liked him. That didn't often happen, as in, practically not at all beyond my family. And even with them, I didn't necessarily like them all the time.

I bit my lip in indecision. "Brody?"

"Yes?" He stopped rummaging through one of the cases he had brought with him, and I pretended not to notice or recognize the window sensors and video disruption device in his hand.

"I would like to apologize." I sucked at apologies, but I'd used him to dig at my brother, and while I hadn't realized it at the time, I could see that my comment was rude and could have been considered demeaning. "I didn't mean to offend or embarrass you this morning in front of Keene, nor did I mean to imply that I thought you would be unprofessional enough to sleep with a client while on the clock."

His eyes went wide in surprise. "I didn't take offense," he mumbled, looking slightly confused. "It would take more than you using me to make a point with your brothers to upset me."

"Oh." I couldn't seem to stop worrying my bottom lip, trying to figure out what was going on, but I drew a blank. "Then ..." I trailed off, not knowing what else to say.

"I'm sorry if you spent the day thinking I was angry." He rose, his hands full of equipment. "I took my cues from you."

He didn't say anything more, but I knew what he was talking about. Ice-bitch Alessia had been front and center today, partly because having him constantly watch me made me nervous and partly because someone on our flight had recognized me, leading to several people sneaking pictures of me while on board and several others trying to engage me in small talk.

I knew I didn't owe him an explanation, but I wanted to. "My job requires me to ... play a certain role ... with the outside world." I weighed my words carefully because they were true in more ways than one, and I didn't want to reveal too much. "I can let that image slip at home a bit, but even then, I have to remember that public image and reputation are a big part of my success or failure. You've seen behind the curtain more than most do, meeting me before we arrived at the airport this morning, but that person you saw in Texas is not the person I can be while I'm here."

The intensity in his green eyes flared as I spoke, and just like yesterday, he actually listened and thought about what I said—didn't ignore my words like my brothers did in their bid to attempt running my life or successful businessmen did when trying to lure me into their beds, believing me to be nothing more than a hard-to-get airhead who secretly wanted nothing more than to have them heaving above me and pretending they were a god in bed. I could see the understanding, and maybe even a hint of sympathy, in his expression.

"So, basically, if you want to keep your contracts and status in the community, they can't see you as a regular person," he mused. "How can you be the face of the goddess of sex and sin if the world sees you as a flesh and blood human being?"

"Pretty much." I gave him a small smile. "And I don't market sex and sin, just clothes."

He gave me a small smile in return. "Tell that to anyone who's seen your work."

I drew in a breath, but before I could respond, he whirled around, heading back to where I assumed my room was located. "Give me a few minutes, and I'll have your room ready for you," he called over his shoulder.

A curse had me following him down the hall. A teddy bear, holding a red rose, sat on top of the bed, placed between two decorative pillows. Oliver had charmed his way in. Probably paid off a maid with a twenty and a story about romantic love or some shit.

"I was focused on making sure there wasn't a person hiding," Brody explained. "I didn't pay much attention to the bedding."

I shrugged, knowing what he was talking about but also understanding why he was upset. True, a person was the most common threat he would have to worry about—especially knowing that a fan was starting to go off the deep end, but the stuffed animal could have been something much more sinister. I waited until Brody had taken a picture, knowing he needed to document the scene, before grabbing the bear, stomping to the kitchen, and tossing it into the trash.

"Do you want to change rooms?" Brody asked, shadowing me as I walked from the room.

"No need." I waved a hand dismissively. "He's long gone, and it'll cause them a headache of massive proportions if I ask for another room. The hotel's booked solid." I knew I should have played up my concern or fear the way a normal person with a stalker would, but it was far from my first security concern, and I hated playing the damsel in distress. For whatever reason, I also didn't want to pretend in front of Brody. My brothers might see me as Bimbo Barbie, but I didn't want him to, even for a second.

He gave me an unreadable look, studying me carefully before slowly nodding his agreement. "Let me do one more sweep, just to be sure."

I let him sweep the room twice and change the sheets—better safe than sorry with that one, considering what else Oliver could have left behind—before he finally gave me the all-clear.

As soon as he let me into my room, I practically sprinted for it, needing a shower in the worst way. I had yet to figure out why airplanes had their own stink when they controlled the air, filtration system, and seat materials, but I felt completely disgusting. Brody had thoughtfully placed both my suitcase and purse—which was big enough to be considered a shoulder bag—on stands, and I ripped them open, carefully studying the contents to see if someone had rifled through them, but nothing was out of place. Grabbing my pajamas and my bathroom kit, I paused and looked over the room. My need to check and recheck my security was too ingrained for me to let it go, even though I knew Brody had it covered. While I ensured Oliver didn't leave anything else behind, I cataloged my bedroom. The hotel was old and charming, in an upscale grandeur kind of way, and my room was no different. A large king bed took up most of the room, the frame made of what looked to be antique hand-carved wood that matched the floors, which, despite their polishing, were clearly original and had the marks, nicks, and stains to prove it. The widows were old as well, the frames latching with an old-fashioned lock that a three-year-old with a knife could jimmy, but Brody had secured them with sensors that would trip if anyone tried to enter or exit. I walked to the window, looking as if I were pulling open the drapes an inch so that I could see into the darkness of the evening, trying to see if I could get around the devices if needed. But it was apparent that he'd either gotten the tech from A.T. or had his own contacts because they were not the cheap, easily fooled sensors I'd hoped for. Turning away, I pretended to examine a small black box on the dresser. Deciding I had better keep up my civilian cover, I sighed.

"Brody, you forgot something," I called, hoping I sounded as ignorant as I was supposed to be. He appeared in the doorway a few seconds later, a kitchen knife in his hand. Seeing what I was looking at, he shook his head.

"That's a jamming device. It prevents video or audio transmissions from working."

I drew the clothes I still held to my chest. "You mean someone could have been watching me?" My eyes opened in alarm, and I whirled around as if to walk back to the window, but he stopped me.

"Keep the drapes closed," he barked as I reached for them. "I have the windows secured so that no one can enter from the outside. The drapes will keep anyone from seeing in. This box will stop anyone from being able to set up a camera or listening device in here, just in case I missed anything in my sweep."

"What about the bathroom?" I whispered, trying to think about what a civilian would do if they were in my shoes.

"You can talk normally," he said with amusement. "No one can hear, remember? The device will cover your room and bathroom, so use them as you normally would."

"What about my phone?" I picked it up from the side table and waved it for emphasis. "Can I still get my phone calls? Instagram? Twitter? How about Facebook?" I channeled my concern from the unease I still had at the thought I wouldn't be able to reach out to anyone in my room, already knowing the answer to my question.

"I'm sorry to say that your phone and anything else that runs on data or Wi-Fi will not be available to you while in your room, but you can use all of them once you're out of range. The living room is far enough from the device that you should have no issues using your apps."

"What if I have an emergency?" I asked, looking disconcerted.

"That's what you have me for." His patient answer was firm as if he was waiting for my outburst but not about to change his mind.

"What are you making?" I changed the subject, looking down at the knife in his hand. Frowning, I continued, "I'm not an expert or anything, but is a kitchen knife the best weapon?"

I could kill someone twelve different ways with a spoon, but he didn't need to know that. "Wouldn't a gun be a better choice?"

He snorted. "I was cutting up some vegetables that were stocked in the refrigerator. I figured you'd be hungry. You had two cups of coffee, a bottle of water, and a bag of pretzels today. I was going to make you some dinner, but the options are a bit ... sparse."

I bit back a grin, knowing what he was talking about. If I had to guess, the fridge was stocked with still and sparkling water, celery, carrots, and lettuce—and no dressing or vinaigrette of any kind.

"The pretzels are our little secret," I said, narrowing my eyes at him. "Salt causes bloating. I'm also supposed to fast for the shoot tomorrow, so I'm afraid they don't stock anything that might cause me to slip from my diet plan today. But if you're hungry, you're more than welcome to call room service. I'm sure you need protein to keep in top form. At least, my brothers always say they do. And I fully intend on eating at least some veggies in there tonight, diet or not."

I knew he'd ingested meat at every meal today, so he shouldn't feel deprived of anything like I was. I'd reluctantly waved off the prepared meals served in first class, but he'd feasted on eggs and bacon for breakfast and roasted chicken with potatoes for lunch. He'd also snacked on a meat stick that he'd gotten from a vending machine when I asked him to get me a bottle of water. He looked relieved as he realized he was not required to eat the same rabbit food I was.

"What are you going to live off of for the next few days?"

"Mainly water, my fat stores, and a piss-poor attitude," I replied without missing a beat. The expression of horror on his face rivaled that of my brothers' when I had announced at Sunday dinner a few years ago that I was debating on going vegetarian. I had no such intention, but the family discussion had been a fun one until Gia had ruined it by giggling, the only one to realize there was no way in hell her aunt could survive without burgers, ribs, and briskets. "I'm warning you now. I'm not responsible for my actions if you come within ten feet of me with a cup of coffee upwind of my position."

He smiled at that. "No coffee, got it. I brought energy drinks, so I should be safe from at least a five-foot distance ... They don't smell as good as a cup of joe."

I wrinkled my nose. "Do you know how many chemicals are in those things? It's liver disease in a can." I wasn't sure about any of that, but they sure all tasted like shit to me. Why mess with caffeine in its most perfect form—coffee? Hell, if I could get away with it, I took it as black sludge that replaced my blood with brown tar. As far as I was concerned, it was a sacrilege to add cream and sugar.

Brody shrugged, clearly not concerned about his health. "Caffeine is caffeine."

I gasped in outrage that was not altogether faked. "You take that back!"

He raised an eyebrow. "If I promise to sneak you a cup in the morning, will you forgive me?"

"Can't," I said mournfully. "They'll know. They always know. I even snuck a cup before I brushed my teeth one day and got reamed out by the seamstress, set director, and photographer who claimed I had coffee stains that he would have to air-brush out."

Wincing, he gave me a pitying look. "My sympathies. I promise to get you a cup as soon as they call the shoot done with, okay?"

I started, realizing that during our exchange, we'd leaned closer to each other. I could feel his body heat, even though there was still a polite distance between us. God, the man was a furnace. I stared into his mossy green eyes, getting distracted as I gazed into them. That time it was him who pulled back, and I cursed internally, trying to control the flush that wanted to rise from my neck to my face. I'd done it again, relaxing in his company without intending to. Damn it. I needed to get a grip on my emotions. Clearly, it had been too long since I'd had sex, and it was messing with my body chemistry. It was the only reason I could think of for having issues when it came to Brody. Or maybe I was just lonely? The thought made me frown. Was I lonely? I never lacked companionship when I wanted it, though I didn't fuck nearly as much as everyone thought I did. Matteo was a constant presence in my life, and my trust in him was absolute, but I didn't know if I would call him a friend ... more of a partner that I knew had my back no matter what—just like I had his. I loved my family, but they'd stopped looking for the real me years ago. Sensing my change in mood, Brody excused himself to go back to the kitchen as I turned to the bathroom for the shower that called my name.

Stepping into the claw-foot tub, I didn't even wait for the water to warm before sticking my head under the cold spray, needing the jolt. I sputtered but forced my body to stay under the needle-like barrage. I felt exhausted, mentally dragging at the thought of having to go to the shoot tomorrow. For the first time, I let myself look at my life, really look at it. I hated being a model with a passion as strong as my love for my duty to my country. And while I delighted in flying under the radar—of no one knowing what I was capable of and what I did—I equally hated that my secret had placed such a huge wedge between the rest of my family and me. I wasn't sure when my life had turned into such a tale of contraries, but they warred within me in equal and opposite amounts. Did I even like myself, the person I was becoming? Because, other than a handful of times here and there, the person I was in the past was being replaced with a fake. Was fake even the right word anymore if I was that person way more than I was the true me?

I toweled off, more than ready to put the day behind me. Between Keene's startling apology that morning and the revelation that I might just be becoming someone other than myself, I was done overthinking. I threw my pajamas on and padded to the kitchen, where Brody had placed carrot sticks, celery, and cucumber slices on a plate for me. He was sitting on a barstool, decimating what looked to be some kind of sausage in a delectable smelling sauce. He pointed to a small salad that had come up with his meal. "I ordered ranch on the side, in case you wanted to snag it for your," he motioned to my plate, "meal."

I could have kissed him because at least I wouldn't have to completely suffer that night. "Thank you," I said, not able to hide my appreciation as I practically dived for the small container. I stayed silent, not wanting to get into anything else, still focused on my thoughts. Brody kept his scrutiny on his plate, barely looking my way.

My attention turned to him as he rose and grabbed two bottles of still water from the fridge, setting one in front of me before downing his without even sitting back down. I tried to tear my eyes away from his profile as he swallowed the contents of the bottle, his Adam's apple bobbing up and down, head leaned back, but I found it impossible. His jaw had more than a hint of stubble, though he'd been clean-shaven that morning. It practically begged me to reach out and feel the rasp on my fingers. Slamming a door on my thoughts, I looked back at my vegetables, poking at the celery on my plate. I'd kill for some peanut butter, but the fat content wouldn't allow me to even think about it, especially considering I'd already splurged on the cup of dressing Brody had so thoughtfully gotten for me. "So," I tried to distract myself from the vegetable that was really nothing but string and water, "if you know Keene, why don't you work for A.T.?"

He tilted his head. "Does everyone your brother know work for him?"

"Most of the good ones do." I shrugged. "And if you weren't good, he wouldn't have planted you into Valencia's security picks."

He smiled, not commenting on what we both knew, but he didn't confirm my statement. "I promised myself I would never work for someone else ever again. A contract deal here or there is fine, but I won't put myself in the same position the military did."

"What happened?" I knew I shouldn't care, but I was curious.

His eyes turned turbulent. "Let's just say I work well with others, but when you work for the government, we're all just cogs in a wheel. I have a problem trusting higher-ups when they don't see people as anything other than pawns in a game of chess. My unit was sent into a situation we never should have been in because some paper pusher wanted to make a statement in retaliation for another country's stupid move. In the end, I was injured, and many men in my unit didn't make it because two countries were having a pissing match over something on a completely different continent that didn't matter whatsoever to the ones who actually have a claim to it."

I knew he couldn't give me much more than that—classified information and all—but I knew what he was talking about. Politics and politicians were the reason I worked black ops. Even the CIA and other alphabet soup agencies had secondary agendas when it came to assignments, and I wanted no part in them. Of course, my organization wouldn't be able to acknowledge me if something went wrong, but the likelihood of other government agencies doing that either was slim to none, so I didn't let it bother me. I simply killed the bad guy, stopped the awful shit they were doing, and went home. I looked down at my plate, where I was still playing with the celery and trying to figure out if I would suffer through eating them to be polite since Brody had gone through the trouble of putting them on my plate, when my phone rang.

I hopped up from my seat, grateful for the interruption. Thank goodness Matteo seemed to have a sixth sense sometimes. Though I was sure he wouldn't rate saving me from a plate full of celery as highly as the time he notified me of a change in guard, which would have resulted in me getting caught at the villa of a heroin dealer in Mexico. "Hi, Matteo. What are you doing up? Isn't it the middle of the night back home?"

"Couldn't sleep, Belle. I missed you too much." He played his part to perfection, sounding for all the world like a close friend or lover. "How is Germany?"

I gave him a fake laugh. "I have seen little of it yet. We traveled most of the day. I actually just finished dinner." Such as it was. "Anything exciting going on there?"

"Yes, actually." Matteo sounded amused. "Your brother called me today."

"What!" My tone put Brody on alert, but I waved him off, mouthing an apology as I pointed at the phone. He grunted and motioned to my plate in question. Because there was no way in hell I wouldn't take advantage of the moment, I nodded, signaling I was done. I would rather starve than eat celery and starve anyway, considering I couldn't eat a fraction of the calories my body practically begged for. "Who called you?"

"Gideon." Matteo's laughter drifted across the line. "You'll never guess why."

I snarled. "If they're trying to drag you into—"

He didn't let me finish, knowing I would assume they were trying to pull Matteo closer into their fold. They'd been attempting to spend some time with Matteo for years. Of course, it was under the pretense of any friend of mine being a friend of theirs, but it was really just an attempt to get in cozy with him so that they could threaten him to stay away from their little sister. "He called to ask if I would take Gia on as a student in my beginning karate class."

I sat on the couch, leaning back as I took that in, completely stunned. Gideon had been against Gia doing anything active since she was a child. She was born prematurely and had so many health problems as a baby that the doctors weren't sure she'd survive at first. After her last heart surgery—she was four by then—they'd given her a clean bill of health and declared her to be as fit as any girl her age, but Gideon couldn't get past the worry that they'd missed something. In the grand scheme of things, karate wasn't much more physical than her tumbling class, but in Gideon's mind, they were worlds apart.

"Oh my God," I exclaimed, blowing a breath out. "We got a lucky break there with him calling you." Because Gia wouldn't be able to hide the fact that Matteo and I had been teaching her since she was six.

"No kidding," he said in all seriousness. "I convinced him it would better suit her to have one-on-one lessons for a bit until I could catch her up with kids her age since the current class is a few weeks in."

"She's well above kids her age," I replied wryly.

"By the time we get to the point of her joining the class, I'll have firmly planted how much of a natural she is and have her practice at home in her room some. We'll get her to jump up pretty quickly. But if he gets suspicious, I'm totally throwing you under the bus and telling him she's joined us for your self-defense lessons."

"I wasn't expecting that." Referring to Gideon's decision, I continued, "I thought he'd relent at soccer or softball." Had my own experiences with my brothers colored my perceptions of them as adults? I wasn't sure, but it was yet another nail in the coffin of things that had gone wonky in the last twenty-four hours.

"Me neither, but I think he likes the idea of her knowing how to handle herself."

"Keene apologized to me this morning while driving to the airport." I left out the details. "He really seemed sincere, so I'm hopeful things will be different between us when I get back," I said it out loud for Brody's benefit, in case he was making regular updates to my brothers, but I really was. "I hate all the fighting that seems to happen anytime I'm home. I was really starting to wonder if I would have to make some major changes."

"That's funny." Matteo was serious now. "My dad said something along the same lines when I talked with him."

My blood froze, and it took everything in me not to drop my casual tone. "How so?" Matteo had never met his father, so I knew he was talking about our handler.

"You know how much he loves you," he said. "I think he's worried that you're pushing yourself too hard. And this problem with your brothers can't be helping."

I swallowed, trying to pick my words without sounding like I was having anything other than a normal conversation. It was a lot harder than people thought to talk in code on the fly with someone else listening. "I think I'm getting burned out in some parts of my job. But other parts, I don't know." I blew out a breath. "I think I love the other parts so much that they've been holding me to the path I'm on a lot longer than I would have without them. I don't want to give them up. But I miss being home, being able to eat what I want, and not having to worry about getting stuck with pins," I teased about the last part, but seriously, I was pretty sure torture with sewing needles should be added to the Geneva Convention.

"I think we all have to have a get-together when you get back. You know, talk things out and see if there's something we can do to help. You aren't alone, Belle, don't forget that." His voice was soft and contemplative, and I knew he was trying to come up with a solution. I just couldn't see one. Modeling gave me the access I needed to reach the monsters humanity pretended didn't exist. I could hardly continue to do what I did without the cover it gave me.

"Maybe," I hedged. "Look, I need to be up early for photos tomorrow, and you need to get some sleep if you're going to be on your game to keep up with my niece. Talk to you tomorrow?"

He yawned so hard my jaw hurt and made some sort of sound of agreement before hanging up.

"Sure, Lessia, talk to you tomorrow. Sweet dreams," I impersonated Matteo. Jerk never said a proper goodbye over the phone, and it drove me nuts.

"Everything okay?" Brody asked, coming over to sit in an armchair near me.

"Yes." I pulled my feet under me, leaning against the arm of the couch. "Matteo just called to check in and fill me in on what's going on at home."

"He's not your boyfriend, is he?" He phrased the sentence as a question, but it wasn't. It was an observation. I schooled my expression, hating that he was so intuitive. My brothers had been trying to get an answer out of me for years, and in the space of one day, he'd ferreted out that secret.

"You heard my discussion with Keene," I said, but Brody was already shaking his head.

"What is he to you?" he asked, and I knew I needed to stop his curiosity from continuing down Matteo's path. I knew with his training, he'd catch a lie, so I told the truth. Or as much of the truth as I could give him.

"He's the only person in the world who gets to see the real me. And my brothers would be both hurt and confused to hear that, so it's easier to give them the story their assumptions led them to."

Brody nodded in conformation, seeing the honesty in my statement. "And Gia?"

"Aren't you supposed to pretend not to hear my private conversations while officially guarding me?" I complained before answering him, keeping with Matteo's story. It really wasn't a story; it just wasn't exactly as ... professional ... expert ... as it was in real life. "Matteo really is my personal trainer, but he teaches way more than yoga and meditation." I trailed my finger down the arm of the couch. "He also teaches karate, as you heard, and self-defense. And, possibly, mixed martial arts for those who need some private lessons. He might teach me when I'm home from time to time."

Brody barked out a laugh. "You mean to tell me you get self-defense lessons from a yoga instructor instead of your own company? The one that trains SWAT officers and the Secret Service advanced hand-to-hand combat and martial arts? Hell, you probably have at least ten instructors on payroll who could take on tier-one operatives."

I narrowed my eyes at him in irritation. "Matteo wasn't always a yoga instructor. And just because someone is former special forces doesn't mean they have to continue working in that field when they get out. He was in the Army, not the Marines, but just because he doesn't continue to shit red, white, and blue doesn't mean he's forgotten his training."

Brody's smile was genuine now, happy. "I knew you had more training than your brothers said."

I waved him off, really not wanting to get into that conversation. "Anyway, Gia might have hung around with us and might have been shown a thing or two necessary for a girl to know growing into adulthood. And, quite possibly, her father doesn't know about it."

"You mean—"

"I mean, on Saturday, Gideon dropped Gia off early for our spa day, and she spent a few hours with Matteo and me learning how to throw him." I couldn't help the smirk. "My brothers, for all of their skills and experience, have zero observation skills when it comes to me. They constantly think I'm this airhead with no idea of how dangerous the world can be. They forget our daddy taught all of us how to shoot a gun before we could drive a car and that I grew up listening to them discuss tactics and rules of engagement at the dining room table. I'm not complacent about my safety. I have ... had ... people in place to keep me safe, but I didn't rely on them as my only line of defense." Shrugging, I continued, "I grew up not only seeing warriors coming in and out of our home, our offices, and our training center, but was raised by them as well. They might not see me as anything other than a harebrained little sister, but I'm a hell of a lot more capable than they realize."

Chapter 11

Brody

She was an enigma. A sexy riddle that I couldn't get my mind off of. Alessia was hot one moment, cold the next, vibrant and full of energy, then jaded and closed-off. I couldn't figure her out, couldn't figure out why I wanted to. Yes, I hated mysteries, but she was wrapped in a blanket of lies and truth, intertwined into a fabric of her own making, and I couldn't figure out if she'd created a safety net around herself or a noose that was slowly choking her to death.

I'd spent the entire time since she'd gotten into her brother's car studying her, my senses niggling at me that something was not quite right. Keeping up my vigilance throughout the day, I had noticed twice during our trip from one plane to the other that she had noted a potential threat and positioned herself on the balls of her feet in reflex until they passed without incident. Again, just like the restaurant, she'd noted all escape routes and kept an eye on everyone around her. I couldn't help keeping on high alert as well, too used to working within a team and trusting my teammates to alert me of danger I might have missed. I figured since Alessia was used to being alone, she must automatically keep herself sharp since she had no one to watch her back. Until me, that was. I was also positive she could drive herself from our hotel back to the airport, turn for turn, although she had buried her nose in her phone the entire drive. Why she didn't own up to her abilities was another mystery.

Her act with the jamming device on her table was just that—an act, though a very convincing one. She hadn't been kidding about her strict diet, though I couldn't see where she had any weight to lose. Even with her dedication to doing what was needed for her job, she didn't seem wrapped up in counting calories or cleansing, or whatever it was that people did when they were obsessed with their weight. The first thing she did when she entered a room was case it—noting exits and occupants, though she hid it as making a statement, striking a pose for the room to fawn over her, for pictures to be taken, before she continued on her way.

At the photo shoot the next day, she didn't interact with anyone if she could help it, barely speaking unless they asked her a direct question or she needed something. Her eyes, which I was used to seeing filled with humor, were so icy I felt frostbite creeping up my limbs from my place behind the crew. She stood on a platform, a circled step up from the floor, while seamstresses clucked around her, tightening her into the cream dress with incredible gold threading until I wasn't sure she could breathe. They continued to pick, motioning to her waist, breasts, pinching her arm as if evaluating her for fat. Through it all, Alessia ignored them, letting them rant and rave in Italian. I couldn't understand a word the two workers were saying, but I didn't have to know the language to know what they were complaining about.

She let them go for close to thirty minutes before she apparently had enough. "Tony, get your ass over here," she demanded, her voice steady and calm, but I could see the fire banked in her eyes. The photographer had come running, a camera in his hand. Snatching a cloth measuring tape out of the hands of one of the women, she ran it along her hips, waist, and over her breasts, telling Tony to snap a picture of the measurements.

"Do not delete them," she dictated quietly, not afraid to be overheard but more trying to contain her temper before she dismissed him with a nod.

She waited until he was on his way back to his table of equipment before turning her wrath on the two women in their native tongue. I never wished I could know Italian before, but by the time she was finished, both women were submissive and silent for the rest of the day.

After they strapped her in and put her feet into the heels that added a good several inches—and did some amazing things to her toned thighs—she managed the minor miracle of staying upright in the pencil-thin stilettos as she walked in the middle of the woods that had been requisitioned for the shoot. I thought the worst of the morning was over, but it was just beginning. Tony, the photographer, was English, though British, not American, so unfortunately, I had to listen to him demean Alessia over and over, berating her for every muscle tremble or body position that wasn't what he demanded. She was forced to hold certain positions for long periods, my own muscles burning in sympathy, leaning back as she stood in those ridiculous heels on a dirt path in an inverted "C," trying to look sexy while I was sure her stomach, leg, and neck muscles screamed through the torture.

They eventually stopped for lunch—only Alessia didn't eat. Instead, she stood off to the side, sipping water carefully from a straw as the crew ate sandwiches and cookies the caterer had brought in. "All right," Tony called after stuffing himself with two sandwiches and several cookies. "Let's change the look."

They'd changed out the lighting and Tony's camera equipment, and I was relieved to hear him declare the heels had to go until I realized Alessia would be forced to walk through the woods barefoot, stones and fallen twigs left where they were to ensure the set felt "natural."

She did it all without complaint, a trained animal performing on cue, giving the photographer what he demanded, though I saw her hide a wince more than a few times as her feet came down on the odd sharp rock or twig. The look of the whole shoot was regal, aloof, and expensive, playing right into Alessia's haughty stare, which got more and more frigid as the day progressed.

Toward the end of the day, a car appeared, and two men got out. One was obviously hired muscle, his suit doing a poor job hiding his weapon or the tattoo creeping up his neck. The other was suave, neatly put together in an understated suit that only old money could pull off. His pale-yellow hair was thinning, but vanity had him combing it over in an attempt to hide it instead of resigning himself to age and genetics. It was apparent that this was someone important. The support staff all stopped what they were doing to kiss up to the newcomer. It was Alessia who alerted me that all was not what it seemed. She'd been largely ignoring everyone all day, barely glancing at any one person in actual recognition.

"Alessia?" Tony asked when she suddenly froze, her gaze looking at the stranger as if she was looking into his very soul. "Alessia?" he asked again when her eyes didn't move. "Alessia? Can you do your job for once? If I have to add another day to our schedule because of your performance issues, I will make it clear to Valencia who's to blame for it," Tony snapped, pulling her attention back to him and breaking her spell over the older man, who had frozen when she'd locked onto him.

I took another look at the stranger, wishing I could run identities the way I had in the military. He had the look of a pampered socialite, his body thin and slightly frail, but he wasn't old ... Maybe early fifties at the latest. He wore his suit like I'd worn my uniform, completely at home with where he was and how he looked. Her gaze had clearly affected him, and he fidgeted with his tie before reaching up to pat his hair. In German, he said something to his companion, who sniggered and replied. Something about their exchange made me stand at attention.

"Excuse me." I waved at a man who Alessia had introduced as her agent, a short, stout man who had largely ignored the work going on around him. He was one of the few besides the photographer who spoke English, and I needed some answers. He looked up, frowning as he set his phone aside, which had only just been snatched back up after greeting the newcomer.

"Who's the gentleman who just arrived? Do you know him? I thought this location was secure?" I played up the concerned security breach, figuring that would be the most logical reason I'd be asking questions at all.

"He owns the property." The agent, Randy, frowned, thinking. "I know it's his security that we're using on the photoshoot. I believe he's a businessman of some sort. I know he's a fan of Alessia—it was her name that Valencia used when they asked permission to use his land. Karl Albrecht, I think. He's connected. That's all that matters in the grand scheme of things, and he's certainly not a security concern."

I committed the name to memory.

"How has she," he motioned to Alessia, "been? Any issues?" He grimaced as he asked like it was a loaded question.

"No issues at all," I replied, but Randy continued as if I hadn't said a word.

"I know she can be a bitch to work with, but she values herself too much to do anything stupid, so don't worry about her bailing out on you or something." He was earnest in his words as if trying to convince me she wasn't as much trouble as she was being.

"I haven't seen any ... bitchy ... behavior at all," I said honestly, not that I couldn't see where he got the impression. She had warned me yesterday that her public persona wasn't who she was at home, and I could see that undersold it. I just hadn't done anything that warranted her turning her ire on me.

He let out a breath. "You must not hover. That's good, fantastic. She hates it when her guards hover. Just let her have her space, and she'll keep you around. It's easy money for men like you if you can toe the line."

He was still speaking in riddles, but I distinctly got the impression he wasn't only talking about her guards but himself as well.

"You give her free rein, then?" I asked casually, wondering if he would actually relax enough to make small talk. He was a fidgeter, constantly jumping and moving around, even so much as squirming in his seat like a three-year-old needing to pee while he sat to answer texts or emails on his phone.

"You bet I do," he answered immediately, turning around to sneak a peek at her as if afraid she would surprise him from behind. "She's my best model—my best money-maker. Not only that, she's normally my easiest ... at least, from a distance. I don't need to babysit her or entice her to do her job. She's no drama as long as no one pisses her off. No drugs, no stints in rehab, no daddy issues. She's as smart as a whip, too. She negotiated her own contract with Valencia and got twenty percent more than I would have been over-the-moon to get. Honestly, I'm window dressing for her, which is an appreciable change of pace for me. The only issue I have to contend with is her brothers, but for what I make from her, it's more than worth the price." He looked green around the gills at the last part, and I had a feeling fear was the foundation of that relationship.

"Has she always had such control over her business dealings?" I didn't know much about the fashion industry—as in zero—but I was pretty sure agents handled most of that stuff for their clients.

"Yep." He pulled at his expensive-looking shirt, frowning as he realized he'd gotten mustard on it. "I'm telling you, the more you leave her alone, the better she likes it. Just," he looked around, "don't piss her off."

I would have laughed, but he looked almost terrified at the admission.

"What am I missing?" I murmured, unsure what she could have possibly done to put that look in his eye.

"Let's just say I used to talk to her like Tony does. Once I did it at a time when she considered it off the clock. She might take what's expected in this industry when she's working, but when she isn't ..." He trailed off, but I got the drift.

"She isn't afraid to stand up for herself," I said, nodding since it made sense—at least to me. When I was enlisted, I could ignore the shit people threw at me that would have sent me into a fit of rage had I been a civilian and not been representing anyone other than myself.

He swallowed hard before nodding. "Her brothers might be scary, but I tell you, I know now why the feared warriors, the Amazons, were women."

Before I could respond, Alessia called out to him, and he scurried like a rat aboard a sinking ship.

Yet another piece to an already fragmented puzzle, I thought, wincing as I saw her step on a sharp rock. She didn't so much as flinch, just pulled her foot up and placed it next to her original footprint, but I swore I saw a bit of red smudged on the stone. The aristocrat who had caught her attention strode past, ignoring me and everyone else completely as he stepped onto the set and took her hand in his to raise it to his lips. She smiled, the first one I'd seen that day, but the warmth still didn't reach her eyes.

"It was so wonderful for you to open your grounds to us." She'd pulled out her accent slightly, just enough to soften her syllables and round the edges of her words. Her accent had almost completely disappeared on the plane, something that had startled me the first time she spoke, but it had come back fully when we were talking the night before. "You've shown us true hospitality. I feel so much safer here than I would out in the middle of the woods." She shuddered softly, and the man's eyes dropped to her bare shoulders. "I'm sure you're aware I have some ... unsavory ... fans who are being a bit overzealous of late."

"Anything for you, Miss Accardi." He practically bowed, his hand still holding hers.

"Please call me Alessia. All of my friends do, Mr. Albrecht."

He turned, enfolding her hand in his arm in a practiced move, escorting her to a chair I hadn't seen her use the entire day. I wasn't sure she could even sit, considering how tight her dress was. "Please call me Karl," he replied. "We have a long history at this estate of guarding what is considered dear. This estate is all part of an *eine Festung*."

"A castle?" she murmured, leaning into him slightly. "How fascinating. I love history. Europe is so full of it."

"Germany has more than its share," Karl said sagely. "And what girl in the world doesn't dream of becoming a princess?"

Alessia raised an eyebrow, reaching her hand to touch the forearm that still held her other in his grasp. "A queen," she said quietly, letting her fingers linger on his skin suggestively.

I cleared my throat, needing to get her hands away from his body before I forcibly removed them. "I'm sorry, Miss Accardi, but they need to take your dress, and your feet need attending." I tried to sound professional, helpful, even, but the look she sent my way told me I'd missed my mark.

She winced, wiggling her toes. "I do detest being barefoot," she told Karl, pulling back slightly as she acknowledged the two attendants waiting to assist her in removing the dress. "But beauty must override pain." She sighed, smiling up at him before attempting to step back.

Karl jolted, gripping her tightly before relaxing his grip, though he didn't let her go. "What did you say?" he asked, his attention riveted on hers. I took a step forward, not liking his hold on her.

Alessia tilted her head in confusion. "My ruined feet hurt but were worth the sacrifice if Tony got the pictures he needed." She rephrased her last statement, and if I didn't know any better, I would say she was trying to be considerate of the language barrier, but her body language betrayed her. Somehow, she thought she had made some sort of misstep in her words. She patted his arm one last time, deftly removing her arm from his grasp.

"You have a wonderful evening, Mr. Albrecht." She didn't look back as she followed the two women to a tent, more akin to a canopy with sides. Karl didn't look away as she left, and I noted she added just a hint more sway to her step than normal. Karl's guard finally said something to him, pulling the man's attention away. With reluctance, Karl walked to his vehicle, looking back one last time at where Alessia had vanished before getting into it. Judging by the look on his face, it wouldn't be the last we'd see of him.

"What was that?" I asked once I'd escorted Alessia to our hotel suite at the end of the day and cleared the room.

Alessia hobbled into a chair, her steps slightly stilted after her cuts had been cleaned and bandaged. "The shoot? A normal life in the day of a model," she said grouchily. "But according to my brothers, I just stand around all day, looking beautiful and trying on pretty dresses."

"Not the photoshoot. The Prince Charming you hooked today." I pulled out two acetaminophen from my medical kit and handed them to her with a bottle of water.

"Just doing my job," she said before popping the pills into her mouth and chasing them with half the contents in the bottle. Wiping her mouth with the back of her hand, she continued, "Networking is a huge part of what I do. My contacts—the demands and desire by others to have me at their parties, events, and even political functions—keep fashion houses like Valencia interested in me.

They dress me for those events, get more people with eyes on their designs, and I continue to increase in popularity."

What she said was reasonable, but it still rankled. "That wasn't like any business networking I've ever seen." My tone had her back up instantly, and I knew I'd pushed too far.

"One, you are my PSO, not one of my brothers, so back off. Two, you have no right to judge what I do and how I do it—you've known me for about a minute and have no knowledge of the circles I move in. And three," she pointed at me, "Karl is a very handsome man for his age. I could do much worse than someone that rich and good-looking paying me a bit of attention. As you've found out, it's not like I have a boyfriend at home, so I'm not doing anything wrong by looking at my options."

I saw red, imagining her in the arms of that egotistical—"He's too old for you," I snapped, not caring that I had no right to say anything. She was right. I was her PSO. I was supposed to stay in the background, unseen and ignored unless necessary. I wasn't supposed to converse with her or argue with her over her life choices. Hell, she could bring any man she wanted into the hotel and have screaming sex, and the only thing I could do was to ensure the man she chose didn't have a weapon or kill her in the middle of their midnight acrobatics.

Alessia snorted. "He's not that old. I'm sorry to say that models are pretty well known for having a type." She frowned. "Or people have a type about models."

I was saved from a retort that I might have regretted when we both heard a knock at the door. I wasn't angry enough to forget why I was there to begin with, so I was cautious as I approached, careful as I looked through the peephole. Not recognizing the well-dressed man, I slowly opened the door, keeping myself between him and the rest of the room so that he couldn't see inside.

"Mr. Albrecht has sent me." The heavily accented English was hard to understand. "I have an invitation to eat," he continued, "for Miss Accardi."

"Let him in," Alessia's sultry voice called from her spot on the chair. I did a quick pat down of the man, noting he was younger than he appeared, before letting him enter the room.

"Hello, miss." The man turned bright red when his eyes met hers, looking down at his feet. She gave him a moment to remember his purpose, and I couldn't help but smirk at her over the kid's head at his obvious loss of composure. She gave me a look of warning, reminding me we both had parts to play, before turning her attention back to the young man, who seemed to recover his wits.

"Mr. Albrecht has sent me to fetch you for dinner. He says he looks forward to getting to know you more." He frowned, and I'd bet my passport that wasn't exactly what he'd been told to say. Likely, seeing Alessia in person had his young brain cells scrambling amid his hormones kicking into overdrive. "He sent a car ... for your protection," he finished, looking at her expectantly. My hands gripped into fists, but there wasn't anything I could do while we waited for her answer.

"Please give my deepest apologies to Mr. Albrecht," she said kindly, the look in her eye earnest and sincere. "But, unfortunately, I have to decline his request." She motioned to her feet, wiggling them to get the man's attention off her thighs. I couldn't blame the kid for almost swallowing his tongue at the glimpse of her mile-long legs, but the wrapped feet were hard to miss. The doctor had bandaged both of Alessia's feet, making it look like she'd walked over hot coals and been treated at a burn center. "The doctor on set gave me strict instructions not to walk or wear shoes until tomorrow morning, or he won't sign off on my medical release to complete our shoot. Since I have another engagement after this, I can't risk delaying my business here. Perhaps there'll be time tomorrow after shooting if Mr. Albrecht is still available and willing to forgive my absence today."

I let out a breath in relief, but the boy only frowned, clearly upset.

"But he requests you come now," he said, looking confused as if declining the request wasn't something he'd considered. I looked over at the landline of the hotel, seeing a pen and paper sitting by the device that looked like it had been around since the nineteen forties.

"Would you like to pen your admirer a note?" I asked, keeping my tone bland. The remark went completely past the kid, but Alessia narrowed her eyes almost imperceptibly.

"What a great idea," she said with a smile. "Whatever would I do without you?" She batted her eyelashes at me, my body hiding her expression from our visitor. She penned a quick note, signing her name at the bottom with a flourish before handing it to me, allowing me to stay between her and the kid. He still looked a bit shocked at her response but took it gamely with the promise to give it to Albrecht. I followed him to the door, locking it securely behind me before returning to the kitchen. Alessia had placed her feet on the stool next to her, keeping them elevated and causing her to recline backward at an awkward angle to rub the backs of her thighs.

"Do you have a swimsuit?" I asked. She gave me a wide-eyed look.

"Uh, yeah." The unspoken why hung in the air.

"You can't get your feet wet, but I bet you'd kill for a soak in a tub. Your muscles have got to be sore. If you can manage the suit, I can assist you in and out." I couldn't believe the words coming out of my mouth. Again, I placed myself in a totally inappropriate situation with my primary, but I couldn't seem to help myself.

Alessia lit up, looking at me like I'd just offered her the keys to a kingdom. "That would be—"

Another knock at the door cut her off. Again, I approached it with caution. "Can I help you?" I asked the blond-haired man who tried to look around me as soon as the door opened. He looked older than the last kid, probably in his early twenties, which put him only about five years or so behind Alessia and ten behind me. He, too, was well dressed in tan pants, loafers, and a patterned button-down that was neatly tucked. His hair was freshly styled, his brown eyes star-filled and love-struck. He looked like a prep-school trust fund kid, and I wondered absentmindedly if anyone there owned a pair of jeans.

"I'm here for Alessia—I know this is her room." British accent, very proper pronunciations adding to the upper crust vibe. He held up a fist full of flowers for my inspection. "Red roses are her favorites. I had to go to two different places to get the correct variation, but I know she'll be pleased."

My eyes narrowed, remembering the teddy bear holding the rose on the bed and wondering if he was the stalker I was hired to protect her from.

I waited for a beat, but Alessia didn't call from her place, hidden out of sight in the kitchen. Whomever he was, she didn't want to deal with him. "Sorry, dude," I said, not at all sorry. "But this is my room. What's your name?"

He looked put out. "It's Oliver Wright." Hopping up on his toes, he still wasn't tall enough to see over me into the room beyond. "My father is Harold Wright. He is a Valencia executive from the London office. It's okay. I'm not some random fan. I know Alessia personally, and I know they reserved this suite for her specifically." He tried to walk through me, but I held firm, letting him literally bounce off my frame.

"I'm not sure where you got your information, kid, but this room belongs to me. Someone broke in here before we arrived, and management demanded Alessia move to a different set of rooms. I only guard her during the day, so I'm not sure where she is right now."

Oliver bristled. "You let the other man in. I demand you let me into your room. For all I know, you're holding her hostage."

I laughed, knowing there was no way in hell the kid would get through me. "Listen," I crossed my arms over my chest, "I called Alessia when the other man insisted he contact her. She's on bed rest after the incident on set today."

"What happened?" His voice rose two octaves as he brought the flowers in, hugging them to his chest. "Is she all right? What hospital is she located in?"

I held up a hand. "Calm down. She's fine, just cut her feet, is all. But the doctor gave her strict instructions to stay in bed and rest until tomorrow morning. She gave me firm instructions to be left alone for the rest of the night. I'm not making any more phone calls—I value my job too much to disturb her in the mood she's in. If you know her like you say you do, then you know what she can be like." I stepped back to shut the door, slamming it for good measure before locking it with a resounding click. He pounded on the door, but before I could decide how to handle him, I heard other voices in the hall.

Poking my head out, I saw two hotel security personnel detaining Oliver as he tried to bluster his way past them. "I was just about to call you guys," I called out, getting their attention.

"Is this gentleman disturbing you?" the first one asked.

"Yes, actually. I've been on set all day and was hoping to turn in early. I've had more visitors in the last ten minutes than Grand Central Station."

He blanched, clearly upset that security had been breached not once but multiple times. "I'm so sorry, sir. I'll ensure you have no more unwanted visitors tonight."

Over Oliver's protests, they physically escorted him down the hall to the open elevator.

Alessia hadn't moved from her position on the stool, looking more than a little curious as I came into view. "Is he gone?" she asked.

"Oliver the creeper? Yeah, hotel security has him." I grabbed a water bottle out of the fridge. "Would you feel more comfortable changing rooms? He was holding some roses, and I thought he might be the one who left that stuffed animal in here for you."

She shook her head, not looking at all concerned. "Oliver isn't a danger to me. At least not in his present state. I'm not saying he's not going to be in the future," she continued before I could protest. "But he's still in the adoring stage on his fixation. The bear was him, but if we're at the gift-giving stage still and not at threats, delusional notes, or scary-as-shit crap being left for me to find, we're fine for the moment."

"The fact that you know he's a delusional stalker and not worried about him is a little disconcerting." I couldn't lie. She was a lot more accepting of the situation, and she was the focus of this guy's attention, not me.

She shrugged. "He's not the first one I've had, and he likely won't be the last. He has a little more access to me than most others just because of his dad. His parents think it's puppy love, but they aren't stupid. With any luck, they will realize his obsession with me and get him the help he needs before he escalates too far."

Chapter 12

Gideon

With Boone sick, the three of us were swamped with our work, plus another the next day. Besides Boone's shitty timing—literally—a bug had broken out in our on-site daycare, and many of the parents of the children who usually took advantage of the work benefit had to call out to work to stay home with sick kids.

It wasn't until the next morning that I could corner them all in our private gym. Keene and Royce were at the bench press while Boone, who still looked under the weather, was attempting to jog on the treadmill. Royce had a white stick in his mouth, his cheek popping out on one side like a squirrel packing in acorns. He'd come in yesterday sucking on a damn sucker and hadn't gone more than a handful of minutes without having one in his mouth since.

"Y'all are fucking idiots," I said as I reached earshot, my fury at them only building over the last day instead of winding down. "You realize Lessia is only going to tolerate your shit for a little while longer—assuming she hasn't already hit her limit—before she permanently moves to New York City or Milan or wherever the hell she's been spending most her time over the last few years?"

Keene carefully placed the bar back on its perch before sitting up. "I will not apologize for looking after my baby sister. I did, however," he continued before I could rip into him, "apologize to her for how I went about it."

That pulled me up short. Maybe I had allowed myself to get worked up over nothing. "You said you were sorry to Alessia?" I hated gray areas in anything. The world ran smoother when everything was black and white. Having to clarify every detail was a habit so ingrained in my DNA it didn't even piss off my brothers anymore.

"Yes," Keene said simply. "I apologized for how I went about working around her and asked her not to sleep with Brody in retaliation."

I felt my eyebrow lift. "You think he would let her?" Whether or not she would fuck Keene's friend to make her point wasn't even a question in my mind. I was more curious if it would have worked. Sleeping with Brody so she could get back at Keene was something I wouldn't have put past her at all. Brody was the outlier in that plan. I would have thought he would keep his hands to himself, considering Alessia was Keene's sister, but even as mad as I was the other morning, I could see the interest in his eyes before he could mask it.

Keene wiped the sweat from his brow with a towel before flinging it aside. "If you'd asked me that a few days ago, I would have laughed in your face. But he got that goofy look watching her when I drove them to the airport yesterday."

"The one that men always get when they fall under Alessia's spell?" Royce asked.

He hesitated. "Brody might be interested, but he's not one to be led around by his cock. No way in hell will he let Alessia run wild over him."

I saw the thought hit him as surely as a cartoon light bulb going off over his head. I knew my brother enough to know that he assumed that, while Brody wouldn't be led around by his dick, our sister might be easier to handle if she was distracted by her interest in the man.

"I should call him and give him some inside—"

My fist flew into his face before I comprehended my impulse. In typical Accardi fashion, Boone and Royce jumped in, but even two against one, they were no match for me. I didn't let the beast in me slip his leash often, but between Alessia, Gia, and the minx who invaded my dreams, leaving me waking up bathed in sweat night after night, my hand wrapped around my erection and her name on my lips, I couldn't control myself. "You're not giving your friend pointers on how to gain our sister's favor. You're not interfering in her life anymore. None of us are going to meddle in her life any more than we would in each other's." My fist didn't slow, didn't differentiate between the three of them, determined to knock sense into them equally. "Our sister is a grown-ass woman, not the snot-nosed teen she was when we left home. Every time you make a decision on her behalf or otherwise try to run her life, you're telling her without words that you don't trust in her ability to live her own life. We will no longer tell the females in our lives that they are somehow not qualified for or otherwise unfit to do anything they set their minds to. Is that clear?" I laid the three of them out on the ground as I loomed over them, breathing hard, my hand flexing with still pent-up anger. The pain in my knuckles felt good, the minor discomfort giving me a slight release, just enough to keep me from blowing up completely, though not nearly enough to clear the anger from my system.

"Is this all about Alessia?" Royce always was a shrewd bastard.

"She's most of it." But not all of it. I threw a few towels down to where they were still sprawled out at my feet. "Gia's opened my eyes to how we've been treating them, her and Lessia. I didn't mean for it to turn into a gender thing—I know none of us have an issue with a capable woman, but with Gia being so sickly when she was born ... I guess I've coddled her in some ways. It had nothing to do with being a girl, but she and Alessia took it that way, especially given how we've handled our sister until now." I blew out a breath. "Alessia pointed out to me that just because her choices aren't ours doesn't make them wrong. We've belittled her job, her life, and then get our noses out of joint when she puts space between us. And because she pulls away, we turn into rat bastards and interfere even more. No wonder she doesn't talk with us."

"She talks plenty," Boone protested.

"Does she? What's going on in her life? Where did she go for her photoshoot? Do you know what she's planning on doing if she's going to pull back from modeling? Hell, for all we know, she has a steady boyfriend in Europe—she's certainly there more than she is here. She has property we didn't know about. What other things is she interested in?

She tried to hide her excitement about spending the day with us at A.T.—she might not have experience enough for teaching classes, but there's plenty of work on the business side of things she could take on. Hell, I don't even know if she graduated college. She was taking online classes after she graduated high school since modeling required her to travel so much, but do any of you know what she was majoring in?" I shook my head at the matching blank expressions staring up at me.

"From this moment on, everyone in our family, no matter whether they served, no matter whether or not they have a dick, will be treated equally. The Accardi siblings might stick our noses in each other's business, but we do it with more than just superior attitude and misplaced intentions." I thought about my past clusterfuck. Lord knew I had enough experience thinking I knew best, given the hellish road I paved with all my best intentions.

Chapter 13

Alessia

My feet weren't as bad as Brody or the doctor made them out to be, but they would certainly be tender for a few days. They served as a good excuse to forego dinner with Karl—I was afraid I might have hooked him a bit more than I'd intended. The bad thing about the rich, fixation types was that they liked who they liked and ignored the rest. I needed to get into his residence. My original plan to go in covertly to ensure I stayed out of his crosshairs was no longer possible because I couldn't be sure I could ditch Brody to do what needed to be done. Karl Albrecht had expressed more than a passing interest in me during our previous interactions, and just his gaze on me made me want to scrub myself down with bleach. He wouldn't be my mark, dammit, but the least I could do was get as much intel as possible to help whoever was chosen for the assignment. He'd popped onto our radar a few months ago when an Italian opera singer had gone missing. She ran in some of the same circles I did, and whispers of unwanted attention from Karl Albrecht, paired with the same people looking at him with fear in their eyes, had put me on his trail. We found seven other missing women over the past ten years—two of which were Americans—and Matteo was still digging. We uncovered more than rumors as well—forensic evidence, police reports, and even a few eyewitnesses who eventually vanished. It all confirmed that Albrecht was too connected and wealthy to be touched by the justice system. When he fixated on a woman, he owned her—he didn't just keep her for a few days before killing her. He spent weeks or months torturing the women, turning them into something less than human, stripping them of their dignity, hope, and humanity before he discarded them like trash, not even bothering to give them the respect in death that he denied them while they were alive.

Oliver was an annoyance as well, but I hadn't lied to Brody when I said he wasn't a danger to me yet. How soon it took him to escalate into more than an irritant, I didn't know, but I sincerely hoped his family read the writing on the wall before that happened and I had to take care of him. I wouldn't kill him, but depending on his actions, I couldn't help if I "accidentally" cut something off that wouldn't grow back.

I checked in with Matteo by posting a photo of my feet on my private social media. My friends replied with sympathy, and Matteo liked it, letting me know he'd seen it. Brody's offer to assist me in the tub had certainly gotten my attention, and I wondered if I should play up my feet—indulge my girly side and let him play the hero—or do what I usually did and suck up the pain. A few trash bags, some duct tape, and a shot of whiskey, if I could sneak some, and I would be fine to shower and sleep. Being a damsel in distress wasn't my style. But the other part of me argued that any chance to get Brody's hands on me was a good one I shouldn't waste. Especially if it involved me, a tub, and some bubble bath.

"Done eating?" The man in question brought my attention back. I looked down at the lettuce I was picking at—without dressing. I'd eaten a bite of an apple, a carton of plain yogurt, and the sorry excuse for a salad that day. The two witches in charge of dressing me had made it abundantly clear that they believed I was putting on weight. I wasn't, but I didn't want to give anyone ammunition by eating something with more substance. Tony knew not to delete the pictures I had him take of my measurements—which were spot-on, thank you very much—and that was my ace up my sleeve if Valencia executives came calling. I was not taking the fall for someone else not doing their job correctly. As it was, I was pretty sure my internal organs were going to bruise from being squeezed into the dress that day, and I warned the two women that they better have the correct dress size for tomorrow's shoot, or I would be the one causing problems for them. Clothing for shoots was always insanely tight, but squeezing into one a size smaller was even more difficult.

"Yep." I grimaced. "My brothers always wonder why the first thing I do is stuff myself with red meat."

He gave me a sympathetic look. "I don't blame you. How long does the shoot go on tomorrow?"

"Just until around lunchtime, thank goodness. Tony needs the morning light or whatever for the next bunch. Then we're done." I hesitated, not sure how much to fill him in on Karl. "If Mr. Albrecht asks me to join him tomorrow afternoon, I won't say no." My chin jutted out, and I gave him a challenging look. "I can't afford to offend him or ignore this opportunity to network. But I won't let him dismiss you." He scoffed at that, but the seriousness on my face had him pausing. "I don't want us separated while I'm in there, even for a minute."

He straightened. "You're afraid of him."

Now it was my turn to scoff. "Not afraid, but I'd be a fool not to be cautious. Karl Albrecht is not a man to take lightly, and while I would benefit from spending the afternoon with him, I'm not about to get into a personal entanglement with him, no matter what I said to you when we discussed it earlier."

"What aren't you telling me?"

I both hated and appreciated how observant he was. It was refreshing to have someone look beyond the surface—and incredibly dangerous.

I looked away, giving him a layer of truth. "There've been ... rumors regarding Albrecht. He doesn't always think societal laws apply to him. He's not the only rich man to take what he wants, regardless of the opinions and desires of others. But he's certainly one minefield I don't want to navigate any more than needed."

"You mean rape," he said flatly. Rape was the least of it, but I couldn't divulge any more than I already had, so I stayed silent. Brody swore. "And you want to visit the man?" He got up from his seat, leaning both hands against the counter to level an incredulous look at me. Seeing I was serious, he swore again.

"You realize how crazy that sounds? Like certifiable crazy, right?"

He had no idea.

"Since you've already seen some really grand examples of my mental state, I'm not going to dignify that with an answer. In the last week, I've signed my brother up for every dating service, prostitute, and phone sex operator I could find, poured out close to twenty thousand dollars of alcohol, and dosed Boone with something that probably required him to sleep on the toilet, cleaned Royce's fountain in the most public way possible, replaced his condoms with suckers, and powdered Keene's underwear, sheets, and towel with itching powder and stole his coffee supply. I think we both know I'm not exactly normal."

He looked at me like I had grown two heads. "Why did you replace Royce's condoms with—you know what, never mind, I don't want to know."

I got up, wincing as my feet touched the floor. "You don't know him well enough, but Royce is a bit of a man-whore. He thinks I don't know about it because he tries to keep it low-key when I'm in town. And I'm not discussing Karl with you anymore. I'm trying to give you a heads-up for tomorrow because I'm sure he's going to put me in a position where I can't say no. But I'm counting on you to have my back, and having an engagement in Monte Carlo will give me the excuse I need to keep it short. The private plane will give me an opportunity to get ready. The party there should only take a few hours, and we have our flight back home at seven the next morning."

"What about your feet?" he asked, looking down at them even as he walked around the counter to extend a hand to me, ever the Southern gentleman.

"I'll wear flats when I'm able, but unfortunately, heels are part of the uniform," I joked. "Seriously, though, they aren't that bad. I have a few cuts, but mainly it's just bruising. They'll be tender but nothing more than a minor irritation." I changed the subject. "Are you really planning on helping me in and out of the tub?"

"As long as you wear a bathing suit," he said as if it was no big deal. His grip was firm around my waist, his arm easily taking most of my weight even as I walked down the hall. His strength was impressive. I might be thin, but I wasn't a lightweight. I had little in the way of fat, but muscle weighed more.

He left me in the bathroom, starting the water and even getting a bathing suit from my bag, so I didn't have to move. The bikini wasn't my most revealing, but it still left little to the imagination. The wine-colored material made my eyes pop and complemented my skin tone to perfection. After changing, I pinned my hair up, not wanting to bother with drying it.

"Come in," I called when he knocked. He carried several bags and a roll of tape in his hand.

"I thought—" His words cut off as he looked at me, sitting on the counter as I waited for the tub to fill.

"You thought?" I prompted when he didn't continue. I raised an eyebrow and crossed my legs. The move was practiced. I knew what I was doing, drawing his eyes to my legs.

His gaze heated as it traveled down my long, tanned skin, but I'd forgotten about my bandaged feet. He frowned. His desire changed to concern. "Are you sure your feet are all right?"

I blew out a breath, exasperated. Did he have to be so darn honorable? "If I promise to let you play doctor, will you stop asking?" There I was, practically naked in front of him, and all he could think about was my damn feet.

He grunted, setting the tape aside to use both hands to open the small trash bags. Touching me as little as possible, he secured my feet inside the plastic and taped the top all the way around to seal my injured flesh from the water. He had kneeled to attend to my feet, placing him at just the right height to be eye level with the juncture of my thighs. I knew I should have squeezed my legs together at the knee, but modesty was never one of my attributes. Glancing up, he was about to speak, but his eyes caught on the strip of burgundy material that lay between him and a part of me that hadn't quite gotten the memo about Brody's obvious attempt at keeping it as professional as possible.

The wicked part of me wanted to egg him on and jump his bones. My sore feet weren't the only thing throbbing, and a quick fling would certainly fix whatever was askew with my body chemistry. But the clearer voice in my head reminded me that not only was he Keene's friend, but he was someone I needed to keep at arm's length. Girlfriend material I was not, and Brody didn't strike me as someone who would be satisfied with one night in my bed.

Sighing, I gently pulled my foot from his grasp and closed my legs to wrap one plastic-encased foot around the other equally encased ankle. Brody followed my cue and rose to his feet, spinning away from me to turn off the tap before pouring a small, complementary packet of bath salts into the water and swirling it around with his hand. Steam rose from the water, quickly filling the small room with the smell of lavender. I inhaled deeply, grateful that he hadn't chosen the rose one—contrary to Oliver's belief, I hated roses with a passion.

"So, what's the plan here?" I asked, relaxing against the mirror behind me.

"Simple," he replied, placing two rolled-up towels on either end of the tub. "I'll pick you up and put you in, then take you out when you're ready. You keep your feet out of the water, relax your muscles, and I get a chance to show off my manly strength, so it's a win-win."

I liked his teasing side. He let it come out every so often, but he seemed more comfortable with me now that we knew each other better. "You're going to get soaked," I pointed out.

Giving me a wicked look, he pulled his shirt up over his shoulders and head, revealing a lean torso, his six-pack highlighted by a scattering of hair. I swallowed hard. I was surrounded by male bodies, mostly naked, tanned, and living, breathing Adonises. Hell, I'd done shoots that practically required me to use them as my personal jungle gym. None of them had ever affected me the way he did. Heat flooded my body, setting my nerve endings alight. I tried to make my brain engage, to say something witty, but I couldn't hold a thought.

His smirk grew as he saw my expression, and he walked toward me without pause. He picked me up, swinging me into his arms like every trashy romance novel I'd ever read. Before I could decide if I was pissed, embarrassed, or girlishly pleased at the high-handed gesture, he plunked me down into the hot water.

"There." He certainly looked satisfied with his handiwork as I sputtered around the water that splashed onto my face with his not-so-smooth move. "I'll let you get to relaxing. Just call out when you're ready for me to extradite you." With that, he whirled around and left, leaving me speechless.

I stayed in the hot water until my muscles were practically a pile of goo. The extreme positions I had to maintain for the shoot had my back, thighs, and calves screaming at me even hours later. No one ever looked at pictures they saw in magazines and actually thought about how their own body would feel holding the same stances we did for even a few minutes, let alone an hour or more at a time, with very few breaks in between.

The exhaustion from the day fell over me like a wave. It was always like that for me ... Full tilt until I hit a wall. I snuggled back into the makeshift headrest, closing my eyes as I let myself doze. I never slept well when I wasn't in Texas, could never let myself drop my guard. Like my military brothers, I could sleep so lightly that I could practically hear a leaf drop outside of my window, but unlike them, the deep, unfettered, any-time, anywhere coma they could put themselves in at the drop of a hat was not something I could afford anywhere else but the safety of my own home. I drifted, letting my mind center and calm, spending long minutes doing nothing but listening to my own soft breathing.

A quick turn of the door handle had me lurching upright, reaching for the knife that I didn't have because Brody-the-white-knight was now stuck on my ass. "Don't you know how to knock?" I asked, catching myself just in time from springing to my feet in a fighting stance.

"Sorry," he muttered, clearly not in much of a better mood than I was. "I wasn't sure if you were sleeping since I hadn't heard much in here in a while and didn't want to wake you."

That he'd been that close to the bathroom, had even put a hand on the door before I heard him, was enough to have me grit my teeth. Less than two days of having a PSO, I was already losing my edge and focus. If that kept up, I would have to have Matteo put in a request for me to go through some retraining courses.

Pissed at the thought, I snapped, "Well, how did that work out?"

He ignored me, grabbing a towel and laying it on the floor to mop up the water I'd spilled.

"Ready to come out?" His tone held leashed frustration. I cocked my head, realizing something must have happened for his mood to take a one-eighty in the hour or so I was soaking.

"Are you going to strip for me again?"

Brody shrugged, but his attitude shift told me I wasn't getting another peek. "I'll dry."

"What happened?" I asked, my temper calming. "Did Oliver try to sneak back here?"

He shook his head. "No visitors."

"Then ..." I let the word hang in the air.

"Your brother called," was all he said as, in a move as sudden as when he dumped me in the tub, he reached in and pulled me out. Acting like I weighed little more than a sack of potatoes, he set me on the rug a few steps away from the tub, making sure my feet were under me before letting me go.

"Keene?" I asked, grabbing the towel he handed me and wrapping it around my torso.

"Yeah."

"And? Is everyone okay?" He didn't look worried, so I didn't think something had happened, but with the jammer in my room and without Wi-Fi, the alarm at my house could have been triggered, and I wouldn't have been aware of it. It wouldn't be the first time a fan had tracked down my address and tried to break in.

"Yeah."

"Was he trying to get updates on me?" Indignantly, I turned to walk out the door, intending to give him a piece of my mind, but Brody stopped me.

"No." He ran a hand through his hair. "He was just checking in on me."

That took the wind out of my sails. "Oh." I paused, studying him quizzically, clearly missing something but unsure what. When Brody didn't get my subtle hint, I prodded, "Then what—"

"Talking with him just reminded me you're complicated. And complicated is the last thing I need right now."

Frowning, I tried to understand. "So, you're mad because I'm complicated? Aren't all women complicated? And what does that have to do—"

He cut me off again, clearly agitated, looking for an escape from either me or the conversation—or both—but the place he dumped me had me blocking his only exit. "I like you." He stated it as if that said everything, but to me, it explained absolutely nothing.

"I like you, too, but what does that have to do—"

"A relationship with you is way more than I want to handle." His cutting me off and making assumptions about what I wanted was starting to piss me off, but I tried to shrug it aside. Maybe I'd pegged him wrong when I thought he'd want a relationship. Hell, I might get what I wanted after all.

"So, you're saying you don't just like me as a friend, but as someone you're attracted to?" I wanted to make sure I understood what in the world he was talking about. He nodded. "And you assume I need or want a relationship and that Keene is going to be pissed because I'm his sister." I tried to put the pieces together. He looked exasperated at me, clearly thinking I wasn't keeping up with the conversation, but only nodded again.

I brightened. "Well, that's an easy fix."

He looked at me as if I had two heads. "It—it is?"

"Well, yeah." I smiled up at him. "We just sleep together and work it out of our systems. One night that no one needs to know about."

Chapter 14

Brody

She was crazy. Her brothers had tried to warn me, but I hadn't realized they were underselling her. How in the hell would sleeping together fix what was developing between us? Did she not realize that sleeping together would start something, not end it? It wasn't a quick flash of flame. It was the start of something hot, bright, and long-lasting. "You think sleeping together once will get this attraction out of our systems?" Maybe I hadn't heard her correctly.

"Yep," she said, nodding as if to back up her idea.

"And you don't think that by having sex, we'll be more attracted to each other?"

Doubt flashed over her expression, but she quickly pushed it away.

"Why would it?" She cocked her head, thinking. "I'm complicated—you said so yourself. That isn't going to change. In fact, you've only skimmed the surface. That's not something you want." Tapping a finger to her lips, she continued, "And I'm not looking for any kind of relationship. Even this friendship?" she questioned, looking at me in confirmation until I nodded. It was as good a description as any. "It's not normal for me, and it's not something I'm completely comfortable with."

That surprised me. I wasn't biased enough to think every woman wanted a gold band and white picket fence. But the thought that she, who appeared to be lonely and alone most of the time, didn't want a friend tugged at something in me. *Well, damn*, I thought, realizing she was pulling me closer even while she was trying to push me away.

I shook my head. "Both of us need to think this through," I said finally. "As much as you're all gung ho about this, we're both the kind of people who think things through when it comes to the major details. And despite the bull you're trying to shovel, this isn't going to be quick or meaningless. We both need time to wrap our heads around what this means and get to know each other, so we're better prepared for the consequences."

She looked like she was about to argue, but I brushed past her to make my escape, leaving her to deal with removing the plastic bags and the short walk to her bed.

Making sure I shut her door firmly behind me, I strode to the kitchen, stopping to check on the door out of our hotel rooms to ensure that the prick Oliver hadn't gotten past security again and was trying to pick the lock or something. Finding the door secure, I practically bolted to the fridge, standing in front of the open door, letting the cool air wash over my damp clothes.

Keene's phone call had come at the best time—or the worst. I'd gotten caught up in the moment, or the situation, or whatever. I'd forgotten I was on a job, not there to get friendly with Keene's baby sister. Even if she was drop-dead gorgeous, had a wicked sense of humor, and a mouth that wouldn't quit. Luckily, Keene hadn't realized anything was amiss and had kept his questions non-invasive and to the point. Regardless, I had some major thinking to do, and I wasn't the only one.

Finally cool, I shut the door to the refrigerator, then grabbed my laptop to open the camera software. Making sure I had good video, I checked each of the six cameras before making my way to my bedroom, needing a shower desperately. Turning the water on as hot as it could go, I placed the laptop on the counter far enough away to keep the steam from killing the technology but close enough that I could monitor it from the shower if needed.

Washing the day away, I let myself half-drown under the spray, willing myself to stop thinking. Sputtering water, I thought back to Alessia almost drowning when I walked into the bathroom. Had she been reaching for the side of the tub to stabilize herself, or had she been instinctively reaching for something else? *Puzzles*, I thought, *I hate puzzles.*

The next morning, I was no closer to resolving my feelings for Alessia or her mysterious behavior. Surprisingly, I'd slept pretty well the night before and woke early enough to get a quick workout in my room before showering. I made coffee for myself, making an iced one in a travel mug for later while I sipped the hot brew. Alessia came out a few minutes after I'd washed out my mug. She sniffed the air mournfully but said nothing as she grabbed a plain yogurt from the fridge. She was walking better than she had yesterday, still a little stiff, but her normal grace had returned a bit.

"Is that damn photographer going to make you walk barefoot again today?" I couldn't help but ask, even knowing it wasn't any of my business.

She shook her head as she sat on the stool and dipped a spoon into the carton. "I'm supposed to be sitting most of the day."

"That should make things easier," I commented. I couldn't figure out how sitting in a chair in the middle of the woods made sense, but if it made for a better day for her, I certainly wouldn't point it out.

She hummed, taking a bite of yogurt. I'd learned yesterday she wasn't exactly a verbose individual in the morning, assumingly because of the lack of caffeine. I didn't take it personally, keeping up a light conversation that didn't make her think overly much.

We got to the set without trouble, but I noticed Oliver arguing with someone at the entrance to the estate. It was obvious he was trying to get in but wasn't on the list. I made a mental note to keep my eyes open in case he managed to get around the security at the gate, but I hoped he'd give up and go home.

Despite my hope for a stress-free day, I quickly learned Lessia was required to sit atop a horse for the shoot—one with more hair than brains, and the half-wild beast struggled on more than one occasion to bolt, rear, and even buck Lessia off. It was apparent she had some previous horse experience because she managed to stay on his back—barely—much to Tony's relief as he spent more time worrying about the possibility of getting the dark red gown dirty than about Lessia's safety. As expected,

Albrecht's bodyguard came up to me mid-morning with a scowl on his face, ensuring I knew her invitation to his estate was expected immediately after the shoot was done and pretty much mandatory without coming right out and saying so. I kept my attitude in check, only nodding my agreement.

The only excitement I had for the day was when Oliver snuck through the woods and tried to insert himself into the photo crew. I'd caught sight of him almost immediately and enjoyed escorting him—with the help of a local police officer—off the property. The officer turned a blind eye toward my slightly-more-than-necessary force and warned him in broken English that if he attempted to get in again, they would arrest him. I ignored the look of absolute loathing Oliver threw my way, eager as I was to get back to Alessia. Not that I could assist her in wrangling that godforsaken horse she was on, but I felt better keeping a close eye on her regardless.

The last hour of the shoot went fairly smoothly, and the boredom Lessia had mentioned I would experience finally set in. The entire crew—minus Tony—seemed overjoyed when he finally called the set a wrap, setting off a flurry of activity. One group of people started packing up equipment, and another raked the ground, in charge of restoring the property to the way it had been before everyone arrived. Lessia practically ran into a tent when a staff member announced they would be tearing that down as soon as the camera equipment was packed.

She came out a few minutes later, wearing what I assumed was the model equivalent to traveling clothes. She wore a dark blue jumper-looking thing that left her arms and shoulders bare but clung to her breasts and torso before draping loosely down from her hips, making her legs look a mile long. A long, chunky necklace hung almost to her navel, and the wedges on her feet looked sky-high. A matching clutch completed her ensemble, aside from the black flats she held in her other hand.

"How are your feet?" I asked as she approached, ushering her to the waiting car.

"Fine. Well, as fine as they're going to be. I brought flats for the plane but have to settle with foam inserts until then. Was that Albrecht's guard talking to you earlier?" She hurried to the sedan, her long legs eating up the ground.

"Yeah, you still want to go over there?" I didn't think she'd change her mind, but I could hope that common sense would kick in.

"Yep, we're still going over there." Her chin rose in stubbornness. "One more thing," she said as I opened the door to let her into the car. She looked around before saying softly, "The driver is a local, so we can't talk freely while we're in the car. Just don't let them separate us unless I say otherwise, and I mean it. And if I touch Karl meaningfully at all, that's your cue to get us out of there."

Before I could comment, she slid effortlessly into the back seat. I rolled my eyes, half thinking she was playing with me and half wondering what the hell she was mixing herself up in. I followed her into the car, seeing the travel mug I'd placed there that morning was still in its cupholder.

"Here," I said, picking it up and shoving it at her. "I promised you this."

She took it suspiciously, smelling the container before her eyes lit up. "Coffee?"

"I put ice in it this morning, so it's probably watered down by now, but yeah." I shifted in my seat at the look she gave me. The pure unshielded happiness made her look younger and made me realize yet again how guarded she normally was.

She drank the watered-down, room-temperature coffee like someone who'd been lost for a week in the desert would drink their first bottle of water. "You," she said when she came up for air, "are a god among men."

"No one's said that to me outside of the bedroom before," I quipped, then immediately wanted to slap myself. *So much for staying professional, McCallister*, I thought, then quickly tried to cover my mistake. "Could you even taste that?" I motioned to the now-empty container.

She laughed, sitting back. "Who cares what it tastes like? Coffee is all about the caffeine. My daddy and all my brothers served in the military. Coffee was the consistency of sludge in our house, and heaven help you if you wanted cream or sugar. Now, I have a hard time drinking it anywhere but at home, because everywhere else makes it so weak. You should see the baristas' faces when I order four or five espresso shots in a travel mug of coffee and down it in one go."

I stared at her, making sure she wasn't joking. "Do you know how much caffeine is in a shot of espresso? It's a wonder your heart doesn't jump right out of your chest."

We turned into a manicured circular drive, passing an open gate at the entrance. I noted the two men in the guard shack, the high wall circling the, well, shit, it really was a castle. Old stone walls, turrets, and even arrow slits illustrated in vivid detail that this wasn't a modern replica but a living part of history. It was well-maintained, and everything from the stone drive to the plants, even the structure itself, was straight, regimented lines and angles, with no softness to break up the severity of the estate. There wasn't so much as a blade of grass or a leaf out of place. It was impressive, but it also had the hair on my neck standing straight up. Between the oppressive atmosphere and the security designed to keep everyone in, my gut screamed at me that it wasn't a good idea. Once those gates closed, there was no way in hell I could get us out without major backup. I didn't like it at all.

"Stay here for a second?" I asked Alessia as the car stopped and the driver placed it in Park. I didn't wait for her to respond before hopping out and motioning for the driver to roll down his window. Before he could say anything, I reached inside and cut the ignition, then took the key and put it in my pocket. No way were we staying there without at least a vehicle I could access. The driver exclaimed in protest, but I cut him off. "You will stay in this car," I barked orders like the marine I was, though at a fraction of the volume of my instructors at boot camp. "You will not exit this vehicle for any reason until we return, and then you will continue to drive us to the airstrip that Valencia has already paid you to deliver us to. Is that clear?"

"But I am supposed to just drop you off here—"

I shook my head at his protest. "No, Albrecht is not your employer right now, and Valencia has told us you alone are to be Alessia's driver." They'd told me no such thing, but it wasn't the time for straight honesty. "You will stay here until she returns. Yes?" I wanted no chance of him not understanding me.

He looked at me, then over at the castle nervously, but nodded once the situation dawned on him. It wasn't like he could go anywhere without the keys unless he was willing to walk. "Yes, okay. I'll stay right here."

"Good," I said, tapping the window frame once before turning back to where Alessia was waiting. I opened the door, extending a hand to help her exit before taking my position a step behind her and to the side, wanting a clear view of what we were walking into. She strode to the front door like she owned the place, putting off the vibe that she didn't have a care in the world, but I noticed the tension in her body—she wasn't any more comfortable than I was.

Another man opened the door, clearly a butler or valet, greeting Alessia and ignoring me completely, which suited me just fine. He escorted her to a sitting room just off the door, letting her know Mr. Albrecht would be right with her. She waved the man away, pretending to be entranced by the priceless pieces of art scattered around the room. Everywhere you looked was an expensive, fragile, and in my opinion, gaudy piece of artwork designed to impress upon you just how important and wealthy Karl Albrecht was. Alessia ate it up, though. Or, maybe that was an act, too, I wondered, seeing a seriousness and sharpness in her eyes that didn't match the wonder on her face.

Footsteps echoing down the hall alerted us to the fact we were no longer alone. "Alessia, my dear. How glad I am for you to join me today." Karl Albrecht's voice held a bit of censure, despite his words. He was dressed in another impeccably tailored suit, as clean-cut and perfect in his appearance as his estate was. And just as empty and off-putting.

"Mr. Albrecht, I'm so grateful for your understanding yesterday. My doctor just refused to sign off on anything other than going straight to bed rest, or I wouldn't be able to work this morning. I pride myself on my dedication to my work, as I'm sure you do. I wasn't about to let pleasure get in the way of my obligations, no matter how much I wished otherwise."

She laid it on thick, but Albrecht seemed to eat it up, mollified by her words.

"Shall we start our tour? After all, obligations will tear us apart again soon, no?" He extended an arm to her, but instead of linking her arm around his, as was his intent, she laid her forearm on top of his, linking their fingers in an old-world gesture. He appeared charmed, but I wondered if she had done it to lessen their contact or because she could get free of the man quicker if needed. "You," he didn't bother to look in my direction, his voice cold and harsh as opposed to the congeniality he'd bestowed on Alessia, "can now go."

I shook my head. Not that he could see it. "I have strict instructions from Valencia. No one, not even Miss Accardi herself, may dismiss me from my post until she has safely returned home and my assignment is completed. I'm sorry, sir. I will do my best to remain as unobtrusive as possible, but the model does not leave my sight."

He turned to me, looking at me for the first time. The shock and anger that I, an underling, refused to do as I was bid didn't surprise me, but the cold calculation and anticipation did. I steeled myself. He was a master chess player, and somehow, Alessia and I had made our first move. I didn't pretend to understand everything at play, but somehow, by attempting to stay safe in a sea of sharks, we'd gotten the attention of the largest one.

"Very well," he murmured, but his lips drew into a tight line.

"Come now," Alessia said soothingly. "You'll never know he's there. Surely you must be used to the trials of having a guard. An important man like yourself must have someone to watch his back. Let us start this tour. I don't have much time, and I don't want you to waste a minute on someone who isn't me." That got his attention, as did the smile on her still-red lips.

For the next two hours, I followed them as Albrecht led Alessia through every hall, corridor, passageway, staircase, battlement, parlor, and sitting room imaginable. Through it all, she played her part, looking and exclaiming over every piece, gushing over its history or letting Karl drone on and on about its worth. But despite her act, she never dropped her guard. Her eyes never stopped as they took in every detail of every room we entered. Her wariness and unease triggered my instincts as well, and I felt like I was back on a mission, every moment seeming to both take an eternity and a blink of an eye as adrenaline pumped through me, keeping my instincts sharp when a mind might normally fatigue.

I kept to my word, never letting Alessia leave my eyesight nor letting us get separated by more than a few feet, much to Albrecht's annoyance. The walk had circled us back almost to where we'd started, and Alessia's limp had progressively worsened over the past fifteen minutes, telling me she was wearing out.

"Let us go into the garden patio for refreshments," Karl said, the gleam in his eye returning as his guard from earlier stepped into view.

Alessia patted his arm, and I wondered if that was the signal she'd been talking about. "That sounds wonderful," she said, turning to take a step in that direction.

I cleared my throat. Regardless of whether I was supposed to break it up, I would. "I'm sorry, Miss Alessia. But you will delay the flight if we don't leave immediately."

She frowned. "Is it that time already?" Opening her clutch, she rifled around until she drew out her cell phone. The screen was lit up with notifications and messages. "Goodness," she said, ignoring Albrecht while she looked at her phone.

Albrecht looked beyond ticked at being ignored. "You have several hours before your event," he tried to protest.

She looked up. "It's going to take a while to get ready, and the executives have some meet and greets they need me to do," she said earnestly. "But I really appreciate you taking the time to show me through your lovely home. I love being able to see history like this, so preserved and maintained."

It was clear Karl didn't quite know what to do in the situation. He wasn't the kind of man to be left or placated, yet she was attempting to do both. His manners wouldn't permit him to make a scene, yet it was apparent he would have preferred that to what society demanded of him. "Of course," he gritted out. "Perhaps next time we will have more time together." He raised her hand to his lips, kissing it perfunctorily before waving a bewildered butler over from his position at the door to escort us out.

Alessia made the last of the excuses, and we exited the residence with much less resistance than I'd feared. I waited until we were both inside the car before handing the driver the keys, telling him we were running late and to hurry. Even the guards at the gate, which was still open, looked confused as the driver waved at them through the window as we passed.

Before I could say anything after we hit the main road, Alessia typed in the password to her phone and handed it to me. "Can you text the pilot and let them know we'll be there soon?" She kept her head down, not looking me in the eye. "I need a minute if you don't mind."

"Are you okay?" I asked as she stayed occupied, trading her shoes for the flats she'd left in the car.

"Oh, yeah." She darted a glance at the driver, who looked very interested in what we were talking about. "I feel bad leaving so suddenly on Mr. Albrecht, but I'm glad we could tour the estate. Though I like Demetri Melnikoff's art collection better, Karl's estate was much more impressive, don't you think?"

I froze, the Russian name sounding familiar, but I couldn't quite place it. "I'm afraid my training didn't extend to arts and architecture."

She shrugged, still avoiding my gaze. "If you don't mind, I need a few minutes to meditate. I'm a nervous flyer and need to get centered, so I don't freak out on you during take-off."

That was an outright lie, but I let her have it, thinking she needed a few minutes to calm down. If I felt like I was coming off of a mission from that visit, I could only imagine what she felt, being a civilian. "Of course." What did she think I would tell her? No?

Sure enough, she closed her eyes, taking deep, steady breaths in and out, totally ignoring everyone and everything as she shut out the world. When we arrived on the tarmac next to the plane, and the driver parked, I wasn't sure what to do. Were you supposed to interrupt someone meditating or wait until they finished? The driver and I looked back and forth, uncomfortable and unsure, but said nothing as several more minutes passed.

Finally, just as I was about to speak, her eyes popped open. "Are we there?" she asked, craning her head around to see out the window.

"Yep," I said, "just waiting on you." We all got out, the driver popping the trunk and preparing to pull out our luggage, but I stopped him, grabbing all but the smallest case. She grabbed it, waving absentmindedly at the driver before heading up the stairs and into the small jet.

I followed, careful not to hit my head before stepping inside the door and straightening once I was inside. A flight attendant slid behind me to close the door, clearly eager to get on our way. The number of people inside had me pausing. I'd assumed the jet was for Alessia, the flight attendant, a pilot, and me. Instead, I saw six other individuals surrounding Alessia, fussing over her as she greeted them with a smile.

"Who?" I asked as I placed the luggage on a rack. The flight attendant shrugged, clearly not caring who else was on board as long as they could get moving.

Alessia came back, a glass of water with lemon in her hand, and grabbed the last suitcase from me. "If you need anything, just let someone know," she said hurriedly. I put an arm on her elbow, stopping her before she could run off.

"Who is everyone?"

"Oh." She looked around. "My hairstylist, makeup, wardrobe, and their assistants. Plus the pilot and flight attendant." She gave the male attendant a brief smile. "I don't actually have enough time to get ready for the event once we land, so we're taking advantage of the jet's privacy to get ready while we fly."

No sign of nervousness now. She was back to being her normal self. "No problems flying?" I couldn't help but ask, and she waved a hand in dismissal.

"None. I just needed a few minutes to get myself back together." Alessia tucked a stray lock of hair behind her ear. "I'll be sure to leave you time to change. You'll need a fresh suit, and I'm sure you wouldn't pass up a shower either. We'll be at the event for a few hours before heading to my apartment in Nice, a few miles away, so we can get some rest before our flight leaves in the morning." She gave me a knowing look. "The apartment has great security, so you can get some actual sleep."

I'd gone days without quality rest while I was serving, but the thought of decent sleep was welcome. The memory of past missions brought the lingering thought back, a name coming to me in a flash. "Demetri Melnikoff, the arms dealer?" I practically yelled the question.

She caught herself before flinching, just barely, before turning to me, her eyes narrowing. "Demetri Melnikoff is not an arms dealer. He's a wealthy businessman who runs in the same social circles I do and was kind enough a few months ago to give me a tour of his childhood home." She sniffed, then continued in a lower tone that only the two of us could hear. "Besides, it's his father, Demetri Melnikoff Senior. He's the arms dealer." With that, she took her entourage and left me fuming while she disappeared into the back bedroom.

Chapter 15
Alessia

I don't know what possessed me to poke the bear, mentioning D.M. Senior, but I blamed it on the fact I'd had only one cup of caffeine in days paired with too little food. As soon as they gave us the all-clear to move around the jet, we headed straight to the bathroom. I let the women chatter around me as I pulled off my clothes, modesty stripped from me years ago, and jumped into the tiny shower. Taking another moment to go over everything in my mind, I made sure I cemented the floor plan, points of exit, security, and best lines in and out of the estate to memory. I had done the same in the car but was afraid I'd missed something. Too bad my home in Nice didn't have a secure line or encrypted computer. I would have to keep everything fresh in my mind until I arrived home tomorrow. I didn't even want to put pen to paper until I was safe in my basement.

The women—I could never remember their names no matter how often they said them—were used to me ignoring them, and they did the same. I might as well be a prized poodle the way they moved around me, fussing with my hair, makeup, and dress, but never looking at me, seeing me as an actual person and not just a canvas for them to decorate.

With difficulty, I got us all out of the back rooms so that Brody had time to shower and change before we had to strap in for landing. He'd barely glanced at me since we'd taken off, and I refused to be disappointed that my flaming red dress didn't get so much as a double take. It was pretty kick-ass if I said so myself. Normally, I didn't care what they put me in, clothes were clothes, and I couldn't care less as long as they were comfortable—something I could never obtain while on the job—and kept me from being arrested. However, the one that evening tickled me a bit. The corset top was a little tight, but since, for once, I didn't have to worry about my breasts spilling out, I was fine with giving it a pass. My arms and shoulders were bare, aside from a single diamond bracelet on my wrist and a matching one at my throat. In contrast to the top, the skirt was as loose as the corset was tight. It moved like water around me and had a sexy vibe, and—even more important to me—it was super easy to move around in. The slit on the side went nearly all the way to my hip, giving everyone a scintillating view of my left thigh, and the hem just barely skimmed the floor in my four-inch matching heels that wrapped around my ankles to my mid-calf. The red matched my nails perfectly, saving me from yet another torture session with a manicurist, as even Tony had cooperated for once and let me keep them for the photoshoot.

My stomach growled, and I put a hand to it in sympathy. I hadn't had anything but a carton of yogurt, a cup of coffee, and a glass of lemon water the entire day. I promised my digestive tract actual food after the night was done, possibly before I even changed clothes. Movement next to my chair made me look up ... and up. I whistled softly as he took his seat. "Damn, Brody, you clean up nice." His solid black suit and white shirt fit like a glove.

"You fill out that dress pretty well, yourself," he whispered back, buckling his seat belt.

"How do you know? You've barely glanced at me once since we walked onto the plane." I wasn't pouting. Or whining, or ... whatever the hell I was doing.

"Which is one glance more than I should have," he said under his breath as the wheels of the jet touched down.

I was still trying to decide what to say when we pulled to a stop, and he rose, extending a hand to me. "Shall we?"

Hours later, feet killing me, head aching, and my stomach pretty well convinced that someone had cut my throat at some point during the day and was physically incapable of providing substance to my body, I was beyond ready to call it a night.

I hated events like what we were attending. There were too many people, too much alcohol and drugs, and fake-ness was spoon-fed to the masses in spades. I couldn't breathe properly, drowning in perfume and cologne. Movement was hard. There were so many people that even in the large space, you ran into someone trying to take more than one step at a time. Brody was solid, staying close without crowding. He did a good job staying visible when I needed him to be and invisible when he wasn't.

Finally, having circled the room twice and kissed up to the executives from Valencia, I knew I'd done my duty and could leave without raising eyebrows. I caught Brody's eye, motioning to the door, and he nodded. I knew he would alert our assigned driver and have the car pulled around.

"You didn't think you were getting out of here without saying hi to me, did you, *krasotka*?" The voice drifted through the background noise.

I whirled around with a friendly smile on my face—the first real one of the night. "D.M., what are you doing here?" I let him pull me into a hug, kissing both cheeks before pulling back.

"I was in the area and heard you were here." He shrugged. "What else could I do but see the woman who continues to break my heart?"

I scoffed. "Dramatic much?"

Demetri looked like a brawler, standing out from the well-polished, soft aristocrats surrounding us. True to his Russian roots, his blond hair was so light it was almost white, and his blue eyes were piercing and hard. His knuckles were scarred and rough, and his nose had been broken more than once. His suit was just as expensive as anyone else's, but no one could mistake Demetri for anything but what he was ... Russian Mafia.

I hadn't lied to Brody. Demetri Senior was the driving force in international arms dealing, but his son was no angel. His mother had been the daughter of a high-ranking member, and he'd been raised in that life. That being said, he didn't directly deal in human trafficking and had never harmed a child, so he was safe from me.

Demetri looked amused. "I'm Russian, my dear. Passion is in the blood." He snagged a glass of champagne from a passing tray.

"So I've been told," I said lightly.

"So you could experience for yourself," he said suggestively, reaching for my hand and rubbing his thumb over my knuckles.

I gave him a slow, assessing smile. "I'm well aware." Pulling my hand away, I sighed. "Too bad I never mix business and pleasure."

Irritation crossed his face, a shadow of a scowl before he pushed it back. But Demetri was well used to this song and dance. The only reason he tried at this point was that he knew I'd turn him down. We were better off as pseudo-friends than lovers; of that, we were both sure. We recognized that we both wore masks, though try as he might, Demetri couldn't crack the reason for mine. His need for one wasn't that original, but it was personal. I didn't blame him for keeping that part of his life hidden. In his profession, any weakness would be exploited if his enemies found out about it.

Brody caught my eye, his professional appearance barely concealing the irritation I knew was brewing beneath the surface.

"Well, then, I'm afraid that's my cue to depart. My driver is holding up the line," I said in the way of apology. "But it was good to see you."

Demetri gave me a wry look. "I'm always the highlight of your day."

"That you are." I gave him a sexy grin as I turned and made my way to the car. I palmed the drive he'd slipped me during our exchange, waiting until we were in the car, where I could rifle around my clutch, pretending to look for my compact while I dropped it into the bag.

"What was that?" Brody asked as I pulled the compact out, using the mirror to check my makeup.

"What was what?" I countered, using a finger to wipe away a bit of eyeliner. It took every bit of my skill and will not to freeze at the accusation. I'd thought our handoff was undetectable, but Brody wasn't an ordinary civilian, and he was close to us to boot.

"You give everyone the standard greeting tonight, but the one person you're actually happy to see is an arms dealer?"

I sighed. Demetri didn't have a scheduled handoff tonight, meaning that whatever he had was extremely time sensitive or important enough he didn't feel comfortable having the information for longer than necessary. At least Brody hadn't noticed the exchange. It would be enough of a pain to explain the Russian's presence and my reaction. The added confusion to the mess was that Demetri thought he occasionally handed off information to me to be passed along to my brothers, who in turn filtered the info to the American government. He didn't realize that I, in fact, was the American government.

I waved a hand in dismissal. "I already told you, Demetri is not an arms dealer. His father is. Demetri's harmless." Well, to me, he was. I wouldn't say he was to the general population, though.

"So you say," he scoffed.

"So I know," I vaulted back. "You know, for someone who hadn't even met me a week ago, you're getting pretty high-handed over what I do and who my friends are." I knew it was a low blow, but offense was the best defense. "You come over here, all judgy about my friends and my life, when I've done my best not to hold your association with my brothers or how you even came to be here against you. If you have such a problem with who I am and what I do, just do us both a favor and quit."

The driver pulled in front of my apartment, and I mourned the lost opportunity to have him swing by someplace to grab food because I sure as shit didn't have much in the way of groceries. I let Brody escort me from the limo and into the apartment lobby. A doorman was already holding the door for us, and another held the elevator. Once we entered, a palm scan was required before it allowed me to choose my floor. The elevator opened directly into my apartment, so I didn't bother waiting for it to start its ascent before reaching down to release my feet from the shoes I'd been wearing for the past several hours. Even though he was still fuming, Brody steadied me as I pulled off the second shoe. Wiggling my toes on the thick carpet, I sighed in bliss.

The door opened, and I let Brody do his thing while I waited by the entrance. The apartment was super modern European in design, with all clean lines and shiny surfaces. It was the least favorite of all my properties, but the security was tight, and the other residents were as private as I was, so it worked for what I needed.

I waited for the all-clear from Brody before high-tailing it to my bathroom, overjoyed to finally ditch the glam look and get back into yoga pants and a simple tee shirt I'd stored in my closet. I'd have to dress up again tomorrow, but after the day I'd had, I deserved comfy clothing. I also took the opportunity to place the flash drive D.M. had given me in the hidden compartment of my makeup case.

By the time I'd showered, changed, and returned to the main living area, Brody was in the kitchen making eggs over easy, sliding them on top of brown rice. I wasn't sure where either had come from—certainly not my kitchen, but the night outlook brightened considerably when I realized food was headed my way. He'd also changed while I was gone, looking comfortable in a tee shirt and jeans. I eyed him suspiciously, trying to get a sense of his mood.

Brody set a plate in front of me before sitting next to me to eat his food. Not sure whether I should poke at him again or leave us in an uneasy truce, I quietly thanked him. We ate in silence, the sounds of our forks scrapping against flatware the only noise in the room.

"I apologize. What I said in the car was out of line," Brody said when we finished our meal. "And while I still think what you did, meeting with Albrecht and being friendly with Demetri Melnikoff are dangerous things to do—I realize it's not my business, and I shouldn't have said anything."

He still looked frustrated, but I realized it was self-directed. Feeling a pang of sympathy—the man really was just trying to look out for me—I reached over and patted his hand. "I appreciate that you care, Brody. But I'm a big girl and have been looking out for myself for a long time now. I don't need another male in my life trying to dictate to me or make me feel bad for my life choices."

"That wasn't my intention." His hand flexed under mine as if he wasn't sure if he should pull away or not. "I just see someone so ..." He trailed off.

"Different?" I offered, not sure what word he was looking for but wanting to offer something safe.

"Real." His answer was firm, his green eyes meeting mine in a stare I couldn't break away from. "You are so much more real than anyone else I've ever met. What you have at home, with your family, is the real you. This world," he waved a hand around the apartment, "is empty. And I can see that you hate it—the job, the people, the events. And I don't get why you bother doing it."

I swallowed, the emotion he invoked swirling in my stomach, knotting into one enormous ball of indecision. I couldn't tell him the truth, but I didn't want to lie. Not knowing what to say, I simply shrugged. "I guess it's what I'm good at."

Brody shook his head in disappointment. "You have so many things you're good at, Lessia. Why stick with one that makes you miserable?"

Chapter 16

Alessia

His question still echoed in my head the next day. Sleep-deprived, hangry, and irritated that the flight attendant in first class couldn't make a decent pot of coffee if her life depended on it, I strutted through the airport to arrivals, Brody trailing behind me. Despite his attempts, I was pulling my carry-on, having fought with Brody about toting it around. I'd checked it on the way there, but with the flash drive concealed in it, I wasn't about to let it out of my sight. I claimed he needed his hands free in case he had to protect me—his job was as a PSO, not a butler—and he reluctantly agreed.

I paused mid-stride, seeing Matteo standing at our carousel, watching the already-unloaded luggage whirling around the track. Letting a grin slide onto my face, I resumed my pace until I was in his arms, letting him hold me close for a moment. A few people stared at me, and some of the brave ones pulled out their cell phones to take pictures of me, but I counted myself lucky that no one looked like they wanted an autograph.

"What are you doing here?" I asked, pulling back to kiss him on the cheek. "I thought Gideon was supposed to pick us up."

He matched my grin, rubbing a hand up and down my arm before pulling back. "I told him this afternoon that I could get you. He said something about a meeting today when he picked Gia up, and I was free." He shrugged. "Besides, I knew you were missing me, and I wanted to surprise you."

I hugged him again, sensing Brody reaching for our luggage behind me as I did so. "That you did. Gosh, I can't wait to get this makeup off and change into some comfortable clothes." I didn't over-enunciate, being too well trained for that. But I knew my words clued Matteo into where I'd placed the flash drive. "I need a shower and a nap in the worst way."

He grabbed my second suitcase from Brody, nodding to him in a friendly greeting before motioning to the exit. "Then let's get your pretty ass on the road, Belle."

I let Brody have the front seat again, and Matteo chattered about Gia and how excited she was that her dad was letting her take classes. "I spilled the beans to Brody." My announcement had Matteo blinking. "I told him about us letting her join my private classes with you. And Brody knows your secret about being ex-Army."

"Former." Both men corrected me at once, and I smirked, loving that I could tease both of them at once.

"Whatever." I waved a hand in dismissal. "Anyway, I just wanted to let you know we don't have to pretend Gia doesn't know the basics around him. And I fully intend on coming clean with Gideon, too, so that we don't have that secret looming over us. But I'm not telling them about you."

Matteo blew out a breath, hitting his blinker to change lanes. "I appreciate that, Belle. I admit I'm surprised they haven't run background on me prior to this, but I'm sure they haven't, or they wouldn't have been as upset about us working out together as they are. Don't misunderstand me. I'm not ashamed of my service—it's not a secret, so you can tell them if you'd like—but it's not something I like to talk about."

Brody nodded. "I get that, and I think they would, too. I'm not ashamed of what I did either, but I'm certainly not going to reminisce about it."

Matteo raised an eyebrow, and Brody clarified, "I served in the Marine Corps."

Matteo nodded, no hint of his prior knowledge on his face. "Then you understand." He pulled into my driveway, only to stop short at the line of vehicles preventing him from getting much more than halfway up the drive. My brothers, all four of them, were waiting uncomfortably on the porch.

"I wonder what's up with them," I murmured as I unfastened my seat belt. "They all have codes for my house. They could have at least gone inside."

"Probably worried it was booby-trapped," Brody offered. Because he was probably right, and it was something I certainly could have done, I stayed quiet.

"This is looking like a private party," Brody said, looking over at Matteo. "Do you mind showing me your facilities? We could hit the ring for a few rounds if you want? I haven't got a good workout since we left, and I won't be able to sleep tonight without getting some energy out, anyway."

Matteo looked intrigued. "I don't get a chance to spar with anyone who knows what they're doing all that often. Alessia is my best student, but ..." He trailed off, not needing to say more. His normal day comprised of overweight men and women and little kids. He had a few more experienced people who came in for self-defense, but it was a far cry from what he did in the army. I could, and did, go toe-to-toe with him, but we knew each other so well at that point that while it was still a great workout, it wasn't the same mental challenge as a new opponent.

Brody gave him a boyish grin. "Then let's knock some rust off your skills, brother."

Matteo looked at me, making sure I was down with Brody's plan and didn't need a backup for whatever was about to go down. He should have known better. The day I needed help handling my family was the day someone put me in the ground. "Go ahead," I encouraged. "I'll be fine. But I'm leaving my luggage in your vehicle until you come back tomorrow for my class, so make sure you hang up my good clothes, or you'll hear about it." Understanding that I'd tasked him with getting the info out and handled before coming over tomorrow, he nodded.

I stepped out of the car, my purse in one hand and heels in the other. I'd switched back to flats as soon as we'd gotten into Matteo's SUV and wasn't about to switch them out again just for my brothers' sake.

"Hey, y'all," I called once I was close enough, waving behind me as Matteo started backing out of the drive. "What a pleasant surprise."

I didn't bother opening the door, not about to invite them in until I knew whether they were there to apologize or say something else that would tempt me to kick their collective asses. Instead, I moved deeper into my porch to sit on the swing, putting my feet up to prevent any of them from getting any ideas about sharing. Granted, that left them in the position of power, looming over me, but I was sitting, and they all had to stand, so I was okay with it. Besides, I was pretty immune to being intimidated by the men I'd watched grow up. I had enough memories of them in their awkward teen years to balance out the testosterone they oozed now.

"We came to apologize," Keene started.

"All right," I said, wishing I had something to drink. It was hot outside, the sun was beating down, and the urge to make some sweet tea hit me hard. Momma used to make sweet tea on days like that, taking it outside to her garden to sit and watch the butterflies and the bees. Some days it seemed like she'd been gone forever, but other days ... Other days felt like we lost her yesterday.

"All right, what?" Keene asked, pulling me away from my thoughts.

"All right, I'll listen to all y'all's apology."

Boone rolled his eyes, but I wasn't about to make it easy.

Keene took a breath, clearly running out of patience with me already. "I'm sorry we—I—didn't take your feelings into account when we assigned you a tail while you were in town and pulled some strings to get Brody assigned as your permanent PSO."

"Me, too," Royce said quietly.

"And me." Boone spoke a little more grudgingly, but I figured he was still mad about the liquor incident, so I let it slide.

I blamed the jetlag for not noticing immediately how Boone held himself, as if his ribs were hurting him, and Keene was sporting a red mark under his eye. Royce had a slightly swollen lip, and one of his cheeks looked a bit bruised, and Gideon's knuckles were red.

I looked up at Gideon. My eldest brother was the last to get himself into a scuffle—even as kids, he took his role as eldest seriously and was enough of a lawyer even then to prefer to settle matters with his words instead of fists. But underneath that polished and poised façade was a beast of a fighter when he was riled. He was actually the best at hand-to-hand of all my brothers, and the boys had all learned from an early age not to push him too far. Gideon Accardi might never start a fight, but he sure as shit would finish one.

"Did you beat them up for me?" I blinked up at him adoringly, but he ignored the question.

Instead, he cleared his throat, adding, "And I'm sorry I jumped to conclusions at the office the other day. I knew you had good men watching you, and instead of asking you what I was looking at with that file, I made assumptions."

I blew out a breath. "Since we're all apologizing," I started. Might as well get everything I could out while we were all there and in a reasonable mood. "I owe you one, too."

"Just Gideon?" I heard Boone mutter under his breath, but I ignored him.

"The reason Matteo suggested one-on-one classes with Gia wasn't so she could catch up with kids her own age. It's because she already knows more than her class, and he wasn't sure how to tell you." I looked down at my hands, not ashamed of what I'd done, exactly, but ashamed that it had required Gia and me to keep secrets from him. "She often joins my classes with Matteo, and he's been giving her instruction here and there over the last few years."

Keene, Royce, and Boone all gave Gideon the side-eye, but other than tightening his jaw, he didn't look that upset. I figured he'd started to think something was up over the last few days, at least. "Why wouldn't you just ask me?" he finally forced out, running a hand through his hair.

I scoffed, and he corrected, "Or at least tell me. Jesus, how many years has this been going on?"

I shrugged, unsure what I should admit to and what to hold back. "Gia had been asking for a few months by that point," I dodged. "And you outright denied even talking about it with me. I was afraid if we told you, you wouldn't let me see her anymore." The genuine fear in my voice stopped him short, and he picked up my feet to sit next to me, placing them on his lap.

"Alessia Alina Accardi, there is absolutely nothing you could ever do that would cause me to take Gia from you." His voice was calm, confident, and so full of emotion that tears came to my eyes. "My little girl loves you just as much as you do her. We might sometimes fight as a family. Lord knows we don't always see eye to eye, but at the end of the day, we will always be there for each other."

I shook my head, unable to stop the words from spilling out. "I used to think that, too."

The moment of stunned silence was deafening. "I—I made you think ..." The harshness in Gideon's words, the heartbreak in them, broke something in me, and I shook my head.

"Daddy," I whispered the word as if I could hardly bear to put it out in the world.

They all blinked, frozen with shock, then Boone swore, running a hand over his face.

"When I was a kid, Daddy let me do anything. He showed me how to shoot, drive, fight. He didn't care that I was a tomboy, that I wanted combat boots for my birthday. And all y'all let me tag along when you were home on leave, taking me with you when you went to work out with the men, or if you were going hiking or rock climbing. You taught me how to survive in the woods, how to throw a punch." My smile was small but genuine. "And then Momma died," I sniffed, "and everyone was gone after bereavement leave, and Boone a few months later—not that I blamed him. But Daddy, he wasn't our daddy anymore. He didn't eat, barely slept, he wasn't ... here." My voice was thick with tears, though I desperately tried to keep them in check. "I was so scared that he wouldn't ... that he would—" I cut myself off. "I took all the weapons in the house and buried them in the backyard in the middle of the night," I whispered that like a secret I was supposed to take to my grave, and in a way, I had planned on it to be.

Keene and Royce came closer, getting to their knees in front of me, resting their hands on my legs.

"You should have told us," Boone snapped, clearly agitated.

"And said what? That I was afraid Daddy was going to blow his brains out?" Everyone flinched, but I didn't stop. "What would that have accomplished? All y'all were enlisted. It's not like you could quit your job and leave in the middle of your tours," I pointed out. "Gideon was already starting his paperwork to muster out when he realized that A.T. wasn't being looked after."

Boone shook his head but knew there was nothing to say.

"Once Daddy heard Gideon was coming home, he snapped out of it a bit. Momma had been gone about a year by then, and I thought things were getting back to normal, or as normal as they could." I looked down at my hands. "I asked Daddy if I could go with him to A.T. to go to the range. I hadn't been in so long because I was afraid of what he would do. But instead of bringing me, he laughed and told me ladies don't shoot guns." I shook my head in bewilderment because even now, the phrase was foreign to me. "He'd brought me to that range since before I could remember, brought all of us, and suddenly I wasn't allowed to handle a gun, let alone shoot it. He used to donate his time teaching women self-defense, but suddenly, it wasn't acceptable for me to sign up for classes? Instead, he went with me to the mall and bought me dresses and skirts, even had the sales lady show me how to apply makeup. All my extracurricular activities had fallen to the wayside after Momma passed, and Daddy refused to let me rejoin anything but my riding lessons. Once Gideon got back, he eased up enough to let me sign up for karate, but Gia was born before they started, and I had to quit."

I looked up at Gideon, wanting to make sure he could see the sincerity in my face. "I love that little girl like she's mine—have from the first time you put her in my arms, but Daddy saw it as another opportunity. You were working full time, learning the ropes from him, and that left me at home with Gia. That summer, I did nothing but raise that girl. Daddy called it good practice for when I got married and had my own kids. But while he pulled back at A.T., and you and Keene took over more and more, he became more and more insistent about what I should or should not be interested in. It's like, with Momma gone and A.T. in capable hands, he felt he owed it to her to mold me into this person, this image, he had of me. I wanted camping trips, and I got elaborate parties at fancy restaurants. I came home one day to find he'd cleaned out my closet of anything he deemed unsuitable, replacing it all with clothing I'd never pick out myself. He's the one who invited the modeling scouts to the house, not me. And when he was taking me shopping or driving me to photo shoots, he looked so happy. I couldn't figure out how to tell him how much I hated it."

I was wringing my hands now, and I loathed that I was a ball of emotion, but it was as if it had been building in me for the last thirteen years, waiting for its chance to explode, and it would not be denied.

"Little girl." Gideon lifted my chin, and I hiccupped. He hadn't called me that in years. "If you had told him, I'm sure—"

I pulled away, hating that I was shattering their picture of our father the way mine had. "I told him on my eighteenth birthday." Knowing I must look like a raccoon since I had to make up my face that morning, I wiped my eyes, hoping to get rid of the worst of it. "I told him I was going to enlist."

They all froze. "You were going to join the military?" Keene asked.

I nodded, giving him a sad smile. "It's the family tradition, right? Serve our country, then come home to focus on Accardi Tactical." I wiped my nose. "That's all I ever wanted to do. Ever since I was a little girl, but Daddy wouldn't have it. He told me outright that if I enlisted, he would disown me. No daughter of his would 'sully herself in the dirt or sordid business of war.' A.T. would be passed down to his sons. Daughters had no place there, and my life was destined for modeling." I shuddered. "I'd never seen him that angry or sincere. I have no doubt he would have followed through if I'd enlisted the way I wanted. I'd just gotten my first big modeling job, and Daddy had been over the moon, sure it was a sign from Momma that I was on the right path.

"That's why I try to stay away during shareholder meetings," I whispered. "I know you four had to go against him to get me my shares anyway, and if he thought I was taking even a passing interest ..." I trailed off. "And, to be honest, it's probably better that way." Being a full working partner with my brothers at A.T. was all I'd ever wanted—still wanted if I were truthful. But I couldn't work there without revealing my training at some point, nor would I ever be satisfied with an H.R. or finance position that my brothers would offer out of guilt.

"Why didn't you say anything?" Royce asked, looking haggard. "You had to have known we didn't feel that way."

I shrugged. "It would have just gotten everyone upset. Daddy still had full control of the shares when I was eighteen. He started breaking it up a few years later. And y'all didn't do anything that made me think you disagreed with him, though I knew you didn't feel as strongly. Y'all came back as men with the weight of A.T. and your service on your backs. No one had time for a pesky younger sister. No one had time to go to the range for fun or do the things we used to do when y'all were on leave. And even if you did, the last thing you'd want to do on a rare day off was to hang out with me."

Gideon's eyes were haunted. "He told me he'd arranged for a nanny to be there for Gia while we were working."

I blinked because there had definitely been no nanny, just me, Gia, and a whole lot of baby books I'd ordered off the internet.

"That you watched her for an hour or so most days until we got home."

I shook my head, feeling awful to have placed this on him. "There wasn't anyone but me. Not during the summers or weekends. Someone came in to cover the hours I was in school, but they left as soon as I got there. Thank goodness you'd shown me the basics when she came home, or I don't know what I would've done. She was so sickly when she came home from the hospital that I used to have nightmares that something I did wrong ended up killing her."

"But even the bottles were made up for me at night." He still looked a little shocked.

Shrugging, I admitted, "I set them up for you. You were working all the time, plus had Gia. God knew I was getting a crash course in what taking care of a newborn was like, and I wasn't trying to hold together a business. I just wanted to help cut any time off I could so you could sleep or spend as much time just being with her as possible."

He swallowed hard and, in a move I wasn't expecting, pulled me from my spot on the chair into his arms, squeezing me so tight I could barely breathe.

"I've loved you since the day Momma put you in my arms," he whispered against my hair. "You are the best of us, little sister. Never let anyone tell you otherwise."

I felt a tear slide down my face. For the first time since our mother died, I wasn't ashamed of letting it fall.

Chapter 17

Alessia

After my uncharacteristically emotional breakdown, we all seemed to need some together time. Since I'd never gone grocery shopping the last time I was home, I piled into Keene's SUV—it was the closest, and my feet still hurt—and we followed the parade of cars leaving my driveway and heading to Gideon's. Out of all of us, he had it the most together and had groceries regularly delivered to his house. He pulled out steaks and fixings while the rest of us helped around the outdoor kitchen and firepit. It was too hot to light a fire yet, but Boone and I got one ready since we all knew Gia would want one as soon as the sun set.

"Where did Matteo take Brody off to?" Keene asked, drying his hands on a towel. "If he's over at my place, I should get him."

I raised my water bottle to my lips, taking a sip before replying, "They went to Matteo's gym to beat on each other in the name of male bonding. They know to head here once they're done and showered."

Gideon wouldn't mind the extra mouths to feed, and I was hoping Matteo might give me a lift home tonight so that we could talk without worrying about Brody or my brothers overhearing. I was dying to know what D.M. had given me that he thought was important enough to seek me out. I knew without question I wouldn't be able to sleep if I didn't get to look at that flash drive.

Gia came running up from where she'd been playing on her swing set. "Aunt Lessia." She slid to a stop. "Uncle Royce won't play with me on the slide."

I smiled, tucking a few loose strands of hair behind her ear. "That's because your uncle is too big to get into the fort."

She frowned. "He said he isn't in play clothes."

Grinning, I winked at her. All my brothers had obviously come straight from the office—all were still in suits. "That's just because you haven't found the right game." I got up, heading for the garage while Gia trailed behind.

She smiled as I pulled what I was looking for out of the bin. "That's awesome!" Gia practically squealed, turning on her heel to bolt back outside. I followed at a more leisurely pace, my bruised feet making it difficult to walk in my normal stride. I kicked off my flats, throwing them next to my chair, letting the cool, thick grass cushion me as I stepped onto the lawn.

"Go long," I yelled to Gia, who sprinted farther down, arms out, trying to catch the football I'd intentionally overthrown. It bounced away from her while she gamely tried to figure out where it would land next.

I heard Keene snort. "You never could throw a decent spiral."

Turning, I cocked an eyebrow at him. "Like you could do better?" I challenged, and he rose to his feet, rolling his sleeves up. Everyone had long since discarded their coats and ties in the name of comfort. Gia returned with the ball, tossing it to Keene, who had to reach low to snag it before it hit the ground. It took less than three minutes before Boone joined in, and in ten, even Gideon was tussling around with Royce, turning our ball-tossing into a mostly friendly game of touch-football with Gia, Gideon, and Boone on one side, me, Keene, and Royce on another. Their shoes and clothes might never be the same, but judging by our smiles, it was well worth it.

My heart clenched as Gideon kneeled without a care about the dirt he was getting on his pants, showing Gia where to put her hands on the ball so that she could replicate Keene's pass. He, too, had rolled his shirtsleeves up, revealing the ink swirling down his forearms. Gideon had always been a contradiction. He was a lawyer who fought like a demon, a clean-cut businessman covered in ink from his collarbone to forearms, and who knew how far down his torso. He held us together yet held himself apart at the same time.

Matteo and Brody came around the corner, matching grins on their faces as they saw what they were walking into. "Got room for two more players?" Brody asked. He wore jeans that hugged him in all the right places but were loose enough to show he was a man's man. *No city-boy skinny jeans here*, I thought. His black tee shirt was tight around his biceps, and I could almost imagine seeing his six-pack abs, but I figured it must be mostly my imagination since his shirt was not quite tight enough to reveal what was underneath.

Gia cheered, yelling that she wanted Matteo on her team. Matteo grinned, his khaki cargo pants and blue shirt as dressed up as I'd ever seen him. Gideon looked over, and I saw a look passing between him and Matteo, but they both looked away before I could identify it.

"Looks like I'm on your team." Brody's thick drawl sounded like honey, but he stepped lightly as he approached, quick on his feet. Clearly, someone was glad to join our little game, and it was apparent he and Matteo would fit in nicely with our not-so-friendly version of touch football.

"Good thing," I teased. "Seeing as we're winning."

He grinned. "Any day you and I are on the same side is a good day in my book. Winning is just a bonus." The childish glee on his face made him look younger, and his unashamed interest in me, despite my brothers being within earshot, made me return his smile, unable to help myself. Anyone confident enough to flirt with me despite my family without being arrogant about it was another point for him in my book.

"Well," I matched his drawl, "let's see if we can go two for two today."

Chapter 18

Brody

Matteo wasn't as out of practice as I figured anyone mainly dealing with high-society types and little kids would be. I ducked away from a right-cross, coming back with my own before dancing out of reach.

Sweat poured down my face, but I didn't dare try to wipe the moisture away, knowing Matteo would take advantage of my distraction. We'd been going at it for a while, both of us testing out the other until we realized we were pretty evenly matched. Then we really let loose, enjoying the bout immensely.

"So," Matteo said as I blocked a kick, "what do you think of our Alessia?"

I nearly missed blocking the next jab but recovered enough to land a punch of my own. "She's great." I tried not to pant. "Easy to get along with, funny, low-key. A little stubborn, but she's logical about it." I shrugged, not sure what else to say.

Matteo dropped his hands to his sides in disbelief. "Alessia was easy to get along with," he repeated, watching me to see if I was joking.

I nodded, not understanding his confusion. "She let me do my job and didn't give me flack about it. She didn't whine, complain, or even try to sneak out once. Any change in plan, she gave me as much notice as possible, even demanded I stay with her when some rich guy she was meeting with tried to dismiss me. That's easy in my book, compared to others I've had to deal with in the past."

He gave me an assessing look. "Well, I'll be damned," he said, almost to himself. "She really must like you."

I raised an eyebrow. "I'm a pretty likable guy."

Matteo shook his head. "Lessia might tolerate you if she had to, but she wouldn't make you happy about your assignment."

I thought back to how she was on the photo shoot with the others and winced, understanding what he was getting at.

"I'm happy to report that, while we were alone, I enjoyed the assignment of watching over Lessia the person, not Alessia the famous model."

He nodded, amazement still lingering in his eyes, mixing with what could have been wariness. Was he afraid I'd get between them? Lessia might only think of him as a friend, but maybe he had other feelings?

"You know there can't be anything between us, right? I'm her PSO, so I can't risk compromising her safety. And she made it clear she's not exactly looking for a relationship." I couldn't help but point out the obvious.

Matteo wandered over to the side of the ring, grabbed his water bottle, and tossed one over to me. I caught it, then downed half of it in one go. "Sounds to me like you're making excuses." Okay, so he apparently wasn't upset at us being friendly.

Shaking my head, I threw the bottle back on the floor with a bit more force than necessary. "Not excuses, just fact."

"I've known Lessia since she was eighteen, and I can count on less than one hand the number of people outside her family she actually tolerates outside of work, let alone likes. Trust me, she might have told you she isn't looking for a relationship, but I think she's just scared."

I scoffed. "That woman isn't afraid of anything. She went to a rapist's home because she was interested in looking at the architecture of his house, for crying out loud."

"Emotionally." Matteo pulled the Velcro of his glove off with his teeth, ignoring my second sentence. "She's afraid of committing to someone who isn't just as committed to her. That woman is out until she's all in, and she's aware most people do things in stages instead of jumping in with both feet. Add in that she's got a large interfering family that scares most men, a grueling job that most wouldn't begin to understand, and fans of both the normal and obsession variety that make even going out to get milk an exercise in public relations. You can understand why she keeps her distance from most." He pulled off his helmet after tossing the other glove, raking his hands through his wet hair and pushing it back from his face. "Unless she knows you're sure of what you want, you can bet she's not going to get past the idea of light, quick, and meaningless." He cocked his head, thinking hard. "Honestly, even if she knows you're looking for something serious, she's likely to run scared for a hot minute before realizing that what she wants and what she can have are the same thing. She's been putting up walls for so long. It'll take some doing for her to comprehend that she doesn't have to keep doing it."

I pulled my own gloves off, throwing them to the side as well. "There's still me being her PSO to deal with. I can't compromise her safety."

He cocked a brow. "That sounds like antiquated thinking to me. Look at the Accardi brothers. Even when they have security, I've noticed they dismiss them as soon as they're in the company of another brother. They know they have each other's backs. Contrary to their beliefs, Alessia has gone through a lot of the same training as what A.T. offers. She doesn't need someone to protect her like some helpless damsel. She needs a partner to help watch her back."

I considered his words, letting myself really think about what a relationship with Lessia could look like if we both let go and dropped our guards with each other. I was still thinking about it when we pulled into Gideon's driveway an hour later.

Grinning when I saw the friendly football game, I tossed my worries aside for later. We joined in, Matteo being commandeered by Gia for her team, while I lined up next to Lessia and Royce. Keene hiked the ball, and Lessia took off running, ducking under Boone's arm, snagging the football from the air in a practiced move. Before she could take more than a step or two, Gia, running to her aunt full-tilt, tripped as she leaned forward to touch her out, taking them both to the ground. Lessia dropped the ball as they fell, turning in mid-air to catch her niece, making sure she cushioned the girl's fall.

"Oomph." She hit the ground in a heap, her arms cradling Gia.

Before any of us could panic, Gia arched off her aunt, looking down at her.

"You okay, Aunt Lessia?"

Lessia winked up at her. "Never better, kiddo." She sounded a little winded but no worse for wear.

"Good." Gia paused. "You know that was a fumble, right? 'Cause you dropped the ball, and Matteo got it."

Lessia lolled her head over, spotting the ball nestled safely under Matteo's arm. She glared at Gia in a mock frown. "You did that on purpose." She rolled, pinning her niece under her, and tickled the little girl while the men watched, a soft smile on everyone's faces as Gia's shrieks of laughter and Lessia's playful growls filled the backyard.

By the time Lessia let Gia up, I was afraid the girl wouldn't have any breath left in her, but she sprang up with no problems, running to give her dad and Matteo a high five. Lessia stayed on the ground a minute more, a silly grin on her face as she caught her breath.

"You okay?" I couldn't help but ask, walking the few steps to close the distance between us.

"Sure." She propped herself up on her hands. Dirt streaked her face and covered her arms, as well as her bare feet. Her makeup from earlier was gone, and her jeans had grass stains. I couldn't help but think she looked more beautiful now than in any photo I'd seen of her. Her eyes sparkled with happiness, the shadows and reserve gone from them, and the purple in her eyes made them even brighter, seeming to take up even more of her face.

I extended a hand, clasping hers in mine as I pulled her to her feet. Apparently still pumped up from my round with Matteo, I pulled a bit too hard, causing her to fly into my chest with a whoosh. *I'm officially an idiot*, I thought as I instinctively wrapped my arms around her to steady us.

"Shit, sorry," I mumbled, letting my arms drop as soon as she was stable. She'd raised her hands to my chest when we collided, and I could feel the heat of her touch through my tee shirt. She didn't pull away, didn't do anything but angle her face up to look at mine.

Whatever she was about to say died, and I felt her hands contract as she licked her lips, but before either of us could do something stupid—at least on my side of things—a throat clearing a few feet away broke us out of the moment. Reluctantly, she dropped her hands, patting my chest as she did so, not at all embarrassed to be caught, despite her brothers surrounding us. I took my lead from her, smiling at her softly before taking a slow step back.

Keene was staring at me, an indeterminable look on his face. Boone was frowning, Royce glancing between the two of us like he didn't know what to think. Gideon and Matteo were heading back to the imaginary line, Gia chattering between them as the three of them ignored us completely.

"Come on, y'all." Gideon tossed over his shoulder. "We only have about twenty more minutes before we've got to stop for dinner."

The men stopped looking at us, clearly more interested in continuing the game than thinking too hard about their little sister and me—at least for now. Though Boone got in a pretty good jab in my side as I was coming down from catching a pass from Keene. We were all a sweaty, happy lot when Gideon finally called the game. Lessia had accidentally-on-purpose fumbled the last pass, leaving Gia to grab the loose ball and return it for a touchdown. The little girl doing her special winner's dance was seriously adorable, made even more so when she roped her father, uncle, and Matteo into joining her.

I was a few steps behind Lessia as we all stepped onto the brick patio. Seeing her wince as her bare feet contacted the hot surface, I stepped toward her, sweeping her up into my arms. She squealed, wrapping her arms around my neck. Wincing as my eardrums protested the noise, I kept hold of her as I walked. Her brothers turned, and Matteo's eyes bugged out as Lessia threw her head back, laughing as I swung her dramatically before plopping her onto the chair next to where she'd thrown her shoes.

"I could have walked, you know," she said. Her tone was slightly chiding, but her eyes danced with humor.

"I know," I admitted. "But just because you're capable of walking on your poor, abused feet doesn't mean I could stand to let you. My momma would have been rolling in her grave at the thought of her son ignoring all those manners she tried so hard to drill into me." I winked before pulling back from the chair to stand upright. "But in the name of equal opportunity, I'll let you carry me the next time you find me barefoot, with bruised feet, attempting to traverse hot concrete."

Lessia smiled up at me. "My feet are fine, but I appreciate your attempt at looking out for me."

"If I tried doing that to her, she would have gutted me," Matteo muttered. We both ignored him.

"What happened to your feet?" Royce asked, and Lessia rolled her eyes, launching into a brief description of what had happened at the photo shoot.

"They're fine," she summed up. "Just a little tender, and Brody's a hoverer."

That had Keene snorting as he sipped his beer, but her brother wisely kept his mouth shut.

Dinner was a friendly affair, a major turnaround from the last family gathering I'd witnessed Monday morning at the office. I was pulled into a discussion of battle tactics with Keene, who was in charge of teaching next week's class, and Boone was catching up with Royce on how the last group had fared in the survivalist excursion class. It didn't surprise me to find the family was so hands-on. Despite owning a billion-dollar company, I knew Keene routinely led or took part in almost all the courses offered. His title might lead one on to believe he rode a desk, but I knew better, and his time with me in the ring reminded me he hadn't lost his edge after his military service.

Jet lag hit hard shortly after dishes were washed and put away. When Lessia was yawning more than talking, and I rubbed my eyes twice in as many minutes, Gideon cleared everyone out. They tried to be subtle about it, but I caught the look Matteo shot Alessia as Royce ushered her out the door and into his car. Exhaustion faded as my instincts kicked in. Lessia might be smooth, but I'd caught Demetri's handoff to her at the party. Someone sticking their hands in their pockets was a major red flag for security, military, and police alike. Guns, knives, and an assortment of things that could cause bodily harm were often concealed in pockets, and Demetri had reached into his several times while he made his way around the room in his bid to appear casual in his approach, fiddling with something within it. I'd seen him pull out something silver, but it had been too small to be anything threatening, which was why I hadn't intervened. As a personal security officer, I had no right to inquire what it was, despite my curiosity, but I suspected that was why she'd kept her small luggage case so close on her way home.

I caught a ride to Keene's house, grateful that I didn't have to drive to my apartment tonight and that his house was just a few blocks from Alessia's. Before I could escape to the guesthouse, Keene motioned me inside the main house as we exited the vehicle. He tossed me a bottle of water and grabbed one for himself, settling in against the kitchen counter.

"So," he said casually, "how did it go?"

"Fine," I said, matching his tone as I unscrewed the cap to the bottle and wondered how quickly I could get past the inquisition and on with my plans for the night. "It's the nicest PSO trip I've taken, that's for sure. No one shot at us. I didn't have to worry about roadside bombs, and the food was pretty good—at least for me."

He stared at me, clearly expecting more, but I stayed silent.

"And," he goaded when it became apparent I wouldn't crack.

"And what?" I wasn't about to make it easy for him, for one. And it wasn't like I could talk about my clients. Granted, Lessia was the first I had as a civilian, but my ethical standards weren't going to change, friends and family bonds or not.

"That's all you're going to give me?" He set the half-empty bottle down on the counter in agitation.

I raised a shoulder in a half-hearted shrug. "Not sure what else there is to say. What were you hoping for? We went to Germany. She did a photoshoot. We both did our jobs and came home." I yawned, not having to fake my tiredness. I needed to move this along if I was going to sneak over to Lessia's in time to find out if my suspicions were true. "Do you mind if we postpone the inquisition until tomorrow? Preferably after I've slept eight hours and had at least a pot of coffee?"

Keene didn't look happy but nodded reluctantly. "I had my assistant do an express order to replace the coffee beans Lessia took, so at least we'll enjoy some decent coffee tomorrow." His phone chimed, and he brightened as he read the screen. "And Lessia just texted me with the password to my Netflix account, so I'll be catching up on the couch for a bit."

Glad to have the distraction, I ducked into the guesthouse, taking time to change clothes before quietly making my way down the driveway. Skirting motioned-activating lights on Keene's property, I made sure I passed undetected by Keene before stopping on the street to evaluate my route options. Taking off in a jog, I hoped fervently that I appeared non-threatening and somewhat normal in the upscale neighborhood. The last thing I needed was to be stopped by the police because of an overly imaginative and worried neighbor.

When I got to Alessia's street, I glanced down the road to see if there was any activity but saw nothing out of place. I continued to the next street, scanning the area to make sure no one was around as I jogged. Dusk had set, but it wasn't truly dark yet. When I came up to the house adjacent to Lessia's, I didn't hesitate, turning into the thick brush lining the edge of their property. Thankful for the cover, I paused and settled into a thick hedge. Waiting for over ten minutes, I let the darkness deepen before inching my way down the side of the large lawn, keeping to the shadows as I made my way closer to Alessia's yard, intending to cross into her property in the back. A large stone fence stopped me short. I should have realized she'd have some deterrent in the back as well as out front. After careful evaluation, I noted the security was tight. Sensors were placed along the stone wall, and cameras seemed to miss little of the yard. Even if I could get past the sensors, there was no place to hide on her side of the property. Clearly, someone did regular maintenance, keeping the trees trimmed well off the ground, and the hedges dotting the beds below were small and sparse. And while the flowers that flowed around the yard were beautiful, they did little to conceal anything.

I could barely make it into a position that afforded me a look into the back of the house while still giving me a view of the driveway before I was forced to stop, unable to go any farther without standing out like the stalker I was trying desperately to convince myself I wasn't. Fortunately, I didn't wait for more than thirty minutes out of the hour I gave myself when a man came up from the other side of the yard, not hesitating to step across the lawn and up the patio to the back door. He knocked softly, and regardless of the fact that there hadn't been a single light on in the house to reveal anyone was awake inside, the door opened within seconds. The figure looked around before stepping inside. The moonlight was barely enough to prove I was right, but it was enough. Matteo had snuck into Alessia's yard—and she was waiting for him.

I was just about to break position when movement caught my eye. The hair on the back of my neck stood on end as I watched a shadow break off from the bushes lining the neighbor's yard directly next to Alessia's. It retreated away from the house and, unfortunately, headed directly away from me, making it impossible to see who it was. Whoever they were, they were definitely proof that the Accardi brothers had been right in thinking she needed round-the-clock protection. No matter what Alessia thought, she wasn't as safe as she believed she was.

Chapter 19

Alessia

My body begged for sleep, but unfortunately, I had a job to finish. After letting Matteo in, we retreated to my hidden basement. I let him snag my computer to upload the drive D.M. had given me while I drew the layout of Karl Albrecht's estate, adding as much detail as I could remember to the margins about steps from windows of egress to hidden camera spots in corners of the rooms, possible hidden doors, and my pick for what was most likely the concealed entrance to the dungeon we knew he had hidden. One of the countless tapestries I'd pretended to admire was the perfect size to hide a door and placed in what had once been a stairwell, according to the only plans of the castle we could find—which were originally dated from the late eighteen eighties. Not very helpful when talking about a castle that was likely built in the thirteen hundreds and had multiple updates over its long lifetime, but at least it was a starting point.

It took a few hours to get everything recorded, scanned, and sent to my handler. Matteo had struggled to decode the flash drive, then had to run the entire thing through a program to translate it from Russian into English.

He sat back as he waited for the final translation program to run and stared at me. His intense scrutiny made me want to squirm, so I frowned at him. "What?" I asked, irritated instantly. Jet lagged, tired, and running on empty in the caffeine department since he wouldn't let me brew another pot, I felt justified in my crankiness.

"Have you thought any more about what you want to do?"

His careful tone put me on edge. I wasn't sure what his agenda was, but I knew with certainty he had one. Matteo always had an opinion, and his blank tone and expression let me know he was treading carefully, analyzing my every move instead of focusing on his thoughts and feelings. My answer was important to him.

"Have you?" I replied, half flippant and half serious. I wasn't exactly sure what to say. Of course, I'd been thinking about it. I had done little else for days but had come no closer to a decision. No way would I work without him, and I knew he felt the same way. We were flip sides to a coin, he and I, and I didn't feel right leaving him behind or dragging him with me in my decision-making. It wasn't like I could hand Gideon my résumé—a real one, anyway. And Matteo hadn't given me any sign that he wanted to step away from what we had been doing.

"Sure. To be honest, I've been thinking about it for years now, but the timing wasn't right."

I stilled, surprised. "Been thinking about what? And what timing?"

He raised an eyebrow. "What to do after this?" Waving his hand around the room, he continued, "Having an actual life, with people who know us and who we can be ourselves with. Hell, my interaction with your family today was the first authentic time I've had with them—or anyone else, really, since we were partnered up eight years ago. It's not like we can risk exposing our actual careers to a civilian, and lying to someone isn't the best ground to start a relationship on."

Biting my lip, I fought back the wave of guilt that hit me. He and I had been together so long, been doing this double life for so long that I hadn't thought about whether he was truly happy with his life. I assumed that if he were tired of what the job required, he would share it with me, and he'd never given me a reason to think otherwise. But unlike me, his job was fully hidden. His work required no travel, almost no physical meetings, and little risk of discovery. On the flip side, his hours were more varied and immediate, and an emergency was literally life-or-death. As much as I claimed not to have time for a social life outside of the one work required, his situation was even worse. And he was several years older than I was, with two tours under his belt before I had been old enough even to vote. No wonder he'd thought about changing his circumstances.

"If I were to retire, resign, or whatever, from what I do now—or at least the way I go about it—would you stay with what you do, or would you move on?" I couldn't help but ask.

He considered my question. "You're not the only agent I'm in charge of, just the one I'm most involved with. Part of that was due to your age when you were recruited. Part is because of your family, and the other is because of how visible you are. You know, you are, by far, the most public asset we have. Your modeling career puts your face everywhere, and your last name puts those we watch on edge just because of your proximity to your brother's company. I have to be close enough to you to have easy access to you because of that. The other agents I work with might see me once or twice a year."

I nodded, knowing that what he said was true. His placement in my life—and mine in his—was a non-negotiable point that happened as soon as I signed on the dotted line when I was eighteen.

Leaning back, he folded his hands over his taut stomach. "No, to answer your question, I don't plan on stopping what I do."

"But what you do will change dramatically if we're just friends instead of partners," I finished for him. Without having to maintain my cover, his personal life would change significantly. All the components would stay the same, but his free time would truly be his own, not spending time shoring up my cover here at home or quadruple-checking backup plans for my backup plans. I had to be honest; most of his critical or emergency situations came from me. Between my fame and my proficiency in creating chaos, I probably racked up more problems in a year than his other agents had in their entire careers combined.

He hesitated, then nodded, not able to deny the facts. Being partners was holding him back from having his own life. My gut clenched. How had I not realized how selfish I'd been?

"Stop it right there." Leaning forward in his chair, he continued, "You're not responsible for my life. And even if you were, I wouldn't change it for anything. Think of all the good you and I have done for the world. The countless lives we've saved. And those who will never know what would have happened to them had we not cut out the cancer. Your position allows you to access people, places, and information that others don't. But you can't do the work indefinitely."

It was my turn to hesitate. The longer I was in the game, the higher my risk of discovery was. I was already several years past the average retirement age for most models, too. At some point, everything was going to start crumbling. "I feel like things are changing, whether I want them to or not."

He nodded, obviously feeling it as well. Today was proof of that. Matteo had been in my life for years and had never once taken up an invitation to visit with my family. His coming over was more surprising to me than my breakdown with my brothers that morning—and I hadn't cried since my mother died. "But change isn't always bad. As agents, they train us to hate change because variables are what get you killed, but human nature itself demands change. Maybe we're overdue."

A chime from the computer put a stop to our conversation. I turned around to see what the translation software kicked out as he whistled. "What do we have?" I squinted at the computer to read the swirling text, so tired that the words refused to stay still.

A name on the screen caught my attention, waking me up in a heartbeat. I stilled, rereading the document in front of me to make sure I wasn't making things up in my delirium. "Am I reading this right?"

He nodded, and I didn't have to see his face to know his grim expression matched my own. I blew out a breath as he reached for the desk phone and hit the button to secure the line. My plans for a bed and sleep had just gone out the window.

Chapter 20

Brody

I was up early the next morning, despite my late night and jet lag. I'd waited another hour after Matteo snuck into Alessia's, but they hadn't so much as turned a light on in the house, and there weren't any more signs of unwelcome guests. When the owner of the property I'd been camping in returned home, I left, afraid they might have a dog that would find my hiding place.

Countless possibilities of what Lessia and Matteo had going on crossed my mind last night, but each one seemed as far-fetched as the last. Not my business, I kept trying to tell myself, but damn, did I hate puzzles.

The smell of coffee and bacon lifted my spirits slightly as I came in through the kitchen door. Keene was at the stove, stirring eggs and munching on a strip of the greasy goodness. "How was your run last night?" he asked as I poured a mug and sat down on a bar stool at the counter.

"What run?" I reached over and grabbed a piece of bacon, sticking the whole thing in my mouth.

"The one you avoided my light sensors last night to get in." He gave me a look that told me I was an idiot. "You forgot that I have an entire security system, and seeing as I'm in the security business, at least on a wider scale, I have a tendency to use it." His dry tone continued as he plated the eggs. "You tripped at least four security sensors and the perimeter alarm." Sliding a plate my way, he took his time walking around the counter to sit next to me, coffee cup at the ready by his elbow. "Want to tell me what you were doing at my sister's house?"

I raised my eyebrow. "How did you know I was at Alessia's?"

He smiled smugly. "I didn't, just took a guess. Only thing that can get a man wrapped up in knots is a woman, and Alessia's the kind to do it more than most." Taking a sip of coffee, he looked at me expectantly.

I hesitated, unsure what to admit to and what to reveal about my observations. "I didn't go over to Alessia's last night. At least not to her house. I stayed up for a bit, surveilling her house from a vantage point down the street. I couldn't shake the feeling I needed to watch for a while." All that was true but didn't give any detail.

His lazy amusement vanished, replaced with a laser-like intensity that I remembered distinctly from our shared past. "Gut, hunch, or observation?" He practically barked out the question. Observation meant I'd seen something off, hunch was a suspicion something wasn't right, whereas gut instinct was something any warrior could tell you was a major red flag that something huge was about to go down, with no real warning or intel. Not about to tell him it was a mix of all three, I just shrugged and shoveled food into my mouth.

His eyes narrowed, and I prepared for an interrogation, but my phone ringing stopped him before he could get started. Seeing the number on display, I hurriedly swallowed and swiped the screen to answer. The call didn't take long, but it completely derailed my plans for the next day or two and, more important to me, at least in the short run, would piss Alessia off. Since I was going to be the bearer of bad news and the closest person to her to take that frustration out on, I figured strategic planning would be necessary.

I looked over at Keene, who'd removed the breakfast dishes while I was on the phone and was now waiting for me to fill him in. "That was an executive from Valencia. One of your sister's crazed fans apparently flew across the Atlantic last night without parental permission and is currently MIA. They've tasked me with sticking to your sister like glue until daddy dearest comes to take him home." I wondered if his parents were off on the timeline and it was him I saw last night. I didn't see enough movement to identify him, but the height could have been right.

He stared at me, clearly confused about why a fan would be on their radar.

"The crazy is the son of the executive," I clarified. "And is the one everyone but Lessia would classify as an obsessive crazy stalker."

His expression cleared. "I'll call the brothers," he said, reaching for his phone, but I shook my head, stopping him.

"If we all arrive on her doorstep, she's going to kick us all out."

"She's going to kick you out, regardless. She doesn't particularly like us in her home for long, let alone anyone else. Matteo is the only regular visitor she has, and even then, they spend most of their time in the gym out back," he pointed out.

I bit back my retort about the two of them looking plenty comfortable inside her house last night, but it was a close thing. Pulling out my phone, I clicked Alessia's name and waited for it to connect. I was just about to settle for the fact that I would have to leave a voicemail when she picked up.

"'Lo?" The smokey, sexy drawl was deep and slow.

"We kinda have a minor emergency. I'll be over at your place in ten. Are you up?"

"Can it *kinda* wait another hour? I'm asleep."

I felt the corner of my mouth lift in a smile despite myself. She certainly sounded more asleep than awake, and I wasn't even sure she was tracking the conversation entirely.

"Nope, but I'll bring coffee. Just make sure you're upright and dressed." I hung up before she could protest, looking over the counter at the huge industrial machine Keene had off to one side. "Does that thing make espresso?" I asked, getting to my feet.

He gave me a bemused expression but nodded.

"Can you make six shots for me? I'll grab my go-bag and be right back."

It didn't take me long to grab my gear, seeing as I hadn't unpacked since I was supposed to be going back to my apartment that morning. By the time I came into the kitchen, all six shots were lined on the counter as if they were alcohol, prepared for a college student to down them in a row.

Keene watched as I poured three shots apiece into two travel mugs, topping them off with the rest of the pot of coffee. "I'm all for artificial energy to get one going in the morning," he said, "but if you drink just one of those, the top of your head will blow off from the rest of your body. Or your heart will explode."

I shook my head. "They aren't for me."

He drove us over to Alessia's house in silence, clearly interested in how I would handle the situation. "You can go." I tried to dismiss him as I juggled the two mugs and my bag.

"Hell no, I can't go. This, I've got to see." He grabbed my bag out of my hands, trailing behind as I stepped up to the door and started knocking. After a few minutes later, I alternated between banging on the door and ringing the bell. I was beginning to think I would have to start on the windows when the door jerked open.

Alessia stood in the doorway, her eyes more closed than open. Her hair was disheveled, a wild heap around her face. A crease from a pillow lined one side of her face. She wore shorts that were just on the side of company-appropriate, and her tank top barely covered her breasts, leaving her toned, tanned stomach bare. I jerked my head up, looking at a spot above her head before my body could get me in trouble, but the damage was already done—the image of her seared into my brain for eternity.

"Coffee, extra caffeinated." I shoved the first mug into her hand before she could say anything. "Be careful. It's hot," I added, though I didn't know why I bothered. Without flinching, she downed the entire mug, cauterizing her vocal cords, throat, and stomach lining in the process, I was sure.

Keene startled but ended up watching his sister in wonder as she drank the first mug dry. I pulled the now-empty container from her and shoved it at him without a word. "I have one more. Can we come in?" I was hoping bribery would at least gain me access to the house. It would be harder to get rid of me if I was inside, not to mention keeping the argument I knew was coming private from the neighbors.

And it almost worked. She nodded, her eyes opening enough so that I could at least see the bright purple that made her so recognizable. Taking a step back, she made to let go of the door but stopped at the last second, her gaze landing on the bag Keene held in his hand. "Oh, no," she said, jumping forward and shutting the door in one movement, leaving all of us outside on the porch. Her eyes wide-open now, the realization I was trying to play her waking her in an instant. "I don't know what you two are trying to pull, but no way am I letting either of you inside until you tell me what's going on."

I sighed. If only Keene had the wherewithal to hide the bag behind him, my job could have been easier. "Please," I stressed. "Can we come inside? I'll explain why we're here and give you the other mug of coffee." I tilted the mug from side to side in front of her as if the moving object could distract her.

I don't know why I bothered, knowing her answer before she even shook her head. "I told you before, McCallister. You're a hired PSO for events, travel, and photoshoots.

I do not, and will not, tolerate a babysitter in my own home. So whatever you and my brother are up to, you can just forget it."

Keene raised his hands in the air. "I didn't do it this time." He threw me under the bus. "Brody just needed a ride, and I wanted a front-row seat."

I scowled at him. "Oliver's missing," I said, turning back to Alessia. "He apparently purchased a plane ticket to the U.S. last night and is on his way here, if he isn't already. Valencia has declared you need protection until he can be contained. His parents are already on their way, so with any luck, it should only be for a day or so. He can't be that hard to track down, seeing as his only money source comes from that trust fund of his." I tried to keep my tone soothing and placating.

Her eyes narrowed. "Don't take that tone with me, Brody McCallister. No way in hell am I going to allow you to sit in my front yard, let alone my house. I don't like people in my home. It's my private place, and my security inside and out is some of the best. There isn't any reason I need to change anything." Her snappish tone left no room for argument, but she was about to get one anyway.

"We both know that isn't true. Or should I call Matteo?" I snapped back before taking a breath, really looking at her. My words hit home, but it wasn't obstinacy I saw in her expression; it was fear. Whatever it was, she wasn't worried, or only worried, about her sanctuary being invaded. She was worried about something else.

"What are you hiding in there?" I asked softly, almost missing the barely imperceptible flinch she tried desperately to conceal.

"My dungeon," she snipped. "And since you work closely with the enemy," she flicked her eyes to Keene, "I'm not about to let you in to spill all my dirty laundry to those around you."

Keene winced. "Can we please never talk about your sex life? As far as I and the rest of us are concerned, you'll be a virgin until the day you die."

Lessia raised an eyebrow. "So, someone desecrating my corpse is okay?" She shrugged. "Good to know."

I shuddered at the disgusting thought and saw Keene do the same out of the corner of my eye. "Though," she continued, "is that considered desecration or defilement?"

"What if I sign an NDA for you personally?" I cut her off, not wanting to think about rotting corpses and sex.

She thought for a while, clearly running through all the possibilities, but I knew I had her. Of course, I already had an NDA in place with Valencia, but if she wanted another one, I was willing.

"I guess that would work," she finally said, reluctant but clearly not able to come up with an argument that would pass muster. "Though I wish you luck finding someone who can get one drawn up quickly enough to make a difference."

Keene looked up from his phone. "Gideon has one saved on his computer. He's making a few changes and will have it here in a few minutes. On top of being a lawyer, he's a notary." He pocketed his phone. "He'll be able to get the legal requirements out of the way so that you can settle in. Though, in full disclosure, I don't want to know what goes on in this house. I have a hard enough time stomaching what she does out of it."

Alessia lifted her nose. "Then I guess I don't have to worry about Brody telling you about the handcuffs and assortment of other goodies I may or may not have under my bed."

Dismay lined Keene's face. "Again, I don't want to know any details about your sex life."

She pursed her lips, tapping a finger against them as she pretended to think. "I guess Royce would be the better option if you wanted to know details about that sort of thing. Not that he's that hardcore, but those partners of his certainly look like they know their way around a bull-whip, and not in a cowboy kind of way."

Keene froze. "How do you know about ..." He trailed off.

"The BDMS club Royce invested in?" She snorted. "Please, like there isn't anything I don't eventually find out about y'all whether I intend to or not. Besides, with the free samples vendors send to his house, he could open up his own sex shop. It's hard to miss when his and the business name are on the packages."

She looked wide-eyed and innocent for a split second before her attention turned back to the mug in my hand. "Can I have my second cup now, since I'm being good and all?" The sarcasm wasn't lost on me, but I handed it over without a word. She was pissed, pinned into a corner, and not about to back down from the fight we both knew was coming, as much as I'd tried to avoid it.

Gideon arrived before she could finish the mug, and Keene filled him in on the little he knew while the papers were looked over, signed, and notarized. The brothers, not dumb enough to stay around their little sister while she was cranky, left quickly, leaving us standing outside, staring at each other.

"Well," I finally drawled after a few uncomfortable moments under her scrutiny. "Are you going to let me in, or are we going to stand out here all day?"

She hesitated, clearly torn between letting me in and having us bake out in the Texas sun. It was still early morning, but the heat in the air and the stilted breeze were already making standing outside uncomfortable.

"Are you offended that I asked for a separate NDA?" she asked finally.

Shaking my head, I grabbed my bag. "Nope. Figure you had a good reason for it. After all, it's not like you don't have secrets."

She opened the door but stopped at my words. "What do you mean by that?" Turning to look at me, she gave me her best innocent expression, but I wasn't as easily fooled as her brothers.

"Where do you want to start? The fact that after expressly telling me you weren't involved with Matteo, you invited him into your house for a slumber party last night." I tried to keep the hurt and emotion from my voice, but I wasn't sure I was successful. "Or the handoff that D.M. gave you at the party that I wasn't supposed to see. Or perhaps the over-the-top surveillance equipment you have installed on your property. What are you hiding here, the gold from Fort Knox?"

Huffing, she opened the door, striding into the kitchen, her hips swaying as she walked. "I'm sure I don't know what you're talking about. My brothers installed the security, so if you think it's too much, take it up with them."

"I'm not talking about the visible one they installed. You have a secondary system as a backup." I'd found that last night just before leaving, adding another thing on the list of items that left me with more questions than answers.

She stilled again, her back going tight. "Did you think that, just maybe, it was a way for me to feel secure without my brothers knowing my every move? I can keep their system turned off and still be safe."

"If I didn't know you better, I might believe that," I admitted. "But with you, nothing is ever what it appears on the surface. I'm going to figure it out," I warned. "You might as well tell me now and save us both the hassle."

She shook her head as she looked back at me, meeting my gaze straight on. "I don't know what you're talking about. But even if I had a secret, it doesn't mean I have to share it with someone I don't know and who doesn't know me."

I shook my head. "I might not have known you for very long, but I know you a hell of a lot better than most people you've known for years. Don't play that game with me."

Whirling around, she took a step closer to me, pointing a finger at my chest. "Don't push me, Brody. I promise you won't appreciate the results."

She was close enough for me to feel her body heat through my clothes. Her anger sparked mine, and I closed the scant distance between us, dropping my bag to the floor. "You don't scare me, Lessia. I'm not one of those weak-willed models or agents you hang out with. I'm not blinded by preconceived notions like your brothers either."

Her nostrils flared as I spoke, the hand pointing at my chest curled into a fist. Not about to let her lash out in anger, I grabbed her fist in one of mine, pinning it to my chest, the other wrapping around her body, pulling her the final inch that separated us until we were plastered against each other.

I don't know who started it. Maybe both of us moved at once, but the kiss that followed was full of aggression, anger, and heat. Teeth clashed as we fought for dominance, our bodies pushing toward each other to get as close as possible. I lifted her, needing her closer, and she wrapped her mile-long legs around me, one leg around my waist, the other wrapping around lower so that her foot rested along my sensitive inner thigh.

Feeling her toes tease my inseam, I growled, digging my hand deep into her mass of hair and yanking her head back so that I could assault her neck, leaving nips and bites along her throat.

Her hands stayed busy as well; one fisted in my hair while the other scraped along my back, her nails certain to leave marks on my body.

It took some effort, but I pulled back enough to mutter something about a bed. Her garbled answer meant little in terms of direction, but I took it as acceptance and approval of what we were doing. Palming her ass, I turned to the hallway, hoping to God I was heading in the direction of her bedroom. I almost tripped over my go-bag, catching us both at the last second from falling to the floor in an undignified heap. She laughed softly, her tongue licking my ear before she nipped at it with her mouth.

Forcing off the shudder, I soldiered on, mostly successful during my trek to her bedroom. I considered it a win when I only paused twice to pin her against the wall, needing her closer, fighting off the need to bury myself in her right there in the hall. We fell into bed with a tangle of limbs. Alessia tried to take control, attempting to flip me so that she was on top, but I wouldn't have it. Pinning her hands above her, I used my weight and superior reach to outmaneuver her, my legs wedging between hers to settle deeper into her, my erection pressed against her core. Even through my jeans, I could feel her heat, see it flare in her eyes as she matched me stare for stare. Even though she fought me for it, her dilated pupils and flushed expression told me how much she liked me taking control. She wasn't playing games exactly—it was more a test to see if I could handle it—handle her. She cocked an eyebrow saucily, daring me to keep the upper hand, but I could see a hint of vulnerability in her eyes. With a woman that strong, that capable, I imagined she'd come across more than her share of macho men who thought they could keep up with her, only to let her down. I would not be one of them. I kept staring into the endless pools of purple, so incredibly vivid I would have sworn she wore contacts if I didn't know better. And at that moment, surrounded by the scent of her—sunlight and sin—I realized she was it. *The* one. I swallowed hard but didn't allow myself to flinch. Most men would have run scared at the realization that their life would never be the same, but if my time with the Raiders had taught me anything, it was to accept reality, adjust quickly, and be thankful for everything life gave you. I wasn't sure if it was love, not yet, but I knew without a doubt, with every fiber of my being, that it was just a matter of time. The woman staring at me like I'd lost my mind was my future.

Shaking off the heavy thoughts, I smiled at her smugly. "I like you right where you are, sweetheart." I flexed my hips, and her breath hitched, the desire etched in her face making me feel ten feet tall.

"You just like me at your mercy," she said breathlessly.

Shaking my head, I returned to the erogenous zone behind her ear. "Nope," I nuzzled the soft skin, "I just like that you let me take charge. We can switch for the next round if you're feeling left out. But I'm warning you, I've got a whole lot of need penned up, so pace yourself. We're going to be in this bed a long time."

Blowing out a breath, she lifted her head back, giving me easier access. "A hundred bucks says you'll be snoring like a baby ten minutes after you orgasm."

Grinning at her sass, I pulled back. "Ye of little faith," I teased. "What kind of self-centered, pansy-ass jerks have you been sleeping with?"

"I think I'd better plead the fifth," she said deftly. "Besides, I don't kiss and tell."

I went back to my task, trailing down to her collarbone, sampling and sipping at her skin as I went, not about to rush this but unable to keep my hands—or my mouth—to myself. I focused wholly on her—what lit her up, made her sigh, squirm, or moan. Working my way down, I peeled off her shirt, then shorts, not allowing myself to dwell on her perfect breast or what paradise lay under her lace panties. I found a sensitive area just behind her knee as I worshiped her mile-long legs, going down to her red-painted toes before finally, *finally,* allowing myself just enough rein to head where I'd wanted to go. She lay quiet, submissive for once, below me. I treasured that, too—that she allowed herself that much trust in me to be soft where she would typically be bold. Not that she wasn't fully participating. Her body writhed under mine, her husky voice not shy in telling me what felt good, great, or sublime. But she let me lead, somehow knowing that I needed to this time, our first time.

When we came together, it was red hot lightning and fireworks. Never in my life had I been that turned on, that in tune with my partner. She came around me, clenching waves of liquid heat bathing my hardness, and it took everything in me to still, to wait until her muscles loosened, her eyes to come back into focus until I began again. Alessia gasped against my mouth, surprise and amazement in her gaze as I built her back up, pushing her over the precipice a second time before joining her.

I came back to myself in seconds, or what could have been minutes, picking my weight up enough that I wouldn't be smothering her.

"That ... was ..." she huffed out between breaths.

"Fantastic ... stupendous ... life-changing?" I offered, panting as much as she was.

"Amazing." She patted my shoulder limply, obviously not fully recovered. "I was going to say amazing. Definitely a top five for me."

I raised an eyebrow, not sure whether to be insulted or amused. "Top five? I call bullshit. You called out to God at least—"

She cut me off with what suspiciously sounded like a giggle, my heart lifting at her teasing. "I'll up that to top two."

I lifted my head enough to glare at her in mock anger.

"Hey," she said, humor dancing in her pools of purple. "There's always room for improvement." She paused, realization dawning on her face as she realized I was growing hard within her again.

"You're going to owe me a hundred bucks." Satisfaction rifled through my voice.

She hummed, wiggling her hips. "I'm pretty sure you're going to make it worth my while. But," in a practiced move, she flipped me so fast I barely had time to blink, "I get the top this time."

"Well." I couldn't deny the view. Her jet-black hair was tousled and riotous around her. Wild waves of silk called for my fingers to play. I gave into temptation and speared a hand into it, cupping the back of her head. "I guess it *is* your turn." Wild laughter followed as I leaned up to press my lips to hers.

Chapter 21

Alessia

My mind blown, panting, and lying undignified in a heap on my bed, I felt wrung out, worn out, and well-tended. Brody McCallister was no stranger to sex, and, unsurprising to me, he was damn good at it. I couldn't remember a time I'd come more than once in a night, let alone took part in a sex marathon, but he had succeeded in not only making me lose count of how many times I'd come but turning my mind to mush in the process. How had I lived that long without realizing that multiple orgasms were an actual, real-life possibility and not just something writers made up in romance novels? My past lovers had some explaining to do, that was for sure. I might have teased Brody about being in my top five, but in reality my past bedroom adventures paled in comparison.

"That was fun." I panted, not even ashamed of my exertion. He struggled for breath next to me, so I felt some satisfaction that he was as wiped as I was. "How long do you think before we can do it again?"

He snorted. "I think I just set a record. I don't think I've come that many times since I was fifteen, maybe not even then. I'm not as young as I used to be, you know."

It was my turn to snort. Brody was every inch a man in his prime. Lean muscle corded under his skin, flexing and writhing under flesh as he moved. "I think you can handle a challenge. Besides, I'm sure it's like any other cardio. The more we do it, the more reps we can add."

He laughed, and I smiled, liking the carefree sound. He was so serious most of the time; it was nice to know I could add some humor to his life. We lay there, the sound of our breathing the only break in the silence as I drifted on a post-coital high. My eyes were closed, my body heavy as I floated between falling asleep and resting when I heard him lift his head and felt his eyes studying me.

"What?" I asked, not wanting to open my eyes.

"Are you ever going to admit what you are? I signed your NDA, and I'm sure you're aware of my status in the military. I have a pretty high-security clearance, and it would only help you to read me in on what it is you are."

My eyes popped open, my desire for sleep and another round, or four, forgotten. "What did you do in the Marine Corps? Keene won't talk about it." Rolling over onto my hip, I propped my head in my hand, looking expectantly. An offence was the best defense. With any luck, I could distract him with his own stories. Failing that, there was always sex or food.

He gave me a suspicious look, unsure how to take my innocent act. The trick to maintaining an excellent cover was the mixing of lies and truth. Straight-out lies were easily sensed by those trained to detect them, while too much truth blew your identity to smithereens. Brody knew, or had a very strong hunch, that I was more than I seemed, but as long as I skimmed that edge of giving him something concrete, I could keep him guessing and not break protocol or my oath to keep my job a secret.

"I tried to get Matteo to dig into all of my brothers' files, but he said something about things being classified and going to jail for eternity for breaking into them. He said I should ask them if I wanted to know something." I gave him an aggrieved look. "I think you know my brothers enough to know that, other than an occasional tidbit here and there, they aren't ones for sharing."

He cocked an eyebrow. "You don't know what your brothers did while they were enlisted?" His disbelief was clear.

"Well." I shifted, letting the sheet slip down a bit. His gaze followed the movement, and I took a breath, making sure I didn't exaggerate the movement too much. "I know what branches they were in, and they share stories here and there, mostly with each other that I just happen to overhear. But no, they don't like to talk about it much, and I don't think they want me to know that side of them, you know?" I didn't give him a chance to comment. "So?" I said expectantly.

"So, what?" The sharpness in his eyes softened, and I knew I'd succeeded in shifting his focus.

"What can you tell me about what you did? Where did you and Keene meet?"

Uh-oh. Wrong move. Whatever or wherever they met was either a bad memory or classified. He shook his head, focusing back on me. "We were talking about you, not your brother and me."

I huffed, sliding out from under the sheets. Naked as the day I was born, I didn't bother looking back as I walked into my closet, no longer in the mood for more fun at the looming probability of having to cut Brody loose since I couldn't lie to him or tell him the truth. "I'm a model who doesn't particularly enjoy her work most of the time." Grabbing a pair of yoga pants, I called over my shoulder as I yanked them on, "I'll admit to enjoying the company of some not-so-nice people from time to time. I was raised to be over-vigilant and over-prepared, and I continue to be that way, despite my overprotective brothers' thoughts on the contrary. Though I will admit that I tend to get myself into trouble, so it's a good thing I prepared for the worst outcome." Turning around, I glared at him, pissed that, yet again, I was forced to skirt the truth with someone I desperately wanted to be honest with, especially in my own home. "Something you might not know about me, that my family didn't know until yesterday, was that I wanted more than anything to serve my country, but my father forbade it. So now, I'm the only Accardi who hasn't served in the armed forces." I let a hint of pain come through, letting him know I was speaking the truth. "There was nothing I wanted more than to serve my country, but Daddy wasn't about to let his little girl go play soldier. So I'm sorry if you think there is something to find, but bringing up bad memories and insisting I'm something I would've killed for when I was younger will not get you anywhere."

The distress on Brody's face told me he hadn't meant to hit a sore spot. He wasn't that kind of man, even when he was frustrated. I softened as he ran a hand through his hair, clearly unsure of his next move. "Go shower," I directed. "I'll start coffee and see if there is anything to eat. I'm starving, and I'm sure you are, too."

I didn't even let the coffee finish brewing before pouring a cup, my mind still fuzzy from days of little-to-no sleep. I'd barely gotten an hour in before Brody called that morning. Somehow the morning had faded into late afternoon, and if I was going to stay awake long enough to make the food my body was demanding, let alone eat it, I needed at least a few cups, or I would probably fall asleep standing at the stove.

Rummaging in the freezer, I found a bag of frozen vegetables and started a stir-fry. No chicken or beef, but I found a can of Spam that I cut into chunks to throw in as the protein. I'd just poured the rice into the pot when an alarm sounded, my phone buzzing insistently simultaneously.

Brody came running, gun in hand, hair dripping. "What is it?"

"First perimeter alarm." I didn't bother getting too excited yet. Another noise sounded off, my phone now pulsing in my hand. "And now someone's tripped an inner wall sensor." I nonchalantly grabbed my nine from under the counter, where I stored it, before heading to the family room to turn on the television.

"Where do you think you're going? We need to get you to an interior room. The police would have been notified and should be here shortly." His indignation would have been cute if I had been in a better frame of mind.

I rolled my eyes, queueing up the motion cameras, rewinding a few seconds to see Oliver's not-so-graceful climb over the back rock wall and fall into a heap into the yard. He stood, dusting off his pants and straightening his shirt before picking up the armful of dreaded red roses and gamely starting in the direction of the house.

Ignoring Brody's curse of dismay, I chambered a round in my weapon. "You want to know how I've dealt with my crazy fans in the past?" I walked to the back door, elbowing him in the ribs—hard—when he tried to hold me back. Stepping out onto the patio, I took careful aim before pulling the trigger.

Red sprayed across the lawn as the bullet connected with the top of one rose.

"Jesus!" Brody said behind me, the same time as Oliver cursed and hit the grass with a dive that would have made a swan envious. He put his hands over his head, still holding the bouquet, trying his best to take cover on the open lawn.

"Oliver," I yelled, stomping a few more feet in his direction. "I'm afraid I'm going to have to be more obvious since subtlety and kindness haven't worked with you. I'm not interested in you. I don't care about your family or your so-called devotion to me. You know absolutely nothing about me, apart from what any fan on the planet can find in an internet search, and even half of that is wrong. I'm not your soul mate. I don't love you, and I can barely tolerate your presence, let alone look forward to any time spent together. I hate roses, especially red ones, and detest uninvited company. Your daddy is the only thing we have in common, and he's about to become a memory when I tell him I will not renew my contract with Valencia."

I shot again when he tried to pick his head up, another flower biting the dust as I blew it into a million pieces. "I highly suggest staying exactly in that position until the police come." Sirens rang out from a distance, alerting me that the cavalry had arrived. "If y'all will excuse me, I need to check on dinner."

I turned on my heels, ignoring Brody's incredulous look as I swept by him, leaving him to deal with Oliver. Strolling into the kitchen, I pulled out my phone, opening the gate with a swipe of my finger to allow the police easier access. Though, it would've been entertaining to watch them try to climb the fence. Then I texted Matteo, who apparently had been watching the entire thing as soon as the alarm tripped. The asshole teased me for shooting harmless flowers but agreed to report what had occurred to my handler on my behalf.

Calls from my brothers started next, almost as one. Pulling the rice off the stove, I began fluffing it with a fork as I put my phone on speaker and group-dialed them all—figuring I might as well get it all done at once.

"All y'all need to take a breath." I started before anyone could say anything. "I'm fine, Brody's fine, the kid who jumped the wall in my backyard is fine, and no one got a scratch on them, apart from some flowers. The police are arresting Oliver now, Brody is overseeing them, and I'm trying to save my dinner while I wait for them to come in and take my statement."

"We were told shots were fired," Boone said, his voice booming over the line.

I winced, hitting the side button on my phone a few times so that I wouldn't lose my hearing. "I may have gotten a little upset, but I think it speaks to my maturity that I didn't wing him." Someone snorted. I couldn't tell who, but no one else commented, and I took that as agreement. It was a fact that if that had happened a few years ago, I probably would have shot him. Not to permanently damage anything, but sometimes seeing a small little, Band-Aid-sized wound that you knew could have killed you had it been aimed differently made a man think a little harder about their preconceived notions.

"If y'all are heading in this direction, please head to Gideon's. I barely have enough veggie stir-fry for Brody and me. There is no way I can feed anyone else. As it is, I'll have to give him all the Spam in it, just so I can feel like I fed him a proper meal."

"Spam and veggies are a proper meal?" Royce asked.

"Is Spam even food?" Boone grumbled, but I ignored him.

"And rice. It has protein, vegetables, and a starch." I couldn't help but defend my pitiful dinner, though he had a point. "All the things a proper meal is supposed to have. I suppose serving it on paper plates is crass, but I refuse to do the dishes, and a good hostess shouldn't allow guests to do physical labor while in their house."

"I can do the dishes, and you had no such qualm about the physical labor we just did an hour ago," Brody chimed in as he stepped into the room from the back deck.

The line was quiet for a second before Keene spoke. "Was that supposed to be a euphemism, or are you just trying to get all of us riled?"

"Both," I said brightly. "And let me tell you, I don't think I've ever had my clock cleaned as well or as often as—" They hung up as a unit, and I sighed. "I wish you hadn't said anything. Now they're going to come over here all manly and have to defend my honor for no good reason. All that chest-beating isn't fun when eighty percent of the men doing it are related to me." I wrinkled my nose. "Now, if some of your old marine buddies wanted to come over in their stead, maybe we can add a no-shirt clause."

He raised his hand, cutting me off. "Cut the shit. You and I both know your brothers would've known we slept together in a heartbeat, and I respect them—and my friendship with Keene—too much not to be upfront about it."

I sighed again. "I still wish you hadn't done it. That was clearly a one-time thing. And now that Oliver the pansy is off the streets, little ol' me is safe to live by her lonesome again."

He smirked. "A one-time thing? You're the one who mentioned we needed to increase our cardio."

I leveled him with a look, plating up the food at the same time. "That was before you ruined my afterglow. I have a rule against having sex with buzz killers—before, during, or after." Shrugging, I took a delicate bite of the mixture in front of me. "One of those sorry, not-sorry kind of things. A girl has to have standards, after all."

He leaned forward. "I bet I can change your mind."

Shaking my head, I stared directly into his eyes so he could read the truth in mine. "No, Brody, you won't."

I wouldn't change my mind. Not because of the questions, at least, not because he'd asked them. But because I couldn't answer them, and if he was going to be so pig-headed about knowing every little thing about me, even though I knew he couldn't talk about his classified missions, then I didn't have a choice. If Brody could have ignored the inconsistencies and been content in his ignorant bliss, then perhaps I could've kept him around for a while. But he wasn't going to let it go. I knew he wasn't.

Before he could say anything, a uniformed police officer knocked at the back door. At the same time, Gideon, Keene, and Boone came rushing in, with Royce a step behind them. "I've got the LEOs. *You* get to handle my brothers." I gave my pitiful dinner a wistful look. The only thing worse than eating vegetables was eating cold, soggy vegetables. I kissed my brothers, giving them each a hug before going out the back door with the officer. With any luck, I wouldn't have to go to the police station.

Of course, I wasn't that lucky. By the time my statement had been taken, they'd verified my gun ownership and given it back to me, and I had signed, posed for, and sweetened up the local law enforcement, several hours had passed.

Surprisingly, my brothers had left the station before I was released, leaving Brody his truck. He'd said little beyond giving his statement to the cops and barely grunted when I told him I was ready to go, escorting me to the passenger side door of his truck like a gentleman. The silence in the vehicle on the drive home was deafening. Normally, quiet was welcome, but the cold shoulder was making the ride a bit uncomfortable.

"Are you upset I stole your bodyguard moment?" I asked finally. Brody didn't strike me as the kind of guy who needed to be the hero, but he was a former elite, a real-life hero in every way. Maybe I cock-blocked a glory moment? No, that wasn't right—he wasn't that kind of man. "Or are you mad I won't have sex with you anymore?" That seemed slightly more likely. I knew I was certainly upset about that as well, but a girl had to make sacrifices in the name of protecting herself.

"You shot at someone tonight, Lessia. You could have killed that kid had he flinched in the wrong direction." He practically bit the words out, stilling me in my seat. I'd never heard him that angry before.

"Oliver was never in any danger." Well, not any more than I was comfortable putting him in, anyway. "I'm an excellent shot and wouldn't have shot a gun off, half-cocked, had I been at all uncertain about what I was aiming at." I thought it over. I guess regular civilians wouldn't have reacted quite the way I had. "My brothers will tell you it's not the first time. I think I scared off my first jerk of a boyfriend that way, or similar anyway, when I was fifteen or sixteen." I wasn't sure if that little tidbit was said to reassure him or give him more nightmare material, but it was the truth. When Blayze Williamton III had refused to leave me like a proper gentleman should have at the front door and tried to drag me into my house to have drunken sex, I'd pretty much done the same thing, albeit at a much closer distance and a lower caliber weapon. Boone had gotten me out of trouble with the sheriff and had run interference with the other three brothers, who were all deployed then. Daddy never found out, as far as I could tell. I was pretty sure the sheriff was afraid of what he would have done to the little shit, but that was only a guess.

"It's pretty well-known in my family that I get into these kinds of situations," I continued. "Keene had to have told you about some things I've gotten into in the past, even before you took me on as my PSO. There's that bar fight, that guy who tried to kidnap me when I went to the big motorcycle rally a few years ago, the motorcycle incident that happened the next day—which is why I promised Royce I would never buy or ride one again unless my life depended on it—that time at the beach in Cancun ..." I counted them off on my fingers, trying to decide how many issues to bring up. If I had to remember them all, we might be there all night. "Hell, you saw the whole Mike-the-asshole incident the day you first met me. If Boone hadn't shown up, I would have kicked that guy's ass just as a public service."

His jaw tightened. "I'm your PSO. My job is to protect you."

I bugged my eyes out at him. "And if I were in any danger, I would have let you. I told you before that Oliver was no threat to me. Just because someone yells, 'The sky is falling,' doesn't make it so. I'm sorry if you feel like I stepped on your toes, but I was just a little mad at you and took it out on Oliver since I didn't want to explain to Keene why I shot another one of his friends." I raised a hand at his startled expression. "Story for a different day." I stopped him before he could ask. That was another one of my tales I would prefer never saw the light of day.

"I'm not mad that you shot at Oliver," he gritted out.

"Then why are you mad?" I tilted my head, studying him. The sky was darkening as the sun rode low, but it hadn't fallen behind the landscape yet, giving me enough light to get a good look at him.

"You don't trust me," he finally said, not looking at me once.

I stilled. He sounded hurt, frustrated, and, yes, angry. The frustration and anger I could brush off, but I didn't like that I'd hurt him, even if I didn't have a choice. "So because I didn't cower behind you like a helpless, timid little girl, I don't trust you."

"Don't twist my words." He jerked the wheel to turn, squealing the tires and launching both of us sideways against our seat belts.

"I'm not." It took some determination on my part, but I didn't comment on his driving abilities since I really didn't want to walk the few blocks home. But discreetly, I tried to grab for the door handle to help hold on. "I'm trying to understand where your head is, and I'm afraid I'm having a hard time figuring it out." His speed increased, and I prayed we wouldn't get pulled over. I'd had a long enough day.

"I trusted you enough to let you do your job while we were overseas. When we visited the castle, I let you take point. Hell, I even slept with you just this morning. If I didn't trust you, I wouldn't have allowed you to do any of those things." Again, truth wrapped in lies. I knew what he was getting at, but deflection and innocence were all I could do to ward him off. He knew the average person would never have pulled the trigger that near another person's head. Even the best shooting hobbyists wouldn't have attempted that shot. The first rule of gun safety was never to point it toward another being unless you planned on, or were okay with, killing them. I could profess to be the best shot in my family—which I was—but as the only one who hadn't seen combat, I was also the least likely one on paper to attempt it. Unless I was batshit crazy, which my brothers and others had claimed in the past. My family didn't so much as blink an eye at most of my escapades anymore, mostly because they were so used to them that it didn't dawn on them how out of the norm it would be for anyone else.

He pulled into my driveway, stomping on the brake hard enough to jolt me forward in my seat. Matteo was sitting on my front porch, waiting for me. I didn't wait for Brody to come around, immediately opening my door and jumping to the ground.

"You know damn well what I mean, Lessia. You don't trust me with this." He had circled the hood of the truck already and motioned wildly to Matteo.

That was it, the line in the sand. "Is he coming in?" Matteo asked. We'd started Brody's background checks last night, Matteo and my handler wanting to cover all the possibilities since I couldn't come up with a final decision about my future plans yet. If Brody could replace Matteo to help maintain my cover, it would, at the very least, give Matteo a chance at a somewhat normal life. We both knew he would pass the checks with flying colors, and Matteo was allowing me to bring him in now versus waiting for the official paperwork, sensing that it was a pivotal moment. But I couldn't bring myself to forgo protocol. As much as I played with bending the rules, certain ones were too important for even me to ignore.

"No," I answered, not taking my eyes from Brody's green ones. "He's headed home. His own this time since they caught Oliver."

Matteo gave me a sympathetic look. "I'll just wait in the kitchen," he said slowly, looking between us.

Brody went to reach for me, but I took a step back. "Tell me something about your missions," I dared him, my voice soft on the slight breeze. "Something you're not supposed to tell another living soul, apart from your teammates."

He went rigid, and I knew he understood what I was getting at. For the first time, I admitted, at least to him in a roundabout way, that I was involved in something beyond the surface. But I couldn't divulge my business any more than he could parts of his past. Classified was classified, and without permission, neither of us would breach our vows to protect those secrets. His silence stretched, leaving only the sounds of the early crickets.

"That's what I thought," I said, finally. Taking another step from him, I gave him a sad smile and a half-hearted wave. "You have a nice night." The finality of those words betrayed the meaning behind them. Like I had told him earlier, what was between us—whatever it could have been—wasn't going to happen. Because I was a professional. And Brody was too good of a man only to get parts of me the way my family did. The fact that the ones I loved the most were the ones I had to sacrifice for the greater good had never worn on me as badly as it did at that moment.

I didn't watch as Brody left, afraid I wouldn't be able to let him go without blurting out something I would regret later. Matteo stayed silent as I closed the door softly, turning the alarm back on as the gate at the end of the drive swung shut.

"Are you okay?" he asked.

I sighed. "No, but I don't think I'm supposed to be." My psychologist, the ones we were required to see quarterly, would be pleased with the emotion, even if it felt like I'd been gutted. She always seemed a bit unnerved by my cavalier attitude regarding certain aspects of my job—the wet work, I suppose you could call it. I just saw it as extermination or being the tool society used to remove a cancerous growth or decaying tissue, but she always seemed a little more squeamish. My real emotion would make her happy, even if it made me miserable.

"Any news about what we're going to do with the information on the flash drive?" I asked, trying to change the subject.

"He said to let it play." Matteo didn't seem much happier than Brody had been a few minutes before. It wasn't often that he, our handler, and I were in disagreement about an upcoming assignment, but I understood his reluctance.

If I were being honest, I was surprised at our handler's decision, too.

"Timeframe?" I asked.

He shrugged. "You read the same information I did, Lessia. They'll need time for surveillance and an exit strategy. I'm not sure whether or not it's a good thing that you didn't pull Brody in. He's going to be a problem if he's present when this goes down."

I nodded. "We'll deal with that bridge when we come to it. Hopefully, the mission will be over and done with before anyone realizes something's wrong. With luck, no one will even know I left and returned at all."

He smiled. "We can always hope. I'll do what I can here, but I'm not sure what I can do to hold back the horde if they catch wind of this."

Trying to return his smile, I knew it was a hollow attempt. My mind wasn't where it should be, and we both knew it.

"Well, I'll get out of here. I'm working on getting a team scrambled and ready. I'll let you know when we get everything in place."

He exited as quietly as ever, even his steps silent. I drummed my fingers on the table, not knowing what to do next. Normally, I would bound down to the basement, determined to go over and re-go-over every detail of the next assignment, but I couldn't gather enough energy to care. With my heart heavy, I pulled open the freezer. In cases like that, a girl needed chocolate and ice cream as much, if not more so, than she needed oxygen. Groaning at the empty shelves in front of me, I checked my watch.

Sweet Nothings, my favorite ice cream parlor, would be open for another hour.

I grabbed my keys and jumped in my car. It was an actual emergency, much more so than the whole Oliver issue ever was, and I wasn't about to give anything a chance to interrupt me. It didn't take long to traverse the few blocks, though I had to park down the street from the storefront. By the looks of things, baseball practice for the kids had just let out. I wasn't great with ages, but I'd guess they were a year or two younger than Gia. The parlor was packed, forcing me to dodge running kids and skim past parents talking to other families as they celebrated the end of another game.

"Well, hello, Alessia. Is that niece of yours with you today?" Nancy, the aging owner of the store, asked as I practically slid to a stop at the counter.

"No, ma'am. Just having a chocolate emergency tonight."

She gave me a sympathetic look. "Man troubles?"

I hesitated. "Is it that obvious?"

She laughed. "Honey, there are only a handful of things that can drive a woman to run through a horde of screaming children. Man trouble is the leading cause, so I played the odds."

I gave her a smile I didn't much feel. "Well, you guessed right. What do you recommend?" I learned long ago to bow to Nancy's wisdom.

She smiled sympathetically. "My granddaughter created a new concoction this morning. Chocolate Dream Supreme, I think she called it. Chocolate ice cream with a hint of espresso, homemade dark and milk chocolate mini chips, plus swirls of caramel and marshmallow, topped with chocolate sprinkles."

It sounded rich, over-the-top, and perfect. Licking my lips, I nodded. "I'll take a double scoop."

My eyes practically closed in bliss as I took my first bite. I sucked on the spoon as I exited a few minutes later. The mix of coffee, chocolate, marshmallow, and a hint of caramel swirled on my taste buds. I would have a stomachache and sugar rush for sure, but it was totally going to be worth it.

I was halfway back to the car when I felt it. The feel of eyes watching me caused the hairs on the back of my neck to rise. *Damn it*, I thought, looking down at the half-eaten bowl mournfully. Apparently, Karl was much more impatient than anyone had thought, and my plans for the next few days were about to be fucked to hell. To top it off, I wouldn't even have a full stomach or a night of sleep to tide me over. I kept my attention on my vehicle, resisting the urge to see where the source of the stares were coming from. Three, possibly four, I decided, busying myself by digging my keys out from my purse. Once I had them in hand, I dropped them so I could case the area. I pegged the black sedan with tinted windows parked just in front of my car as the getaway driver—real original there, but they would have to get me out of there somehow with no one seeing. There was still a fair amount of pedestrian traffic a block or two away, but it had cleared out a bit from before.

The quiet in the darkness was almost deafening and further cemented that, although I'd pegged them, the team was comprised of experienced professionals since they weren't making a sound. For the first time in my career, I had to force down a shiver of fear. We'd thought we'd have time to put a team of our own in place. One that could watch from a distance, sure, but be there as backup nonetheless. Now I didn't even have Brody to watch my back. The realistic part of me knew that if he were there, the team circling me would have killed him to get to me, but the human element in me wished I had someone by my side to help steady my nerves. I was used to being the hunter, not the prey, and I didn't like the change one damn bit. Worst-case scenarios flashed through my brain. What if I was totally off base, and this team hadn't been hired by Karl, but by some other unknown threat? I couldn't imagine Oliver having the resources, but he wasn't the only one with an unhealthy fixation—just the one who was currently the most persistent and had the easiest access to me. Would my backup be able to find me? How long until someone realized I was missing? Would my brothers find out, and how worried would they be? If this was Albrecht, was I strong enough to endure whatever was in store for me until I could be rescued? I had seen the reports of what he'd done to his past victims; was knowledgeable enough to know just what the human body could withstand, and what the brain could not.

I was almost to my door when I saw the first man materialize behind me, courtesy of my side mirror. *Sometimes it sucks, pretending to be ignorant*, I mused as I watched him without looking like I was watching him. With an unknown team around me, and if I were to assume it was

Albrecht, my orders had been clear to hold my cover in place. I couldn't take out everyone and it would only help me later to be underestimated. I completely missed the partner, who grabbed me from behind and slapped a hand over my mouth. Panic took over despite my attempt to hold it at bay, and I struggled in the man's grasp, feeling the needle prick my neck as the first man reached us. The drug took effect quickly, and my strength waned almost immediately. For the first time since I was a teen, I truly felt helpless as my movements were easily subdued. Fear ran through me in a cold, metallic wave as I realized just how vulnerable I was. There were no cameras to see what was going on, no people to hear my pitiful struggles. No team for at least hours, assuming Matteo realized quickly I was in trouble, and even that was doubtful. My last conscious thought before darkness descended was of Brody, and my somewhat foolish wish that I would make it through this alive, if only so I could see him again.

Chapter 22

Brody

I was stewing, and I knew it. What was worse, I knew with absolute certainty that if I hadn't opened my mouth and spewed out nonsense that I didn't even believe, I wouldn't be stuck in my apartment in a shitty mood and hungover from the beers I'd drunk the night before. Instead, I could have spent the night with a passionate woman who, believe it or not, had a brain I found even more intriguing than her body. I was an idiot, but I couldn't quite bring myself to voice it out loud. I knew my apology and subsequent groveling were inevitable, but not yet. A man had a right to take his time when he knew the woman he owed an apology to would make him work for forgiveness. Eating crow was nasty any day of the week, but Lessia wasn't the kind of woman to let me pluck, marinade, and grill that meal. She'd make me eat it feathered, raw, and bloody.

I yanked open the fridge, hoping that food was magically delivered while I was sleeping last night because, other than a moldy block of cheese and a few bottles of water, I knew nothing was in my apartment. My phone rang from where I'd left it on the counter, so loud I jumped at the sound, my head hitting the refrigerator. Swearing, I rubbed the back of my head as I retraced my steps, snagging it before it went silent.

"Yeah," I said, not bothering to look at the screen to see who was calling.

"Where are you?" Matteo's voice sounded off.

"My apartment. Lessia sent me home, remember?" Even I could hear the bite in my tone.

"Alessia's been taken. If you want to be a part of her rescue, I need you to leave your phone and get in your truck right now. Her brothers are finding out she's missing as we speak, and they can't know the details of where she is or how we're going to get her back."

Every muscle in my body tightened. "What do you mean, she's been 'taken'?"

"Look," impatience colored every word Matteo spoke, "I have a jet getting ready to take off in less than forty-five minutes. If you want to help save her, you'll get your ass in your vehicle in less than five and haul ass. Otherwise, I'm leaving without you." He gave me a few more details about where to meet, then hung up.

I didn't hesitate, slamming the phone down and running to grab my shoes. Not even bothering to tie them, I snagged my keys. My phone rang again, and I saw Keene's name displayed on the screen. It tore at me to ignore the call, but if Matteo said they couldn't know where we were going, I would wait until I could at least ask the man what had happened, where we were going, and why the hell her family—who had more contacts in law enforcement and the federal government than I could dream of—couldn't be told what had happened.

Glancing at the dash as I started my truck, I noted the time. I had forty-four minutes to get to the airstrip. Tires squealed as I peeled out of the parking lot. With any luck, I'd be able to avoid red lights, traffic, and police while I drove because there was no way in the hell I was stopping for anything.

I didn't know what to expect, but a Gulfstream 650ER parked in a darkened hangar was not it. I jumped up the steps two at a time, acting like I belonged, though I half-expected to find I'd somehow ended up on the wrong jetway. The luxury jet didn't scream "rescue transportation" any more than a stretch limo would have.

"What's going on, and whose plane is this?" I demanded when I caught sight of Matteo. He ignored me for a moment, talking to someone on the phone and signaling to the only other person in the aircraft, a man wearing sweats, a sweaty tee shirt, and a slightly panicked expression as he practically ran past me and into the cockpit.

Matteo motioned me to take a seat and sat next to me as he wrapped up his call, setting the phone down next to him before reaching for his seat belt. "We have three minutes to get this thing in the air before someone notices it's missing," he announced nonchalantly. As if he'd not just informed me we were in the process of stealing what I was sure was a multimillion-dollar jet, he narrowed his eyes at me. "You left your phone, right? Any electronics—laptop, watch, anything that can be tracked?"

I nodded. "I'm clean. Why and how are we stealing a jet? What happened to Alessia, and where are we going?"

Was stealing a plane even possible? Granted, not a whole lot of the population knew how to fly one. Nevertheless, you'd think they'd lock them up or something. Could stealing one result in getting shot down? And how critical was it to have a flight plan filed?

He waved a hand in dismissal. "Once we're airborne, we have nothing to worry about, as long as we get Alessia back safe and sound. Taking this jet allows for two things—one, her brothers can't follow us, assuming they even knew where to look for her since this is the only one they own that has the capability of crossing the Atlantic, and two, it'll get us there and back in the least amount of time possible."

I stilled. "You stole an Accardi Tactical jet?" I looked at my surroundings with a whole new light.

"Not important." Matteo was all business, his tone having an edge I hadn't heard before. He sounded ... worried. "Alessia was kidnapped last night, apparently after going out to get some ice cream. They found her car this morning when Boone grew concerned about not being able to reach her. I'd already started tracking her when she didn't show up at my apartment this morning." He didn't even have the decency to look uncomfortable about that information.

"So, where are we going?" I felt like I was a broken record. "Why can't her brothers know, and why aren't we letting the police deal with this?"

"We're going to Germany." The plane took off, and, apparently feeling like he could fill me in since I couldn't escape anymore, he started answering my questions. "Her brothers don't have the jurisdiction or the relationships to allow for them to circumvent those legal issues, and the local police are in Albrecht's pocket."

"And we do?" I certainly didn't. I didn't have any connections in my own government, let alone a European one. I didn't even have my passport with me, for crying out loud.

He nodded, pulling out a tablet. "Yep. And you're in luck because your clearance came back about an hour ago."

"Thank you?" I wasn't sure what else to say.

He snorted. "You'll regret those words later, I bet. I'm hoping to rope you into Alessia detail, giving me a chance to step back. I don't have to tell you how exhausting that woman is, and it's just a matter of time before she and her brothers go to war. With any luck, I can stay out of the middle of that mess."

The headache from that morning came back in full force. Rubbing my eyes, I leaned forward in my seat. "I don't know whether to be happy I'm apparently about to be read-in on whatever Alessia has been hiding or scared I'm about to be handed Pandora's box."

It was a little of the first and a whole lot of the second, I realized a few hours later. That woman had layers within her layers. No wonder she seemed so guarded. She was wrapped in a web of her own making, walking a figurative tightrope to keep her cover intact and live some sort of life. No wonder she hadn't even blinked at the Oliver situation. Her file read as a mixture of an American version of James Bond and a goddess of chaos and war. Twenty-two kills. Three had resulted in governments being overthrown in the upheaval of their leaders dying—and those three had been declared natural causes despite the proof I held in my hands. There were several drug lords listed, countless human traffickers, and even the girlfriend of some Russian mobster. The file for that one was still mostly redacted, and I took a moment to wonder why, out of all of the assignments they allowed me to view, that one was blacked-out. I didn't have much time to think before my attention was diverted by her most recent kill, which was the day before I'd met her the first time. I tried not to wince at the details of how she'd made a public statement of what the world thought of human traffickers.

We changed gears after I had some time to process, going over plans of Albrecht's castle. Plans I had a very sneaky suspicion Alessia supplied, now that I knew what her job—her real job—entailed. Matteo and I were joining up with the team assigned for her rescue. Matteo hadn't explained everything, like a better reason behind stealing a jet and why the two of us were flying across the world to rescue a woman with an entire team of better-qualified individuals already en route to collect her. But I wasn't complaining, mind you. If anyone was going to pull her out of this situation, it would be me. I still owed her an apology and one big I-told-you-so about hooking Albrecht.

An hour out from our destination, an alarm on Matteo's tablet blared, causing him to drop his glass. It crashed to the floor, ignored by us both, as he pulled up a screen with slightly shaky hands.

"What is it?"

His face had visibly paled. "Maybe nothing." Which definitely meant something.

"What was the alarm for?" I wasn't in the mood to play a thousand questions.

He swallowed audibly. "Alessia has a tracking implant, which is why I knew exactly where she was."

"And?" Dread filled me, waiting for him to continue.

"It just went offline."

"You mean like she's underground? Or it ran out of batteries?"

He rubbed the back of his neck. "The range on these things makes it unlikely. They also rely on the body for an electrical charge."

I needed him to spell it out for me. "So?" I let the word hang in the air.

"So unless she was hit by lightning, someone either cut it out of her," he blew out a breath, "or she's no longer living."

Chapter 23

Alessia

I woke up pissed. Not the I-see-red, burn-the-house-down kind of pissed, the ice-cold, I-will-dismember-someone-alive without so much as blinking or a single regret kind of pissed. The cold detachment cloaked me like a blanket before I even fully registered what had happened or where I was. I kept my breathing slow and regular and my eyes closed, not wanting to let anyone know I was awake until I'd fully evaluated my surroundings. I remembered being taken, the needle jamming into my flesh before being thrown in the back of a vehicle, but nothing after that.

Other than the sound of my breathing, the room was silent, though not dark. The glow from beneath my closed eyelids told me the lights were bright—either I was lying below a skylight or a fluorescent light. I was on my side, my hands tied in front of me, but I couldn't feel the individual rope strands on my wrists, just the rough material against my face, so I could only assume they had foolishly placed fabric between my skin and the rope. I wasn't naked, so that was something, but the restricting movement of my chest when I breathed told me I wasn't in the same shirt and jeans I'd been in when I was kidnapped. With almost imperceptible movements, I checked to ensure I had full use of my extremities. I had feeling in everything, and none of my responses were sluggish, though my feet felt prickly still. I let out a small sigh of relief that whatever they'd drugged me with was clearing out of my system quickly.

Taking a chance, I opened one eye just enough to peek out from beneath my eyelashes. Scanning my surroundings—what I could see of them anyway—would have filled me with dread if I wasn't a trained assassin. I was in a metal room. The floors, walls, and even the ceiling was shiny stainless steel. There was a toilet and sink on the wall close to the foot of the wrought iron bed I was currently on. The bed frame was another sign I was in trouble. From the angle of my face, I could see down my body and about half of the room. The frame was solid tube metal, black, with clips welded to it that could only be meant for restraints in various positions. I moved my gaze to my body. I was dressed in the same damn gown they had forced me to squeeze into the first day of the shoot a few days ago. The creamy-white dress with gold threading was so tight I could barely breathe in it, but it was the shoes that finally had a trickle of fear running through me. The golden stilettos on my feet had been altered as well. Instead of being too small like the dress, a single nail on each shoe had been forced through the bottom, into where my heel rested, leaving my feet above them a solid inch or more from the true bottom. If I were to take so much as a step, my body weight would shove them into my feet. *This is so not good*, I thought as I tried to plan what to do to get out of it.

Best guess, based on the expert team that had kidnapped me, the clothes, and accessories, was that I'd been taken by, or rather for, Karl Albrecht. He'd moved quicker than we expected, but there was good news within the bad. If that was the case, I was likely in the hidden rooms I'd been trying to discover the passage to on my last reconnaissance mission. If that was true, then I knew Matteo already knew I was missing, which meant help would come for me sooner rather than later. The flight to get me from Texas to Germany would have taken a while, which was a positive as at least that had delayed whatever was in store for me, but on the flip side, it added to the time it would take for a rescue. Still, a rescue was coming in hours or, at worst, a day or so, not weeks or months.

I thought back to everything I'd seen in and around Albrecht's castle, as well as the intel already gathered to prepare for my original mission before Brody's presence changed our plans. We suspected Albrecht's primary bodyguard, the butler, and one other guard were the only ones who knew what went under the estate grounds. No way did Albrecht want his proclivities to be common knowledge, even if he thought himself untouchable. We didn't suspect the butler of having anything to do with what Albrecht did other than knowing and not stopping it. So he likely wouldn't be a threat to me until I made it beyond the room and somehow found my way into the residence.

That left me with two guards and Albrecht to deal with if I wanted to get out of that mess. Hopefully. If I was lucky.

I couldn't see the door or the rest of the room from my position, and I wasn't sure if I wanted to move enough to reveal I was coming around. I was sure Albrecht had at least one camera in there, if not more, so even though no one was with me at the moment, I couldn't be sure someone wasn't watching.

Before I could choose my best course of action, the sound of a heavy door opening out of my field of vision made my decision for me. I stayed limp, letting my eye close completely again. I heard someone step into the room, the heavy tread and slight scraping on the ground telling me it was likely a large male, either overweight or with some sort of slight impairment that caused him not to pick one of his feet up all the way when he walked. It wasn't much, but in those few steps, I could identify it wasn't Albrecht or the guard he had with him when he visited our photoshoot.

The door slammed shut with a beep, and I held my breath, forcing myself not to tense as he stopped next to me, touching my wrist as he clumsily felt for a pulse. I couldn't hide my heartbeat, but instead of being reassured, he cursed and brought his hand up to my neck. However, his fingers were too low to feel my carotid artery properly. *Clearly, this one's not winning any IQ contest*, I thought to myself.

His hand pulled away, and a second later, a walky-talky crackled. I couldn't understand German, but the panic was clear in his voice. Without waiting for a response, he pulled me off the bed, laying me on the ground. It took everything I had to stay limp and lifeless. Apparently, he assumed I wasn't breathing and was positioning me for

CPR. *Perfect*, I thought, getting ready to take advantage of the situation. My lungs burned from wanting oxygen. I was still holding my breath, not daring to lose my edge against him, but I was running out of time.

I waited for him to shove my still-bound hands out of the way, positioning his on my chest, before making my move. While he was distracted looking down at his hands, I launched, hitting his head with my own, knocking him sideways. I wrapped my legs around his neck, squeezing as tight as I could and cutting off his oxygen even as I took a breath of my own. My thighs burned with the effort, but I held firm as he struggled, his arms waving around, desperate to find purchase. I grabbed his arm, twisting and pulling at the same time to dislocate it. Normally, I wouldn't damage a person any more than necessary, but I needed to put him down fast and hard, with minimum possibility of him getting the upper hand.

I counted to sixty after he went limp, checking to make sure I'd dispatched him before turning my attention to my feet. I unbuckled my shoes and kicked them off before I started on my bound hands. I'd just barely loosened them when the sound of running feet and the door opening alerted me to my next opponent.

Crouching, I readied myself as much as I could, waiting until the bodyguard rounded the bed to propel myself forward, tackling him to the ground. I rolled as I fell, getting back up to my feet and twisting around to face my opponent. He struggled to rise as quickly as me but was still trying to get up from his hands and knees when I attacked. With my feet bare, I couldn't count on kicking to do any damage, so I used my knee, grabbing his head in my hands as I inflicted as much momentum into my leg as I could. He swore when I connected but grabbed my legs instead of his face, pulling me down on top of him. I screamed, my battle cry loud and determined as we each fought for the upper hand. My arms were still bound, but I used it to my advantage, circling his neck and using the rope to cut off his airway. He was obviously much more trained than the previous man, and he wiggled out of my hold, getting a glancing punch to my face as he did so. We both struggled to our feet, blood pouring out of his nose from where I'd kneed him in the face and staining his teeth pink as he smiled sinisterly.

"You're going to regret this, bitch," he spat, his accent so heavy in his anger I could hardly understand him.

I saved my energy and air, studying every move he made as he tried to circle me. The longer it went on, the less of a chance I would have at beating him, that much I knew. I kept my eyes on him as I continued to wiggle my hands from the rope in subtle movements. The handkerchief or whatever had been used to prevent marks on my wrists—a weird issue when looking at the shoes Albrecht wanted to torture me with—helped slide my hands loose.

The door ripped open a third time, and Albrecht strolled in, stopping short when he saw what was going on. Before he could get a word out, I smiled brightly at him. The guard's back was to the door, and my cheerful response had him instinctively starting to glance behind him, assuming whoever had arrived was on my side. Taking that distraction, I threw the mess of rope at him. Instinctively, he batted the rope away, but his focus on it was long enough for me to spring toward him.

Albrecht moved behind him, not in our direction, but heading toward the guard I'd already taken down. I ignored him for the moment, all my attention on the threat in front of me. I raised my right hand, palm out, connecting with the guard's nose, throwing all my weight behind the move. Cartilage and bone bent and broke in a sickening crunch as I relocated parts of his face into his brain. The girly part of me wanted to cringe. I had no issues with blood or even torture, but hearing bone break was something that had always made my stomach clench.

The guard's eyes widened in surprise—the last voluntary move he would make before his knees gave out. He was dead—his body just hadn't quite gotten the message yet. As he sank in front of me, I caught a flash of movement out of the corner of my eye. I whirled on my heel, raising my arm to protect my face.

My change in stance saved me from a hell of a hit to the face. Albrecht had grabbed what looked to be a baton from the first guard and had tried to slam it into my head. I leaped away, slipping slightly on the pooled blood of the second guard. The stick slammed into me again, right across my shoulders and upper back that time, knocking me to my knees. I rolled away, springing up as quickly as I could manage, trying to ignore the pain as I collected myself into a fighting stance.

"You're going to regret this little escape attempt, my dear," Albrecht said, his voice soft, almost sing-song-like.

I tilted my head. "I really don't think I am." My strength was waning, and I could feel my muscles wanting to tremble with a combination of adrenaline overload and fatigue, but I held position and stared him straight in the eyes, not about to let him see weakness.

He smiled; his eyes as cold and remote as ever. "I love the strong ones. They take longer to break, sure, but the reward when they do." He sighed in remembered pleasure. "It's the headiest aphrodisiac. Turning something so strong into a shell of a being." He raised his arm again, but that time, instead of hitting me with the baton, he barely touched it to my skin.

I couldn't even gasp as electricity raced through my body. I felt like I'd been kicked by a bull and struck by lightning at the same time. My legs gave out, causing me to drop into an undignified heap. I screamed—or would have if my brain could have communicated with my mouth and my jaw hadn't clenched in reflex. Never in my life had I felt such pain. I didn't even realize I hadn't died for what felt like minutes.

Albrecht chuckled softly as my lungs finally re-engaged, forcing labored gasps as I struggled to remember how to move, how to do so much as think, my limbs under me in odd angles. "It's truly the only thing I find entertaining." He hit me with another shot of electricity almost absentmindedly as he passed me, turning his attention to his primary guard. I struggled to crawl, to inch myself away from him, though there was nowhere I could go to escape.

He rose from leaning over the dead guard, shaking his head almost sadly. "Do you know how hard it is to find decent employees?" He tutted his tongue, placing his hands on his hips as he continued to look down, studying the prone body. My arms, still tingling, cooperated enough to drag the rest of me a few feet before I had to stop, my muscles trembling, somehow simultaneously screaming in pain and numb at the same time. Lying next to my hand, I saw one of the shoes strapped to my feet when I'd woken up, the nail sticking out of the sole. It had a stiletto heel. I didn't reach for it, not wanting to show my hand. "I hope you take longer to break than the previous few I've possessed. I have high hopes for you. You're the first one who's shared my thoughts on beauty and pain—though your opinion is only a shadow of my own."

"They're going to find me," I rasped out, gathering the last bit of strength I possessed.

"Your family," he misunderstood my threat, and I could hear the amusement in his tone, "will never find you here. You aren't the first pet to find herself in your position, and you won't be the last."

He came up behind me, leaning over to grab my hair, pulling me up and toward him. I lurched forward, grabbing the shoe to my chest as my body hid my movements from him. My scalp burned as he forced me to stand, my legs shaking as they gamely tried to take my weight. Hunched into myself, I was the epitome of a scared, cowed woman. I leaned back against Albrecht, partly to hinder his response to what I was gearing up for and partly to help conserve energy.

I steeled my breath and gripped the shoe tightly, the nail digging into the palm of my hand. I figured I had one shot before he overpowered me and dealt out his version of punishment and torture for killing two of his guards and trying to attack him. As quickly as I could manage, I spun on my heel, my hair still in his fist, blinding me as I faced him. Before he could mount any form of response, I let my fist fly, stiletto first, toward his face. The high-pitched scream told me I had found my mark, but the pain in my hand and the dizziness the effort cost me blurred what little vision I had, and I hoped my strike was enough to incapacitate him because I knew I didn't have another left in me.

Blinking away the lightheadedness, I realized that the force of my strike had impaled the heel into Albrecht's eye, as well as the nail into my hand. He sank to his knees, his hands reaching for the shoe, making me bend over as my palm lowered with him. Blocking out the pain, I tried to hold the sides of the shoe as much as possible. Blood—his and mine—made the entire thing slick. With one last burst of energy, I shoved into him again, driving my whole weight behind my attempt, and the heel yielded, dropping Karl Albrecht backward and pulling me with him as my legs gave out.

My chest heaved as I struggled to take in air, trying to focus enough to examine my hand and ignore the fact that I was lying on top of what was likely a dead man. The nail had gone all the way through, the blood-smeared point gleaming at me, surrounded by my own flesh. "Damn it," I cursed. Normal first aid would have called to leave the nail in until I could reach a medic or at least find a med kit. But the idea of my hand being that close to a dead man's impaled eye was too much for me to stomach. And it wasn't like I could or would just sit there, on top of him, until someone came along. "One ... two ..." Silly as it was, even though I was the only one counting, I still pulled my hand back on two, not waiting for three.

"Sonofabitch," I ground out, rolling off Albrecht and curling into an involuntary ball as I clutched my hand to my chest. The wad of rope and material loomed at my feet, and I grabbed it, the handkerchief coming free in my palm. Wrapping the material around the wound, I was happy that, despite the blood oozing from it, I could still wiggle my fingers and close my hand.

Satisfied that I'd escaped any permanent damage, I looked around and snatched the lightning-charged baton off the floor before using it to help me lurch to my feet, checking the guards and Albrecht for other weapons once I could get my legs to hold me enough to move. I'd kill for a gun but couldn't find so much as a knife. Resigned to using the devil stick, I hobbled to the door, which stood shut in front of me. It was then that I realized the door didn't have a handle. A retinal scanner was on the wall next to it, silent and daunting as I comprehended my dilemma. I looked at Albrecht, the stiletto still sticking out from his face, and then at the two guards. "Well, damn," I blew out a breath. At the moment, I could barely move my own arms, let alone pick up and hold a full grown-ass man in front of a scanner six feet off the floor. I cursed again at the realization. Unless my backup was still in Texas and I had more than a few hours to recuperate, I would need rescuing after all.

Chapter 24
Brody

With the possibility of Alessia being in real danger, Matteo's original plans went out the window. Somehow, he was able to update his handler and have us outfitted with tactical gear and weapons as soon as we stepped off the plane. Neither of us was willing to wait for the other team. We got in the procured vehicle and made our way to the estate, parking in the forest next to it.

"Any ideas on how to get past the guards if we have to haul ass out of there?" I whispered as we snuck close to the wall. He shrugged off his bag without a word, unzipping a pocket and pulling out what was inside it. I grinned. "That'll work."

"Might I suggest less talking and more movement?" The gravelly voice in my ear just about caused me to jump out of my skin. "You're on a timetable, after all."

I hadn't realized anyone else was on coms besides Matteo and myself. "Who the hell is that?" I whispered to Matteo, who started assembling the C-4. He ignored me, and I got the message loud and clear. As the new guy, it was my job to keep my mouth shut and back him up.

We quickly scaled the wall and entered through the hole in the guard that Alessia had somehow noticed and added to her notes. There was a lot fewer security personnel closer to the house than there had been the day we were there. Someone wanted to make sure no one was the wiser of what was going on inside the house, I figured. The only person inside the castle was the butler I'd met before. Matteo incapacitated him, leaving him tied and gagged in a closet off the kitchen. Falling into old habits, I held position at his back as we cleared each room, ensuring we were alone. When we found the tapestry that we all hoped was the hidden entrance into the basement, Matteo paused, his eyes casing the room for what would most likely be a hidden mechanism to open the door. "Is there anything in this room that looks historically important or ostentatious that he didn't point out while he was with Alessia?" he asked suddenly.

I looked around. "Besides the tapestry?" I thought back. "I was trying hard to keep an eye on him, not necessarily the room. But Alessia seemed pretty interested in the bookcase of rare books. He skimmed over them. I thought maybe he didn't know enough about them to brag efficiently, or he'd gotten them through less-than-legal means."

Matteo looked over the collection. "I don't know much about old books, but I'm going to guess this one," he pointed to one that looked as old but much more ragged than the rest of the collection, almost as if it had been handled so often the cover was wearing out, "is not as important as the rest." He pulled the book toward him, and we both heard a low click. The wall the tapestry hung on jutted out a scant inch, and we yanked it open. I expected stone walls with dank and moldy air and poor lighting. Instead, sleek modern metal walls and floors made me feel like I had walked into the future. I was a little afraid to allow the door to shut behind us for fear it would seal shut. Matteo must have had the same thought because he hesitated at the opening. Thinking quickly, I grabbed what I was sure was a priceless book off the bookcase and placed it in the doorway. Satisfied that we'd secured an exit, we crept farther down the stairway.

Lights turned on as we traversed the steps, our motion triggering the sensors. Humming from above us told me that fresh air was being pumped down. The stairs led to a long hallway with four doors on either side.

"Please don't tell me he has more than Alessia down here," I muttered to Matteo.

He shook his head. "Last intel tells us he doesn't have anyone, which is why we think he jumped on Alessia so fast. Even then, he took us by surprise. We expected a move next week, not now, which is why a team wasn't already in position. I'll be honest, I expected to come across at least one guard by now. And where are Albrecht and his men?"

I had the same thought, dread crawling through me.

We stayed focused, clearing each room as we came to it, and I was starting to panic as we readied to breach the second to last room. Had they really killed Alessia, and we were too late? Or had they realized she had a tracking device and moved to a secondary location after removing it?

The door opened as I slapped the panel on the wall. I didn't know what I thought I would walk into, but Lessia sitting on the floor, back to the wall, dead bodies lying prone around her while she stared at us with bloodshot eyes as we launched into the room, wasn't it. She was tapping the fingers of one hand on the floor with impatience; her other was cradled in her lap, wrapped in a blood-soaked cloth. The white dress with gold trim was identical to the one she wore the first day of the photo shoot, only it had what looked like blood splatter on it, the sleeve of one arm was ripped, and the hem along the neckline had been yanked hard enough to warp the lining.

"It's about time y'all got here. And someone make sure that door doesn't shut, or I'm going to have to forgo waiting on someone to show up and attempt to hot-wire a retinal scanner." She practically vibrated with an overload of emotions ... fear, relief, anger, or some sort of mixture of them all, I wasn't sure. There was a disconnect between whatever she was feeling and what she was showing. It was almost like she'd slammed a wall down on all her feelings. The mask she had in place was a familiar one—it was her professional model mask. Not model, I realized suddenly. The mask was Alessia's professional façade, no matter what the job.

I studied her face. Other than the hand, a bruise along the jaw, and a slightly fat lip, she appeared to be unharmed. Holstering my weapon, I stomped toward her, not sure if I was mad that I needed to rescue her, that she apparently didn't need our help, or that she'd allowed herself to get into this mess in the first place.

"You good?" I asked as I stepped over a pretty gruesome-looking body with a high heel sticking out of his face.

She stuck her chin up. "Yes," she practically bit off, but I noticed she didn't rise from her place on the floor.

I didn't wait for her to try, just grabbed her by the upper arms and hauled her to her feet. She let out an "Oof" and put her hands on my biceps to steady herself, but she didn't flinch, so I didn't stop until I'd plastered our bodies together against the wall.

Using my hips to pin hers, I let her feel me—all of me—before reaching to tip her stubborn chin up. Her eyes narrowed, but before she could comment, I came down for a bruising kiss, not even caring about her damaged lip. If she was going to place herself in downright dangerous situations and make me get her across an entire fucking ocean, she deserved the consequences, and I was pretty sure Matteo wouldn't allow me to wring her scrawny neck after he'd gone through the trouble of flying across the damn globe to keep her in one piece.

Her nails dug in my flesh, matching my kiss and adding to the heat by opening her mouth and allowing me entrance. "Can y'all do that later?" Matteo broke us up from his place at the door. "I would rather get out of here before the cleanup crew arrives. If they catch us still on scene, you know they're going to rope us into demolition or body removal."

Reluctantly, I pulled back, shrugging off my backpack to pull out a tactical uniform that matched my own, combat boots, cap, knife, weapon and holster, and a pair of wraparound sunglass goggle-looking things that Matteo insisted on adding to my bag. She beamed at me as if I'd just given her a diamond ring, snatching up the knife and cutting herself free of the dress.

"Hey, now." I stepped between her and Matteo, trying to hide her from his field of vision. "Could you not strip yourself naked in front of other men?"

She waved a hand in dismissal as I snatched the uniform from the floor and shoved it into her chest. "Matteo has had plenty of opportunities to look over the years. Trust me, he doesn't see me as anything but a pain in his ass."

"Got that right," Matteo mumbled, his back to both of us as he studiously watched the empty hallway.

She shimmied into the garment, looking much sexier than she had any right to, and donned the knife and holster. Jamming her hair under the cap, she placed the glasses on her nose. I scoured her for injuries again, not able to help myself.

"I'm fine." She saw my gaze, and her own softened. "I have a puncture to my hand, a few bruises, and got hit with a hell of a lot of electricity, but other than that—"

I cut her off. "What kind of electricity?"

She huffed, pointing to the club-looking object on the ground where she had been sitting. "Albrecht hit me with what felt like the offspring of a cattle prod and a car battery." She flexed her fingers, grimacing.

"Did you lose consciousness?" I asked, reaching to her neck to feel her pulse.

She batted my hand away and straightened. "If I promise to let someone check me out when we get clear, can we go?"

That she wasn't arguing about getting checked out in the first place had me whipping around to Matteo, who'd already turned around to look at her. She gave him an aggrieved expression and raised her right hand. "I swear I'm fine, apart from the fact that I feel like I was hit by a bus, am still a little tingly in my extremities, and stabbed myself in the hand with a rusty nail. I'm pretty sure I'm up to date on my tetanus shot, but I'm betting because it's not in my file—since I needed it because of a personal incident that I didn't want to disclose—and I can't provide documentation since everything I own is back in Texas, the medic is going to jab me with a needle." She pouted. "As if I need another hole in my body today."

"Cry me a river," Matteo quipped, still watching her as she crossed the room. I did the same, making sure she looked steady on her feet.

"I almost did when I realized they were going to kidnap me before I could finish my ice cream." She followed him, letting me take up the rear as we made our way back the way we came.

"I'll buy you a new one when we get home," I promised.

"Brown-noser," Matteo grumbled as Alessia hummed with delight and gave me a carefree grin that never failed to make my heart tighten.

Our way back to the jet was anticlimactic. We were able to sneak out the same way we'd entered, rendering the C-4 that Matteo had rigged if we needed an exit strategy no longer required, much to my disappointment. The whole rescue had been, if I was honest, anticlimactic. I'd been gung ho about a rescue when, in reality, Lessia had needed a locksmith more than us. Apparently, we'd missed out on the exciting fight, though Alessia hadn't filled in the details yet.

The rescue team was disembarking their plane when we arrived, looking more than a bit disgruntled that Matteo and I had stolen their thunder. They apparently knew Alessia and Matteo well, exchanging hugs in her case and handshakes in Matteo's. It was clear they didn't know Alessia's real identity—the glasses kept her trademark eyes hidden, and they used a codename when they greeted her. Their medic checked Alessia out, even hooking her up to a heart monitor to ensure her rhythms were correct before giving her the dreaded tetanus shot and bandaging her hand. It amused us all that she stoically withstood the cleaning and bandaging of her hand while she cursed up a storm when he pricked her with the needle, even letting me hold her good hand—which she had in a death grip—while he poked her.

Although she was okay, or maybe because of it, I had an overwhelming urge to hustle her ass onto the jet and into the back bedroom so that I could inspect every inch of her. I knew that wouldn't be possible until we were airborne and Matteo debriefed her. Fortunately for me, Matteo and Alessia were in as much of a rush to get out of Germany as I was, though for more practical reasons.

Chapter 25

Keene

I should have known it was going to be a shit day when my assistant called out to work that morning, leaving me without my requisite cup of coffee on my desk when I came into my office. The intern had tried his best, but somehow, the brew looked like swamp water, and it tasted just as appealing.

I winced as I tried to gulp the liquid, not wanting to hurt the feelings of the man looking at me with hope-filled eyes. He reminded me of a puppy, all good-natured and eager to please. "Thanks," I somehow managed to get out without wheezing.

"You're quite welcome, Mr. Keene." He practically bounced on his toes with excitement. "Please let me know if you need another cup made."

I'd given up having him drop the "mister" after the hundredth correction. I just didn't have the energy to waste on banging my head on that particular wall. The man had barely left the room when Boone came barreling in with such momentum that he slammed the door into the wall.

I'd already lurched to my feet in surprise before he could speak. "Alessia's missing," Boone said, clearly panicked.

"What do you mean she's missing?" I came around my desk, not sure what to do, but not able to just stand there.

"I tried to stop by her place last night," he admitted, even though we'd decided as a unit to leave her and Brody to themselves last night. It had been clear the two of them had hooked up and even clearer that they had some sort of issue to work out. "Her car was gone, and when she didn't answer her phone, I just assumed she went with Brody."

I raised an eyebrow. "Unlikely. His apartment could charitably be called a landing pad, and it's not exactly a close jaunt from here."

He nodded. "I thought the same but couldn't think of anything else that made sense. But when she still wasn't answering her phone or at home this morning, I called a friend at the police department and asked if they had seen her car or any suspicious activity."

He paused as Gideon came rushing in, followed by Royce. "Have you heard?" my oldest brother asked. Clearly, I was the last to know.

"Just that they found her car by that ice cream place she likes, her purse by one of the tires," Boone said.

Gideon shook his head. "I tried calling in a favor to get this looked into. Since she's an adult, she officially needs to be missing for twenty-four hours, but someone higher up won't allow them to investigate, despite the suspicious circumstances."

Royce looked down at his phone. "I called the stores up and down that street, offering a reward for any video anyone might have of her or the car. A few are emailing us what they have from around the time the store owner said she came in last night."

We moved as one into the conference room, the group of us too big to fit into anyone's office comfortably. Royce queued up the big screen on the far wall, pulling up his email as it flashed to life.

We watched as one as the ice cream parlor footage came into view, showing her in the lobby, narrowly avoiding some small children running around unsupervised before practically falling into the counter. She exchanged some pleasantries with the woman at the counter, paid for her purchase, and left. No one immediately followed her, nor did it look like anyone in the place paid her any attention among the small crowd of people.

The second email was from a business that must have been next to the parlor because it did nothing more than show her walking past the windows, then returning a few minutes later, a large insulated cup in her hand before she passed out of view again.

We hit pay dirt on the third video. Alessia's face was clear as she walked past, eating a bite off her spoon before depositing it back into the cup. She reached into her purse, clearly looking for keys, when someone jumped out behind her, having been hiding off-screen. Unfortunately, they both walked off the screen at that moment, showing nothing other than a person in black pants and a dark hoodie appearing out of nowhere before they disappeared again.

"Jesus," Boone whispered. Royce pulled up a few more emailed video clips from other storefronts, but we didn't get any more shots of Alessia, her car, or the mysterious men who'd materialized out of the shadows of the alleyway.

Without thought, I pulled my phone up and dialed Brody. Where the hell had he been when my sister was kidnapped? He was supposed to be watching her, for fuck's sake. Yes, the stalker issue had been taken care of, but based on the looks the two of them were throwing at each other, I'd thought he would have stuck around. When his phone went unanswered, I looked at Gideon, all of us with identical looks of dread, fear, confusion, and denial.

Gideon blew out a breath. "Let's tamp down the emotions and work the issue," he said with authority. "I'll call the police commissioner, then go up the chain from there. We have enough politicians and high-level clients to get someone on this. With this video, we should be able to get an investigation opened. Boone, you call your person with the FBI. If this is a kidnapping, we're going to want them brought into this. Royce, you get on social media and press—I want her face plastered on every available network and internet site available. Keene, you scour the videos and see if we missed something." We all nodded, getting our shit together and shoving it in a box so that we could do what we needed to do effectively. I might not know where our baby sister was or why she was taken, but I was sure as hell they would come to regret taking her.

I was still going through the video an hour later when Gideon stormed back into the room. It took a lot to anger our brother, but someone must have really worked to build the inferno because if a person could have steam actually coming from their ears, he would have at that moment.

"What's wrong?" Boone asked. He hadn't been able to get a hold of the Director of the FBI but had talked with another one of his contacts. While it wasn't surprising that the director wasn't immediately available, we held enough contracts and spoke with him often enough that he should have called us back by then. Even Boone's contact, whoever they were, had been suspiciously quiet after the initial conversation. It stumped all of us why the FBI was dragging its feet. Not only was Alessia famous and beautiful, but she was also connected with A.T. Accardi Tactical trained the best of the best. The FBI, Secret Service, and even black ops and military teams trained with us. To say we knew the who's who of D.C. wasn't lying or being boastful. It was the plain truth. Yet all of our connections were failing us.

"The jet's missing."

We all froze. Even Royce, who was still trying to talk to a reporter at one of the local news stations, paused in his explanation.

"What the *hell* do you mean, the jet's missing?"

He gave me a look that clearly said I didn't understand English. "It's not in its hangar. I called to have the crew get it ready. I was going to fly to D.C. since we're all getting the run-around from our connections over the phone. But apparently, you and I took it this morning with a pilot. They filed flight plans saying we took it to your place in Colorado, but the tower noted we headed in an eastern direction before we disappeared off their radar."

"So we've got a missing sister, missing PSO, and a missing jet." Royce summed the facts up, looking thoughtful.

"And Matteo is also missing," Gideon added. "I got a call from a phone service on his behalf, letting all of his clients know he's out-of-town attending his ailing father and will reschedule his appointments when he returns. Gia was supposed to have class tonight."

I added that to the mental list of question marks.

"Where is she?" Boone asked. He was pacing behind Royce.

Gideon ran a hand through his hair. "I pulled her from school and have her hanging out at the training center. I don't want her here with us as we deal with this, nor do I want her at home since we don't know what's going on. Some of my old teammates are in town, so she has several sets of eyes watching her as well as spoiling her rotten. She doesn't have any idea something's amiss."

I went back to the video that showed Lessia about to be kidnapped, backing it up frame by frame before playing it again and again. I'd watched the same twenty seconds of the recording for the better part of an hour, trying to pinpoint what was off. Something about it bothered me, but I couldn't figure out what ...

"Sonofabitch!" I bit out, standing up so fast my chair flew over backward, a steady stream of curses coming from my mouth, some of which I hadn't uttered since I was active military.

"I'll call you back," Royce said into the phone, hanging up before whoever was on the line said anything else. Gideon came over to my side of the table, looking at the now-paused screen, Boone doing the same.

"What did you find?" Royce asked, getting up to line up with the rest of us. All three of them studied the frozen image of our sister, trying to see what had gotten me so upset.

I backed up the image a few seconds, then played the recording. Alessia came into view, eating her ice cream. She walked a few more steps before I paused the image. "There!" I pointed at the screen. "See how she tenses for a split second, and her head starts to look right? She relaxes almost immediately and faces forward again, but you can tell she knows someone's there." Boone and Royce looked doubtful, but Gideon just looked at the frozen image, his lips pursed, a finger tapping his bottom lip.

I backed it up, then played it again and again and again. Eventually, all of them seemed to come to the same conclusion I had. "So she knows someone is sneaking up on her, or at least feels like something is off," Royce admitted. "What does that mean?"

I played the video again, letting it continue to roll. I thought back to Brody's warnings that I hadn't really seen past the surface of my sister. "Let's say she knew someone was targeting her. Why would a smart woman, one with some self-defense and classes in safety procedures for potential targets, ignore her training and not so much as look around at her surroundings and, a few steps later, put her head down while digging into her purse? Hell, even a normal woman alone wouldn't walk down a darkened street with her head damn near in her bag. And what do you think the odds are that the answer to that question ties into why we're getting the Texas two-step from all of our contacts, both here and in D.C.?"

It was Royce and Boone's turn to swear as Gideon's face turned contemplative. "You think she's undercover? That's kind of hard to believe, seeing as everyone knows who she is. And the model part isn't exactly fake—there isn't a fashion magazine cover she hasn't been on."

I shrugged, not exactly sure what I thought our sister was involved in. Despite that, I knew in my bones I was on the right track. "Think about it, the long stretches she's not home, her tight lip about her work. And she's protested at the tops of her lungs since she was a kid that she was more capable than we give her credit for."

"But she mentioned the other day that Daddy wouldn't let her enlist," Boone pointed out.

"Which just makes that make more sense," Gideon replied. "She couldn't serve her country publicly the way we did. Maybe she found a way to achieve her dream, just not the traditional way."

"So, what are we saying?" Royce asked. "That she's CIA? Even if that's the case, why would she let herself be targeted here, without backup, on home soil?"

"Is she really without backup?" Gideon asked. "Both Matteo and Brody are missing. And the jet."

"Sounds like a rush job. No way was Brody supposed to be a part of whatever support system she was supposed to have. And stealing the Gulfstream definitely wasn't according to plan, either." I couldn't help but point out the obvious.

Gideon knocked on the table twice before straightening. "Either way, it gives us a starting point. Between the four of us, we have a few contacts in the CIA. If she's not one of theirs, there's a whole alphabet soup worth of agencies in the U.S. that she could work for. But it's as good of a place as any to start."

"Sounds like I arrived just in time," the voice from the door had all of us whirling around. The man standing there was the last person I would have thought to see, yet I wasn't surprised at all.

Chapter 26

Alessia

I raised an eyebrow at Matteo when he arrived back at the jet. If the scripted A.T. logo on the tail hadn't clued me in, the luxurious and spacious interior would have been a warning that we weren't on the standard plane we would typically use.

"What?" he asked at the look on my face. "Technically, you're a shareholder, and using this thing is one perk of the position."

"Is that the story I'm supposed to go with when I get home? You know my brothers likely know by now that I'm not at home, and I'm not sure I can pass off that Brody and I snuck off for some time alone with you and this thing missing."

Matteo's sheepish expression had me on alert.

"Don't tell me they know I was kidnapped?"

Brody's hand on my back anchored me, pulling me back an inch from my almost-panicked state. "Let's sit down, sweetheart. We need to get this thing in the air, and the three of us have some catching up to do."

Because I couldn't find any argument with that plan and my legs were still a bit wobbly, I plopped down on a chair, snagging a blanket off the back to cover the seat before doing so. I was likely in enough trouble, and I didn't want to add ruining company property to my tally by getting anything bloody while I was at it.

Once we were cloud-high, I motioned for Matteo to continue catching me up, but he shook his head. "Let's get you debriefed and changed first."

Well, shit, I thought. Matteo wasn't normally the kind of man to put things off, and while it was protocol to get the paperwork in order when the experience was as fresh as possible—in my case, the range for that opportunity could vary from hours to a week or longer—but the fact that he couldn't seem to meet my eye for more than a second or so told me he wanted all work-related details taken care of before the possibility of a meltdown occurred. Though with me, meltdown might be the wrong word ... Inferno may be a better word choice?

I almost jumped when Brody touched my shoulder. "Do you want something to eat?" he asked as he handed me a water bottle.

"I ... uh ... not right now." I was hungry, but my stomach was too knotted to eat. My upcoming showdown with my brothers wasn't the only source of my uncertainty. I hadn't anticipated Brody being there, and I wasn't sure what to do. I'd ended things because I couldn't tell him the truth. Now he knew the truth, but I wasn't sure if finding out that the woman he thought he knew was mostly a façade had him feeling differently about me. Not everyone could handle what I did for my job—hell, most couldn't. It was one thing to kill in the middle of battle, but even hardened military types couldn't always accept someone with my skill set. They might agree with it in a distant, someone-needs-to-do-the-job type thing, but to know me as a person, and to be okay with what I did, was a completely different animal entirely. And that I was wasting mental energy being all girly and worried about if a boy I liked, liked me back pissed me off.

"Why don't you go find a TV or something and chill?" I told Brody.

I meant to hack him off, but he only smiled softly at me. "Trying to dismiss me, sweetheart?"

I looked him dead in the eye. "I'm about to admit to letting myself get kidnapped so that I could prove what kind of man Albrecht was. My assignment was to take him out if I had the opportunity to manage it or to stay safe until my team could come to get me. I killed three men in keeping to that order, practically bare-handed, still a bit drugged, and with the help of a stiletto heel-turned-torture device. That's not a conversation I particularly want to have in front of someone who yelled at me for shooting some flowers the last time I dealt with a potential threat."

"I wasn't upset at you shooting," he explained. "I was upset you were keeping secrets from me."

I scoffed. "So, you're mad I was keeping classified information from someone who didn't have a proper security clearance? Something I'm sure you've done so many times you've lost count?"

"I'm not mad any longer, and I admit I might have overreacted."

I wanted to knock the placating look off his face, but I was too tired to stand. "*Might* have?"

"Can we get work stuff out of the way so that I can be somewhere else when you two have this argument?" Matteo cut in, focusing on his tablet in front of him and not on the two of us. He didn't bother waiting for what I was sure would have been a smart-ass reply on my part before putting the tablet down on the coffee table between us and hitting the standard red button to record our conversation.

Brody took a seat next to me as Matteo stated the date and other pertinent information. Brody snorted when he heard my code name but otherwise stayed quiet as I began my report, starting with my arrival at Sweet Nothings and my observations on the street before my kidnapping. When I turned to the more active parts of my retelling, he froze. I was acutely aware of him, barely two feet away, but I kept my emotions locked down tight, my voice calm, controlled, and remote. I couldn't focus on him right now, not if I was going to get through the next hour. My worries about his reaction, about us—if there even was an us—would have to wait. I had a report to finish.

Chapter 27

Brody

It was everything I could do to stay in my seat. Hearing how she killed the two guards and Albrecht cemented just how elite she really was. How quickly she evaluated her options, eliminated the threats against her, and the way she conducted herself, both then and when we'd arrived, clearly illustrated she was a badass. But I also couldn't help but notice how her hands stayed balled into fists throughout her conversation with Matteo and how straight and proper she stayed in her chair, studiously avoiding looking in my direction.

I realized she was nervous, and I was the cause. I thought back to all the conversations Alessia and I'd had over the past week about how she wasn't the woman she portrayed to the public and how true those discussions had been. Alessia, despite being placed between a rock and a hard place, had done her best to be herself with me and to stay truthful. When I had idiotically pushed her beyond what she could actually divulge, she'd cut me loose instead of lying to me.

I shifted slightly, watching as Lessia stiffened almost imperceptibly before making herself settle back in her former position. I wanted to take her hand in mine, to give her that small peace of mind that I wasn't upset with her, that I was happy she was okay, but everything about her body position said I'd better keep my hands off any part of her, lest I wanted to lose a limb.

So, instead, I stayed where I was, able to do nothing but listen to her give the details, watching as she patiently answered when Matteo asked for clarification before I couldn't take it anymore.

"Done?" I asked Matteo as he clicked off the recorder.

Looking up at me, I saw a flicker of amusement behind his stoic expression. "Yes, I believe we are."

Before Lessia could protest, I pounced, picking her up into my arms and heading to the tail of the plane.

"What the hell do you think you're doing?" she asked icily.

A lesser man would have flinched at her tone, but I just glanced at her with an eyebrow raised as if she'd asked a strange question. "Making sure you don't get blood anywhere, for one." I pushed open the door to the bedroom with my foot, not pausing until we were in the surprisingly spacious bathroom. Placing her on the small vanity, I kicked on the water, cranking it up as hot as it could go.

She stayed where I'd placed her. "And?"

"And I wanted you in my arms for a minute." I wouldn't usually admit that out loud—it wasn't the manliest of statements, but I wanted to give her that truth. I needed her to know I would not back down from the honesty she had been giving me. As I stripped, I set my weapons aside. Lessia sat quietly on the vanity, just watching as I pulled off my clothes, one by one. Once I was naked, I went back to her, reaching for her shirt before going to work on the rest. We left our clothes in a pile on the floor and the weapons on the counter as we stepped into the shower. Steam filled the space quickly since, despite the opulence, the bathroom still wasn't large compared to a normal bathroom, though it was worlds apart from the standard broom-closet-sized airplane bathroom. At least I didn't have to duck to get under the showerhead, even though I still hit the side of the shower with my elbow.

I felt her quiet amusement more than I saw it as I wiggled backward until my back was flat against the still-chilly tile, giving her as much room as I could under the spray. As she tilted her head back, I raised my hands, skimming her arms before digging my fingers into her scalp, massaging in what I hoped was a soothing motion. I had plenty of experience showering with a woman but had little experience outside of having sex in it. And while my cock was certainly up to the task, I wanted to take care of her, not *it*, at least not right then.

She groaned in appreciation, leaning into my touch. "Feel good?" I asked, pouring some shampoo into my hand before returning to my task.

"Mmm ..." She leaned into me, her body finally relaxing. I couldn't help but kiss her bare shoulder. I took my time, using the bubbles to my advantage and continuing my massage down her body, down her neck to the tips of her fingers and toes, and everything in between. The water started running cold as I rinsed the conditioner from her long black tresses.

Lessia pulled back reluctantly, giving me an uncharacteristically shy smile before exiting the shower and wrapping a towel around her body. I hurriedly rinsed myself, then turned off the water, getting out before she could even finish drying off. She lingered in the bathroom, seeming as reluctant as I was to break the solitude. Some turbulence reminded us that we weren't exactly in the comfort of a normal home.

Matteo must have left clothes on the bed for us because they sure as hell hadn't been there before we'd entered. Grateful I wouldn't have to walk around the plane in a towel to find something to wear, I pulled them on. Alessia put on the underclothes, jeans, and a tee shirt—everything fitting so well I realized Matteo must have had a go-bag for her on the jet. She padded back to the bathroom, bringing out her weapons, handing me mine as she strapped on her gun and knife as if they were a part of her.

Finally, she looked up at me, determination and uncertainty in equal measure. "I think we need to talk."

Smiling down at her gently, I gathered her in my arms. "I *know* we need to talk," I said softly, wanting to kiss her but knowing I needed to take my time with her.

She bit her bottom lip. "So ... I guess you know everything."

"Well, probably not everything," I teased. "But I think I got the highlight reel."

"Say it, then." She tilted her head up, challenging me.

I raised an eyebrow in question. "Say what?"

"What am I?"

"You're an assassin," I said matter-of-factly, not releasing her from my arms.

She studied me carefully. "And?"

"And, what?" I knew what she was getting at but wanted to make sure we fleshed it out fully. Talking about feelings wasn't my strong suit, and I had a feeling it wasn't Alessia's, either. If we wanted a chance at a genuine relationship, we needed to get it all out.

Lessia looked a bit bewildered at my turning the question back at her. "Now's the point where you tell me you knew I had a secret all along, that you're excited to be a part of the team, and that you're happy we're partners." The disappointment in her words sounded all the world like a six-year-old thanking someone for getting socks for their birthday.

"You think because I found out you're some kick-ass secret soldier, I don't want you anymore? That I want to back off from you personally so that we can work together professionally?"

She shrugged. "Most people don't want a relationship with someone who can kill them twenty different ways while making it look like an accident. And that doesn't account for how I can kill you and make it clear you didn't die of natural causes."

"You think I'm most people?" I let my amusement show. "For someone who hates the fact that people make snap judgments about you, you sure didn't have any issue assuming my feelings on the matter."

She flushed a bit. "I didn't put words into your mouth without cause, Brody."

"You've always been a straight shooter, Alessia. Don't wimp out on me now."

That got her fired up. She put her hands on her hips, the movement pulling her back from me. "I want to know if you're man enough to handle the fact that you slept with someone who can and has slit someone's throat and slept like a baby afterward. That you knowing what I do, really do, doesn't change how you feel about me. And if you still want to—" She ran a hand through her wet hair, swearing when her fingers got stuck halfway through the length, and she pulled them back.

She looked so adorably frazzled I couldn't help but smile.

"Still want to have sex with you? Start a relationship with you? Fall madly in love with you?"

"I—I don't know what to say."

Well, that wasn't what I was hoping for.

I could feel my face falling, and she must have seen my expression because she continued to speak in a rush, "I mean, I want all of that. But I also don't know if I'm going to keep doing the job ... jobs ... I've been doing or not. And I'm not sure if Matteo has spoken to you about an actual job offer or not and if you're still going to want to do it if I decide to resign. Plus, there are my brothers to think about, and what about—"

I pulled her into my arms, forcefully enough that she bumped into me with an "Oomph!"

"You assassins are all the same," I teased. "Have to over-analyze and over-plan everything."

She raised an eyebrow, looking up at me with a cocky glint in her eye. "Because we have to be prepared for every possibility."

"Now you're part of a team," I pointed out. "You don't have to know everything going in. Half the fun is working out the details together … in work *and* with our relationship."

"What relationship?" she quipped innocently. "I don't remember agreeing to be in a—"

I leaned down and kissed her hard until both of us were fighting for breath before I pulled away. "I think," I said in between taking in huge breaths of air, "we can both agree that whatever this is between us can definitely, at the very least, be called the start of a relationship."

Chapter 28

Alessia

The wheels touched down on the tarmac much too soon and way too long for my taste. Too soon because I hadn't yet come up with a plan on how to deal with my brothers, nor had I been able to pin down Matteo about what they knew regarding my disappearance. Too long because if Brody and I had spent much more time together without having sex, I was pretty sure I might've burst. Or possibly disintegrated from internal combustion. We both seemed to have the same reluctance to take advantage of the jet's bed for reasons other than sleeping while coming off a mission, though the heat between us hadn't dissipated. I knew that until we landed, I still felt like I was on company time, even though I wasn't. And I was betting Brody felt like he was returning from the field as well.

I was the first to step out of the plane and onto the stairs, relieved to be back home until I looked up. Seeing the unwelcome welcoming party, I pulled up suddenly, almost causing Brody to run into me. He stopped short, placing a hand on my arm, whether in comfort or to steady himself, I wasn't sure. All four of my brothers stood, side by side, leaning against one of the two black SUVs parked next to the tarmac, looking all the world like four fathers looking down at their daughter returning home two hours past curfew. Squelching the urge to squirm, I straightened my shoulders and met them look for look. Gideon, hands in his pockets, stared at me with an unreadable expression. Keene, his arms crossed in front of him, glowered at me. Royce and Boone were on either side of them with twin scowls.

"Well, shit," I muttered, reading the situation in under a second. "Ain't this a warm homecoming," I drawled loud enough for them to hear. "I haven't even been gone a full day. I don't think a quick trip really rates all y'all taking time to meet me at the airport." Gliding down the steps, I walked straight to them, keeping a smile fixed on my face as if I hadn't a care in the world.

I stopped at Gideon first, reaching up on my toes to kiss his cheek before moving on to Boone, Keene, then Royce. None of them moved a muscle. "Where's Gia?" I asked, looking around as if she would appear out of thin air.

"Home, now that we know she's not in any danger," Gideon replied, his tone mild.

I hated guilt trips. As a kid, I remembered once begging Daddy for a whooping rather than the lecture he'd given me when I'd put blue hair dye in the cheerleader's shampoo bottle during gym class. Of course, no one could prove I was the one who'd done it, but everyone knew it was me. It's not like I'd hidden my snickering and gloating—but even as a teen, I knew better than to leave physical evidence. By that age, I'd figured out how to avoid cameras and carried latex gloves in my pocket, just in case.

I sighed, dropping the innocent act. "I'm sorry if y'all were worried about me."

"If? If we were worried about you." Keene unfolded his hands in a rush, and I wondered for a second if he would try strangling me in his frustration before he pushed back into the side of the vehicle again. I felt Brody move to stand next to me, Matteo on my other side, having my back while I faced down the wall of testosterone. "You let yourself get kidnapped, stole our jet, and vanished for almost twenty-four hours!"

"I wasn't the one who stole the jet." I wasn't about to take the fall for that one. There was enough for them to be angry at me without adding that one to my tally. "That was all Matteo and Brody. I wasn't even in the country at the time."

It was Boone's turn to swear. "Weren't in the—are y'all hearing her?" He and Royce had taken a step forward, the Accardi brothers closing ranks around us in a half-circle, but I wasn't about to be intimidated into taking a step back.

I tipped my chin up. "I'm pretty sure they heard me, Boone."

Gideon shared a look with Keene. "So you admit you let yourself get kidnapped." Keene's statement had me straightening my spine.

"I didn't say that. I was just addressing the biggest issue first."

Royce chimed in, "You think a missing jet is the biggest issue? *You* were missing. We watched the video of a man coming at you before you both disappeared out of frame.

Your car, purse, and cell were left on the sidewalk by your car, and you couldn't even bother to call us on your way home to tell us you were all right?"

Guilt punched me in the gut again. "I'm sorry that y'all were worried. If I had known that you were fully aware of the situation, I would have called. And I'll admit, I had a somewhat eventful day and haven't had a chance to get my bearings yet." I wasn't sure what to tell them about the kidnapping. Yes, I could admit to being blindfolded the whole time and the men rescuing me before anything eventful happened. I could claim I wasn't sure who was behind it all, but I didn't have a story for how Matteo and Brody knew where I was, let alone why they didn't call the authorities and have them rescue me. But in the end, I didn't have the energy to create—and sell—some elaborate story I knew they wouldn't believe, no matter how well I lied.

"I think it's time you came clean, Alessia." Gideon stood to his full height lazily, pulling back from where he was resting against the car, pulling his hands out of the pockets as he did so. "We know."

What did they know? Or, more likely, *thought* they knew? I blinked once, not allowing myself any more time to hesitate, lest they pounce like vultures on a fresh carcass. "If you know, then I really don't think we need to discuss it." I reached up and patted his chest, taking a step back to look over at the two men at my back while still talking to the ones in front of me. "Now, if you don't mind, I've had a really, *really* long day and want nothing more than to face plant onto my bed. Alone," I added with a pointed look at Brody. "Do y'all mind giving us a ride, or should I call an Uber?"

Without warning, the door to the second SUV opened, and a figure dressed in his typical stuffy suit emerged, buttoning his suit jacket as he exited. I couldn't help my inhale of surprise and heard a similar noise coming from Matteo. Brody, obviously knowing whoever this was had caught us both off guard, stepped up beside me, studying him closely.

"I know you're eager to get home, my dear," the rough yet cultured voice said. "But I'm afraid we need to clean this whole mess up—with your brothers, the mission, and your future."

Brody extended his hand to him, closing the distance between them. "I'm Brody. Nice to officially meet you. I'm Alessia's new permanent PSO." He said that with no hesitation as if it was a done deal.

"Harrison Accardi." Uncle Harry returned the handshake. "Your new boss." As Brody stepped back, I came forward, wrapping the older man in a hug. "And Alessia's uncle," he added as he weakly returned my greeting. He never was great at showing affection, but I knew my demonstration pleased him.

"You know each other?" I asked as I pulled back, looking between the two men.

Brody shook his head, motioning to his ear. "We've never met in person."

I nodded, realizing that Harry must have been on coms during my rescue, which wasn't typical, but considering I was the one they were coming to get, it made sense.

"Well," I tucked a strand of hair behind my ear, "I suppose we better get this done and over with."

Chapter 29

Alessia

I stayed quiet in the car, partly because I wasn't sure what to say and partly because I was beyond exhausted. Brody, Gideon, Keene, and I were in Uncle Harry's SUV, with Boone, Royce, and Matteo following behind. The silence was tense, with Keene and Gideon wordlessly communicating in a way that never failed to annoy me. Brody seemed oblivious to their byplay, but I knew better. Ignoring them, he moved his hand to grasp mine, rubbing my knuckles gently in a soothing massage. I left my hand in his, enjoying the sensation his touch provoked. My fingers had finally stopped tingling an hour before, but my nerve endings fired up again for a whole other reason.

When we turned into A.T.'s parking lot, I squeezed Brody's hand before letting it go, unfastening my seat belt and jumping out without waiting for Gideon to open my door. A few days ago, I would have been dreading what was about to happen, but now, I just wanted to get it over with.

Brody split off from our group as we headed to the conference room. Everyone left the chair next to me open, leaving Matteo and me on one side of the conference table and my brothers on the other. Uncle Harry sat between us, pulling out a jammer so that we could talk freely, and I couldn't help but feel like he thought he could mediate this to a peaceful resolution. If everyone thought I would behave myself how I had at Sunday dinner, they had another thing coming. I hadn't done anything wrong. And yes, while lying to my family wasn't exactly right, protecting your cover for the sake of everyone's safety was the only option.

"I am *not* going to apologize." I wanted that on the record immediately.

"For what, exactly?" Boone asked, his attitude hot and scathing.

"Boone—" Royce started, but our brother cut him off.

"No, I want her to answer. Is she *not* sorry for lying to us for all these years? For letting us believe she was someone she wasn't? Or maybe because now we have to deal with knowing that our sister is a cold-blooded killer."

Brody came back just in time to hear Boone's tirade, holding a tray of bottled water and a mug. Setting the tray down, he set the mug of coffee in front of me before turning to Boone. "Your sister might not owe you an apology, but she sure as hell deserves one from you with that comment. Do you think Alessia's the only Accardi who has killed for her country?"

I swallowed hard. I hadn't looked into my brothers' pasts, although I could have. It felt like an invasion of privacy to know about that part of their lives when they could not know mine, but I knew at least one of them had seen action. Raiders weren't the kind of soldiers who spent their entire enlistment on a nice safe base. Boone scoffed but looked over to see Gideon and Keene staring studiously at the wall behind me. Even Royce looked uneasy at Boone's words.

My voice came out shakier this time, quieter than I was a moment ago, but just as certain. "I will not apologize for doing what I do. I made my choice a long time ago, and at a point in my life where I felt it was the only way to stay true to me. My oath required that I keep my career to myself—something I know every one of you understands as you have all done things while enlisted you cannot discuss. I'm not sorry you feel this information came out of the left field because it means I did my job correctly. If those closest to me had no idea what I was involved in, what I am capable of, then the outside world doesn't either." I glanced at Brody. "Though I'm not sure if I can be as certain about that anymore," I half grumbled, feeling his silent amusement.

He set the tray of waters at the center of the table, then moved his chair closer next to me before sitting down. Matteo reached for a bottle, as did Gideon and Keene.

"Don't feel put out, sweetheart. You have to admit, my PSO duties put me closer to you than the average person. And I came into this not knowing who you were, so I didn't have any preconceived notions when it came to you."

I raised an eyebrow. "My encounter with Mike-the-asshole was that impressive, huh?"

He grinned down at me. "It made an impression, that's for sure."

I snorted. "You just think it's sexy that I can take you down without breaking a sweat."

"I'd like to see you try, darlin'." His slow, sexy smile made me want to flush.

Gideon cleared his throat, bringing my attention back to the rest of the room. "Our feelings about this are individual and not something I think we're ready to tackle right now. Each of us needs time to process what we've learned today, and now is not the time to address this." He turned to Uncle Harry. "What I would like to know is how or if this kidnapping changes anything for her regarding her and our family's safety. And what this means for us from this point forward." He looked at me for the first time since we'd sat down. "Were you targeted because you were the perceived weak link of the Accardi family, because your cover was blown, or because of an obsessed fan? If someone kidnapped you because of us, we need to know."

It was Matteo's turn to speak up, looking sideways at me as he did so. "The situation had nothing to do with the Accardi family, and Alessia's cover is still intact, should she decide to continue to work in the field."

Gideon nodded. "Good enough."

"That's it?" Boone asked incredulously. "She puts us through hell, lies to us for years, and that's all you're going to say?"

He looked over at our youngest brother. "As I said before, we all have different thoughts about this. We all need to take time to think about how we're feeling and get past the point of just wanting to react before talking to Alessia one-on-one. Until then, as far as I'm concerned, that's all we need to know."

Uncle Harry waited for a beat, making sure no one else had something to say before turning to me. "That might be all your brothers need, my dear, but I'm afraid we still have one last important matter to discuss."

I looked at my brothers, unsure why we weren't having the conversation in private. Uncle Harry nodded to Matteo as he continued, "Matteo has already informed me about pulling back as your in-field partner to be replaced by Mr. McCallister." I could see the hint of amusement in his eye. "However, I know you've also been contemplating a change. Your advanced age—for a model, anyway—as well as a growing discontentment in your current role are all reasons to think about your career."

None of what he said was a surprise. Ignoring the whole left side of the room made up of my male relatives, he pressed on. "Our organization has been in talks with Accardi Tactical," his eyes flickered to Gideon, "regarding the hiring of someone with a more ... private ... skill set for the express purpose of teaching advanced classes for back-door or prospective back-door operatives within differing levels within the United States. An individual who, on paper, would blend in with the rest of the staff typically hired by A.T."

I felt my pulse tick up a notch, unable to stop myself from leaning forward in interest. Three of my brothers looked slightly surprised as they made the connection, but Gideon stared at Brody with an unreadable expression. If I didn't know better, I would think he was ignoring the conversation, but I knew my brother enough to know that, if pressed, he could recite our uncle's words verbatim.

"Just because she's got the right name doesn't mean she'd be able to blend in—on paper or otherwise," Boone said.

Not about to put up with his snark any longer, I replied, "I have an MBA, as well as degrees in finance, political science, and pre-law. It's widely known I've negotiated my own modeling contracts since I was nineteen, and I play with the stock market for fun from time to time. I can also pass your shooting, self-defense, and physical tests that are required for any position in this company, including yours." I couldn't resist the taunt. "If you want to act like a child, feel free. But until you're willing to act like an adult, I will treat you accordingly, meaning you need to sit there and shut up while the rest of us have a worthwhile conversation."

Boone flushed bright red but kept his mouth shut as I turned back to Harry, who studiously ignored our by-play.

"As discussed," Gideon spoke to our uncle, still not taking his gaze from Brody's, "we have several positions that could fit that résumé. The individual has to do the job created to keep that cover in place for the other employees, as well as take on whatever classes we at Accardi Tactical deem necessary for all class levels, not just the back-door operatives for your specific organization. Essentially," he finally turned his attention to me, his dark blue eyes pinning me in place, "you would work for us, not your organization, and would be required to act accordingly."

For a moment, I felt like I was making a deal with the devil, but I reminded myself that it was Gideon, and he knew me well enough to know I wouldn't meekly fall into line like one of his soldiers. I smirked, folding my arms and leaning back against my chair. "Of course," I agreed.

"Yeah," he said, almost to himself. "That's what I thought." Louder, he said to Brody, "You sure you're up to keeping her in line?"

Brody smirked. "I can only promise to do my best."

Gideon sighed, looking back over at Harry. "Then I guess we better do a two-for-one and take both of them off your hands."

Chapter 30

Alessia

I woke with a start the next morning, a hand gripping the Glock under my pillow and the knowledge I wasn't alone. Before I could pull my weapon, the realization that Brody was next to me had me relaxing back against the bedding. Although I'd told Brody at the airport that I'd be going home alone, he trudged into my house with me as if it were a foregone conclusion he'd be welcome. I was too tired to argue, ignoring him as I performed my usual sweep of my house before collapsing on my mattress. I hadn't even felt him get into bed beside me.

"Sorry," he whispered as he rolled off the mattress. "I didn't mean to wake you."

I groaned, my face buried in my pillow. "Is it morning?"

My muffled words must've been recognizable because Brody answered, "Afternoon, actually. You're due for your antibiotic. Do you want me to make you something to eat with it? I asked Keene to drop off groceries a while ago. He should have food here by now."

Turning my head, I cracked one eye. "I guess feeding me is the least you can do, seeing as I distinctly remember telling you that you were *not* welcome to spend the night."

He looked unperturbed. "What kind of boyfriend would I be if I weren't here to take care of you after your ordeal? Besides, we might as well get used to living together."

That had me sitting upright. "And why would that be?" I asked, drawing the sheet up to cover myself when I realized I was naked. I definitely did not remember pulling my clothes off last night.

Brody stretched his arms to the ceiling, his shirt riding up to reveal his happy trail and the bottom of his six-pack. "The next step in this relationship is moving in together. And your house is way better than my apartment. The gym you have out back is awesome, by the way. I hope you don't mind that I went exploring after I woke up this morning. I got a decent workout in before coming back for a nap."

I narrowed my eyes. "I just agreed to the start of a relationship yesterday. Why the hell would you think I'm anywhere near ready to allow you to move in?"

He gave me a winsome smile, the innocent expression and sparkle in his eye making him look like a mischievous boy. "How can I ask you to marry me if we aren't living together?"

I bolted out of bed. "Hell no." I dragged the sheet off with me, whirling to face him. "I'm not going to marry you—you didn't even know who I was a week ago."

Unconcerned, he shrugged. "Is there an official length of time we're supposed to date or live together before we can decide to get married?"

"First," I stomped over to him, jamming a finger from my uninjured hand into his chest, "we won't 'decide' to get married. You will ask me properly, after talking to Daddy and my brothers, down on one knee and with the appropriate ring. Second, you haven't even taken me out on an official date. I'm not about to let you move in until we've been dating for at least a few months. And everyone knows that getting engaged before you've been living together for less than six months is crazy."

His sexy smile grew as I spoke, and he ignored the finger I was poking him with to emphasize my words. "Well," his smooth drawl was thick and slow, "I guess I can agree to that. Seeing as I only plan on doing this once, I might as well do it right. Your family will do their best to put me through the wringer, but you're worth it, sweetheart."

That drew me up short. "What?" *When have I lost control of this conversation?* I wondered. That was why I really shouldn't argue before I was properly caffeinated and ate a decent meal.

Nodding as if he had the world figured out, he headed to the closet door, turning the light on to peer at the contents. "Do you wear everything in here, or are some of these just in here to maintain your image? 'Cause, babe, there is a shit-ton of clothes in here."

I brushed past him, dropping the sheet in favor of a bra, panties, yoga pants, and a tank top. I only wore a tiny fraction of the garments—the closet itself was large enough to be another bedroom, but until I regained control of the conversation, I wasn't about to volunteer anything. "Of course, I have a diverse wardrobe," I said as I drew the shirt over my head. "I'm a woman and a model."

"I guess I can throw my stuff in a dresser. There's enough room for one in here," he commented from the doorway, staring at the lone, mostly empty wall, where a painting from Gia hung proudly on display.

I stared at him in amazement. "You're not moving in here." The beginning of a headache brewing, I padded barefoot out of the room, pulling my hair up and into a messy bun on the top of my head. "Does Keene know you're certifiably crazy?" Not waiting for him to reply, I continued down the hall in search of coffee.

I turned the corner into the kitchen, stopping short when I saw it was occupied. Keene was sitting at my kitchen counter, a plate of what looked like half-eaten scrambled eggs and toast in front of him. Gideon was on a chair at the head of the dining room table, an empty plate with a few crumbs pushed off to the side in front of him, a tablet in his hand. Boone sat across from him, a mug of coffee steaming by his elbow. Royce was at my stove. None of us except Gideon were especially handy in the kitchen, and eggs were his go-to when it was his turn to cook a meal. A glance told me no one looked especially hostile, so I continued, reaching for a mug in my cabinet. I needed coffee in the worst way possible.

"Brody, crazy?" Keene rubbed the side of his jaw with his finger and thumb as if contemplating my words.

I fished an antibiotic out of the container on the counter, washing it down with a sip from my mug with only a slight wince. My lip was a little more swollen, as was my hand, and my body was sore, but all in all, I was in much better shape than I ought to have been.

The man in question came up behind me, patting the counter next to the sink. I raised an eyebrow but obliged, letting him help me as I jumped up so that I didn't put my weight on my injured hand. "He just told me we're living together," I said to my brother as Brody took my wrapped hand in both of his. "And I told him we had to date for at least a few months before I'd even consider it."

"You said we couldn't get married unless we'd lived together for six months," Brody replied, focusing on unwrapping the bandage. He had all of my brothers' attention on him now. "You can't blame me for wanting to push the timeline a bit. But I'm content to follow your lead. For now. Though I am going to commandeer a space for clothes. You might not want to make it official, but you can be sure I'm going to be at your place more often than I'm at mine." He held my hand up, making use of the early afternoon light streaming in from the window over the sink to inspect every inch of my hand. I wriggled my fingers at his request. A little red, a touch swollen, but overall, I thought it looked good. Brody must have thought the same because he grunted once before reaching for the saline solution and antibiotic cream. "Did you take your antibiotic?" he asked.

I nodded, taking another sip of coffee before turning to my brothers. "Really, none of y'all have anything to say?" I snagged a piece of toast slathered in jam from Keene's hand, taking a huge bite.

Boone was staring at my puncture wound; his face tinged green. "That looks ... painful." He hesitated before continuing, "Were you ... you know." He waved a hand at my injury, looking more than a little concerned. The entire room had gone still. I looked from my hand to his face again before realization dawned.

"Oh, no, I wasn't tortured. This is just an unfortunate consequence of using the tools around me to take control of the situation." Everyone but Brody relaxed as one.

"Brody's always been stubborn," Keene resumed our conversation. "He does his own thing and ignores everything that doesn't fall into line."

"You try to handle me," I threatened Brody, "and you won't be happy with the results."

He smiled. "I wouldn't dream of it."

Sighing, I gave in. "Fine, I guess I can clean out one teeny tiny section of the closet. But you better do your share of the housekeeping. And you still keep your apartment." A thought occurred to me, and I folded my arms over my chest. "But I am *not* sharing my gun safe or weapons collection."

Royce slid a plate of scrambled eggs next to me. "We were looking for something like that while waiting for you to wake up," Royce said, adding a fork to my plate. "The walls all look correct, and we couldn't find any hidden compartments other than a few hidden guns around the house."

Matteo entered the kitchen from the door to the backyard. "She has an excellent collection. And it's not in some piddly little wall safe."

Royce nodded as if Matteo had confirmed his suspicions.

"It's got to be in the floor," Boone muttered, looking at the surrounding surface speculatively. I kept my face blank. What he was looking for was pretty much an entire floor, not in it.

Brody finished re-wrapping my hand, giving it a slight squeeze before releasing it so I could use it to hold my plate. "Not that all y'all aren't welcome," I said in between another bite, "but why is everyone gathering in my kitchen this morning—afternoon?"

Gideon set his tablet aside. "We all took an early lunch and ended up here for various reasons. I came over to check on you. Keene came over for groceries, Royce to make you breakfast, and Boone to apologize for his behavior. I said yesterday that we all needed time to think, and apparently, all of us felt we had enough time to decide how to feel."

Matteo chimed in, "I just delivered your car. Your purse and cell phone are in it." He placed the key on the counter.

Gideon raised a hand before Matteo could make a quick exit. "I know you turned us down yesterday." Gideon had extended a job offer to Matteo, too, who'd quickly given him a "Thanks but no, thanks." "But surely you'll be bored teaching a bunch of kids without Lessia's brand of excitement to spice things up."

Matteo gave him a brief smile. "You're assuming Alessia is the only one bringing me that type of excitement."

Gideon gave him a disgruntled look, realizing that Matteo was admitting to being more than just a handler for me, taking away his trump card. "I'll get you eventually," he threatened.

Matteo just shrugged. "We'll see," he said before turning back out the door, exiting as quietly and quickly as he'd appeared.

Shaking my head, I commented, "Matteo will never work for A.T. He has his hands full as it is, and he isn't the type of man to work in the light. He enjoys doing what he does in the periphery."

Keene smirked at Brody knowingly. "I know another man who swore he'd never work for us." Brody just stared at him for long moments, not saying anything. Suddenly, Keene started laughing. "Oh my God, is that why you brought up marriage?"

Boone and Royce started chuckling, and even Gideon cracked a smile.

"I don't get it," I said, looking between Brody and Keene and waiting for someone to clue me into the joke.

In between chuckles, Keene explained, "If you're married, what's yours is his and his is yours, meaning ..."

I whirled around, punching Brody in his arm before anyone could blink. "If you think that by marrying me, you're going to get my shares in Accardi Tactical—"

Brody grabbed my face with both of his hands. I was still sitting on the counter, and with him standing between my legs, we were almost the same height. His lips closed over mine, his tongue plundering my mouth as if he hadn't seen me for months. My mind went blank, and I couldn't have said my own name, let alone remember I was angry. His hands gentled on my face, angling me for a better fit, getting deeper, fanning the flames even hotter.

A quiet throat clearing broke us apart, both of us panting. I'd forgotten my brothers were still in the room. "You know me well enough to know I couldn't care less about getting anything that belongs to you," he said after a moment. "I'll admit, I wouldn't even consider taking this job if it wasn't for you. But working with the love of my life, with the men I'll call brothers eventually, differs completely from what Keene had in mind when he first asked me to work for A.T. after I was discharged."

I stared at him, stunned. Had he just said he loved me? Without waiting for me to process his words, he bent down and gave me another peck on the lips. "You visit with your brothers," he said. "I'm going to shower. And you," he pointed to Keene, "stop trying to get me in trouble." And then he was gone. I was still looking down the empty hall after his steps faded.

Chapter 31

Alessia

Gideon was the first to talk when I turned back to them, deciding to think more about Brody later. Always the leader, it didn't surprise me in the least when he set his tablet aside, turned his full attention to me, and spoke. "I'm not upset that you kept secrets about your job from us. We've all served our country," he included me in his gaze as he looked at all of us, "and we've all kept our mouths shut to protect others. The past is in the past, but I want it understood that, unless it reveals confidential information, you are to be *you* from here on out." He gave me a rare smile. "I miss our sister. We've seen plenty of the woman you think we wanted, or expected, to see. We want the person you actually are."

Keene added, "We don't run from each other in this family, Lessia. You have an issue with us, you tell us so. We get too far into your business, you push back like you did when we were kids."

Royce chimed in, "I don't think she's completely forgotten how." The amusement was clear in his voice, and I knew he was thinking about my retribution last week. Boone made a sound of agreement.

I tilted my chin up stubbornly because I stood by my past actions—both the confrontational and nonconfrontational ones—but nodded in agreement. "Okay. But you're *not* sticking me with a job in H.R. or finance." Both of which had been brought up yesterday, and I'd promptly shut both down, but it bore repeating.

"We'll, figure something out," Gideon said magnanimously. I narrowed my eyes, unsure if he was humoring me or not. Before I could say anything, Boone cleared his throat.

"I owe you an apology," he said quietly but firmly. He shook his head when I waved him off. "No, I do. What I said yesterday was wrong—it was spiteful and meant to hurt you, and it did. And I'm sorry. I didn't mean it, never even really thought it. It just seemed to spill out."

That was the thing about Boone. He might be hotheaded and rash, but he always—always—owned up to it when he had time to calm down.

"To be honest," I said, "I thought I'd get more of it from more of you." I shrugged. "Kinda figured it would be a default response. I accept your apology."

"We're good?" he asked skeptically.

"We're good. No retribution." I gave him a playful smirk. "I don't think your stomach could handle another round, anyway."

He groaned, placing his hand over his middle in part truth, part fun. "I think you ruined enchiladas and whiskey for me for life."

"Just don't go switching to tequila," I said, only partially in jest.

"So," Royce said, throwing down the rag he'd been using to wipe off the counter.

"So," Boone echoed, both of them giving each other a sideways look before looking at me expectantly.

"So, what?" My voice came out slow and wary, unsure of what they wanted to know and mentally trying to flip through what I could divulge from my past missions and what I had to keep to myself.

"Since you're basically retired and all," Royce said casually, "I guess you could show us where a covert operative might have, at one time, stored their weapons and other tricks of the trade."

I put my hands on my hips. "Semi-retired. And I'm not showing you where I keep the fun stuff. You'd never leave unless it were to head to the range to try out my toys. Besides, they're *mine*."

Boone looked around at the floors again while Royce gave a speculative glance at the walls. "You'd have to hide them someplace unexpected," he mused. "You couldn't have one of us getting suspicious and poking into something we weren't supposed to find."

Keene's eyes widened, and I slammed a mask in place, knowing he'd put the pieces of one part of the puzzle together. "Holy shit." He gave me a wild-eyed look. "Do you actually have a dungeon? You told me—" He cut himself off, turning to our brothers. Even Gideon looked intrigued. "The morning she made Brody sign that NDA, she said that's why she didn't want him... us... poking around. That we might find her dungeon. I thought she meant—" He cut himself off a second time, looking at Royce, who was as stone-faced as I was.

"I don't have a sex dungeon," I protested, trying to turn the conversation. "I don't have any kind of dungeon. All my kinky sex stuff is stored in my bedroom. I wasn't kidding about not looking under the bed." Pausing for dramatic effect, I continued, trying to change the subject. "I guess if I'm going to keep Brody, we're going to have to agree for him not to talk about our sex life while he's in the locker room. All y'all are not going to want that mental picture."

Boone winced. "Good thing he's not one to kiss and tell, but I agree, no sex talk."

Gideon, who had stayed silent through our exchange, stared at me, clearly not detoured by the conversation the way I'd hoped. "Keene's right," he mused, watching me. "I never noticed how well you toed that line between lying and blatant honesty so outrageous we thought you were joking." He turned to the other three. "You aren't looking for an in-ground cubby. You're looking for an entrance to a basement."

Damn it, I thought, hating how well he could read me when he put effort into it. "I can show you the blueprints for the house—no basement permit was pulled, was in the home inspections, or was on the plans."

"I bet not," he agreed. "But I'm right, aren't I? I remember thinking you were going off the deep end with this house. After you bought it half-finished, you went through what, five or six contractors? You said it was because they kept ditching, but I'm betting you didn't want any one company to have full purview of the house design. At the time, I thought you were being high-strung, but you played that shit up on purpose."

I smiled smugly. "I can neither confirm nor deny the existence of a basement. But even if there was," I said, over my brothers' voices, "you wouldn't be able to get into it."

"That sounds like a challenge to me," Boone said, looking like a kid getting geared up for a treasure hunt.

"As fun as that would be," Gideon glanced at his watch with a flick of his wrist, "our lunch hour was over an hour ago."

Boone, Royce, and even Keene looked more than a little crestfallen. *Little boys*, I thought, *they never grow up*. "It's not going anywhere," I assured them, unable to help myself. "Assuming you can even find it."

They grumbled, teased, and otherwise did their best to annoy me as they left as the unit they almost always were. I sighed over the remaining dirty plates, mugs, and silverware, putting them all in the dishwasher. That, at least, was back to normal. And, I mused, everything else was going to settle into a new normal eventually. I had one more obligation to Valencia, but nothing else to hold me back from doing what I'd always wanted to do—work at A.T. with my brothers, being able to eat what I wanted when I wanted. And, maybe, I thought as I padded down the hall, listening to Brody sing—badly—in the shower, get the chance to live happily ever after with a man strong enough to handle me. I dropped my clothes as I walked, not bothering to pick them up as I opened the shower door, my smile growing as I took in the sight of the sexy, grinning, naked man in front of me. *Not a bad life*, I thought as I walked into his arms without hesitation. *Not bad at all.*

Chapter 32

Epilogue—Keene

I was going to strangle my sister. I wouldn't miss her—much—I didn't think. Over the past month, we'd been working pretty much side by side. Gideon had always run the show, Royce and I were the details men, and Boone was our hands-on, in-the-trenches instructor and overall liaison with just about every branch of government agency I could think of. Alessia was the fire and passion, that was for sure. But sometimes, I just wanted to wrap my hands around her neck.

"What do you mean you told Maria I would take on the survivalist class this weekend?" I pinched the bridge of my nose between my fingers, hoping to starve off the brewing headache.

Lessia looked at me innocently. "I mean, I told Maria that your calendar was clear and since she needed someone to take over the class because of Cal quitting—"

"You mean since you caused Cal to quit," I said flatly.

Her eyes flared in memory. "I mean, since Cal quit because I kicked his egotistical, misogynist ass after insulting me for the thousandth time. If he can't back up—or at least live up to his own mouth—then that's his own damn fault."

Because I agreed with her, at least in principle, I returned to the class. "Why can't you take it over?"

She gave me an aggrieved look. "Because I haven't had time to pass my qualifications on teaching the survivalist class, as basic as it is. And I haven't been camping since I was a teen."

I closed my eyes. The survivalist class was definitely one of the most basic—more like camping with a ton of "what to do ifs," thrown in. If it weren't for the exorbitant fees we charged for it, it wouldn't even be worth our time. But there was nothing rich men loved more than bragging about how bad-ass they were unless it was bragging about how they'd been taught by the best in the world how to be the bad-asses they thought they were.

"It's one weekend," she consoled, patting my shoulder in mock sympathy. "And you'll have Brody and me for company."

I brightened at her mention of her boyfriend. "Brody could—"

She shook her head. "Brody hasn't had time to take his qualifications in this class either. He's had his hands full taking over and revamping the Tactical Firearms courses." He'd officially taken over as the head instructor of those classes a few weeks before.

I sighed, resigned to canceling my plans to fly to my cabin in Colorado that weekend for some R&R. "And I'm guessing all our other siblings are otherwise occupied?"

Lessia shrugged. "They called not-it before I could do anything."

Bastards, I thought, but I knew I would've done the same thing in their place. "Fine. I'll plan on babysitting rich assholes this weekend."

She grinned, the mischievous look in her eye making me pause. "You forgot, there's a potential hire going on this trip, plus Brody and me, as well the rich assholes."

"Just remember they're paying clients." I felt the warning was necessary. "It's bad enough you've been tossing around employees. The last thing I need is to deal with you punching some bastard who said something out of line."

Instead of warning her off, she seemed to brighten at the thought. With my headache worsening, I yanked open my top drawer, pulling out the almost-empty bottle of aspirin. It was my third bottle since Lessia had begun working at A.T. "Cheer up." She handed me a bottle of water as I tossed down two pills. "Brody will be there, and with any luck, this new person will work out. I think they're angling for this trip as their regular gig if I remember correctly."

I thought back, trying to pull the file from memory but coming up foggy on the details. "I think Boone did the initial interview. But you're right. I think they're supposed to take over the basic camping and survival classes, assuming they know their stuff."

Her smile grew. "We can always hope."

"As long as no one leaves in an ambulance or a body bag, I'll call this weekend a win."

Shrugging, she looked unconcerned. "No problem. If we end up having a casualty, I'll have Brody bury them in the woods." Her laughter followed her out the door.

With any luck, whoever Boone had interviewed would know their stuff, and I could put them in charge of the weekend, all in the name of making sure they were the right person for the job and put Brody on Alessia detail. Maybe it would be a peaceful trip after all. I tried to think positively, but my churning gut told me I'd better strap in for a wild weekend.

About Author

K.C. is the alter ego of a thirty-something dreamer who lives in the heart of small-town USA. Seriously, cows outnumber people four to one and she has to drive almost an hour to visit the grocery store! Business owner and farm girl by day and writer by night, she keeps herself busy. When she's not working or writing, she's playing with her countless dogs, riding her horses, or reading her favorite authors. She writes what she loves to read—primarily protector romance and romantic suspense. You can count on her to provide entertaining stories filled with strong women, hot alpha men, and love forever after.

She loves to hear from her readers! Please reach out at authork.c.ramsey@gmail.com, and check out K.C. Ramsey's Readers on Facebook for upcoming releases, giveaways, and bonus content.

Made in the USA
Monee, IL
31 May 2024

59214170R00215